PHILIPPE RICHE

THE ALLIANCE OF THE
CURIOUS

HUMANOIDS

Philippe Riche
Writer & Artist

Natacha Ruck & Ken Grobe
Translators

Alex Donoghue
U.S. Edition Editor

Jerry Frissen
Book Designer

HUMANOIDS

Fabrice Giger, Publisher
Alex Donoghue, Director & Editor
Jerry Frissen, Senior Art Director
Edmond Lee, Rights & Licensing
licensing@humanoids.com

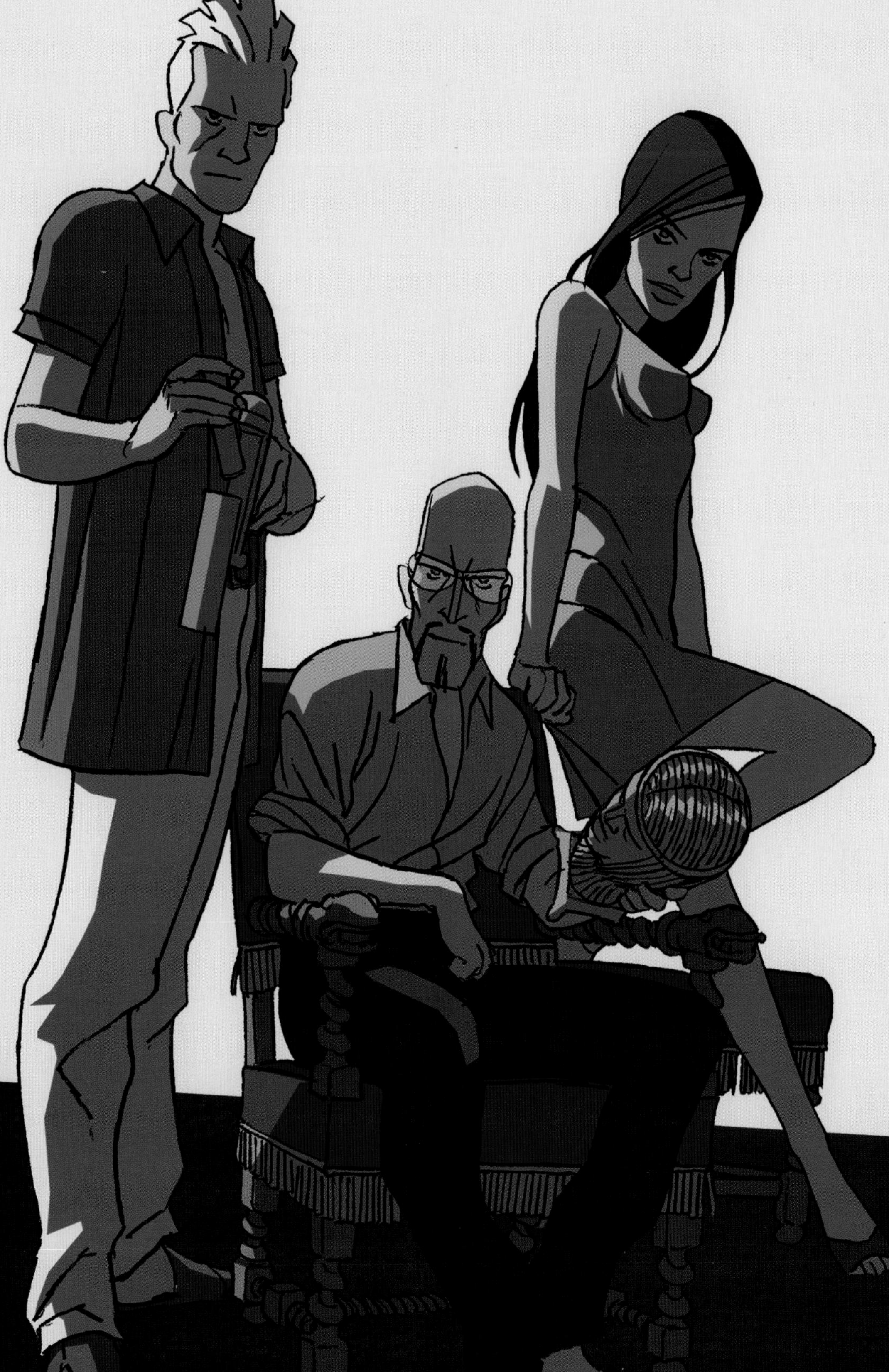

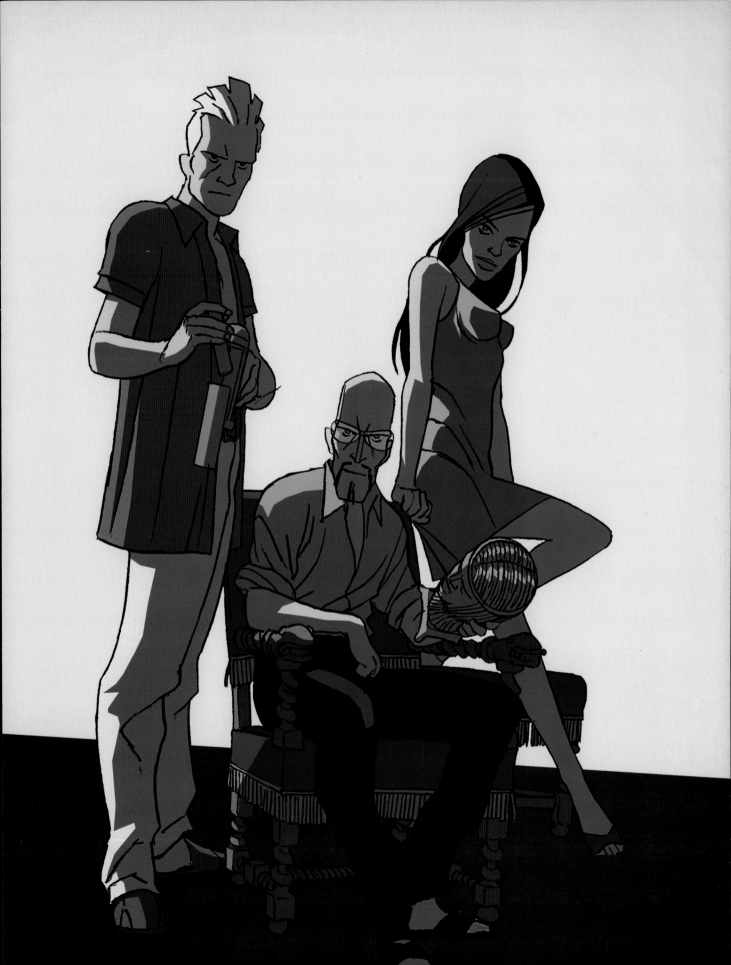

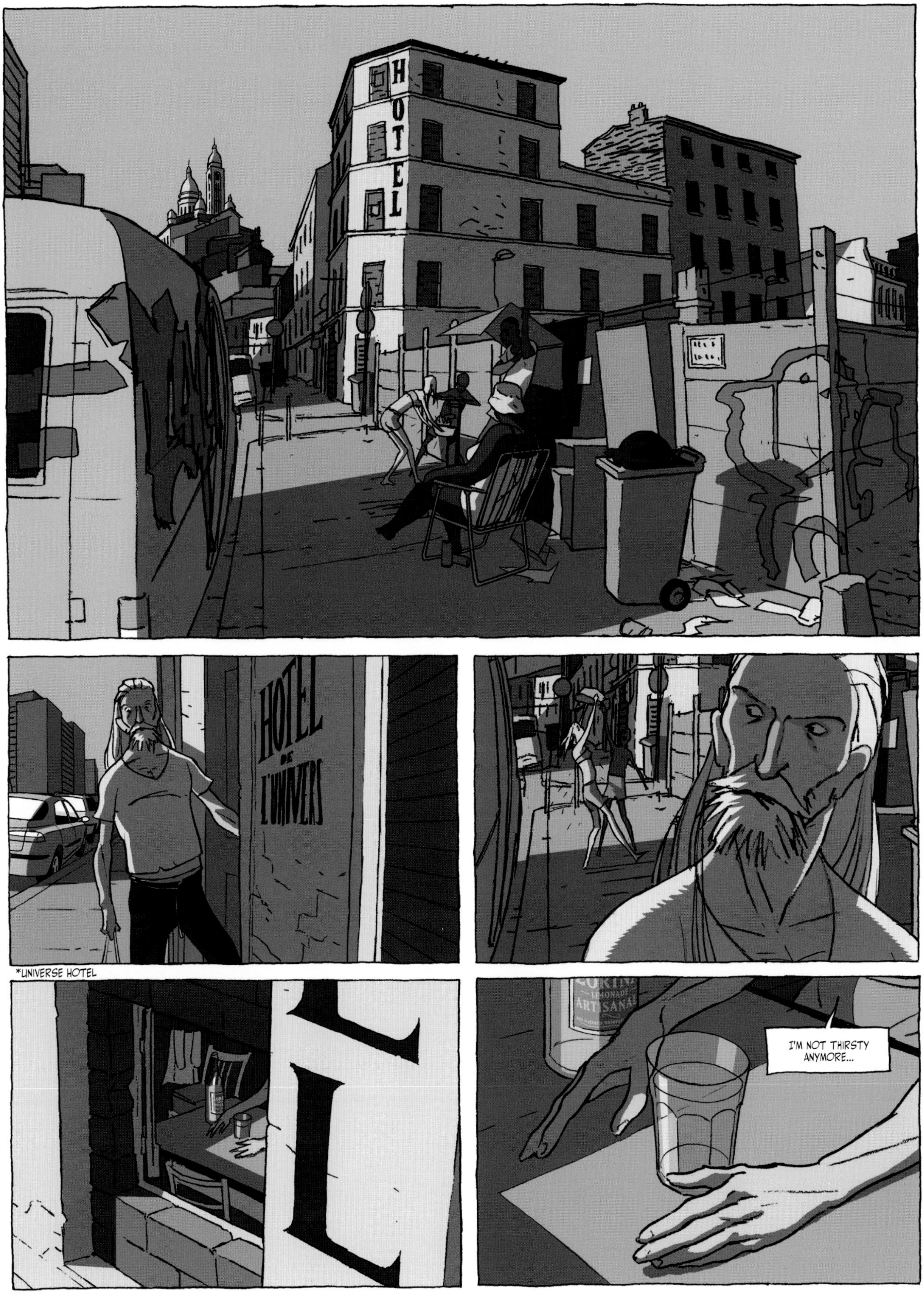
HOTEL
HOTEL DE L'UNIVERS
*UNIVERSE HOTEL
I'M NOT THIRSTY ANYMORE...

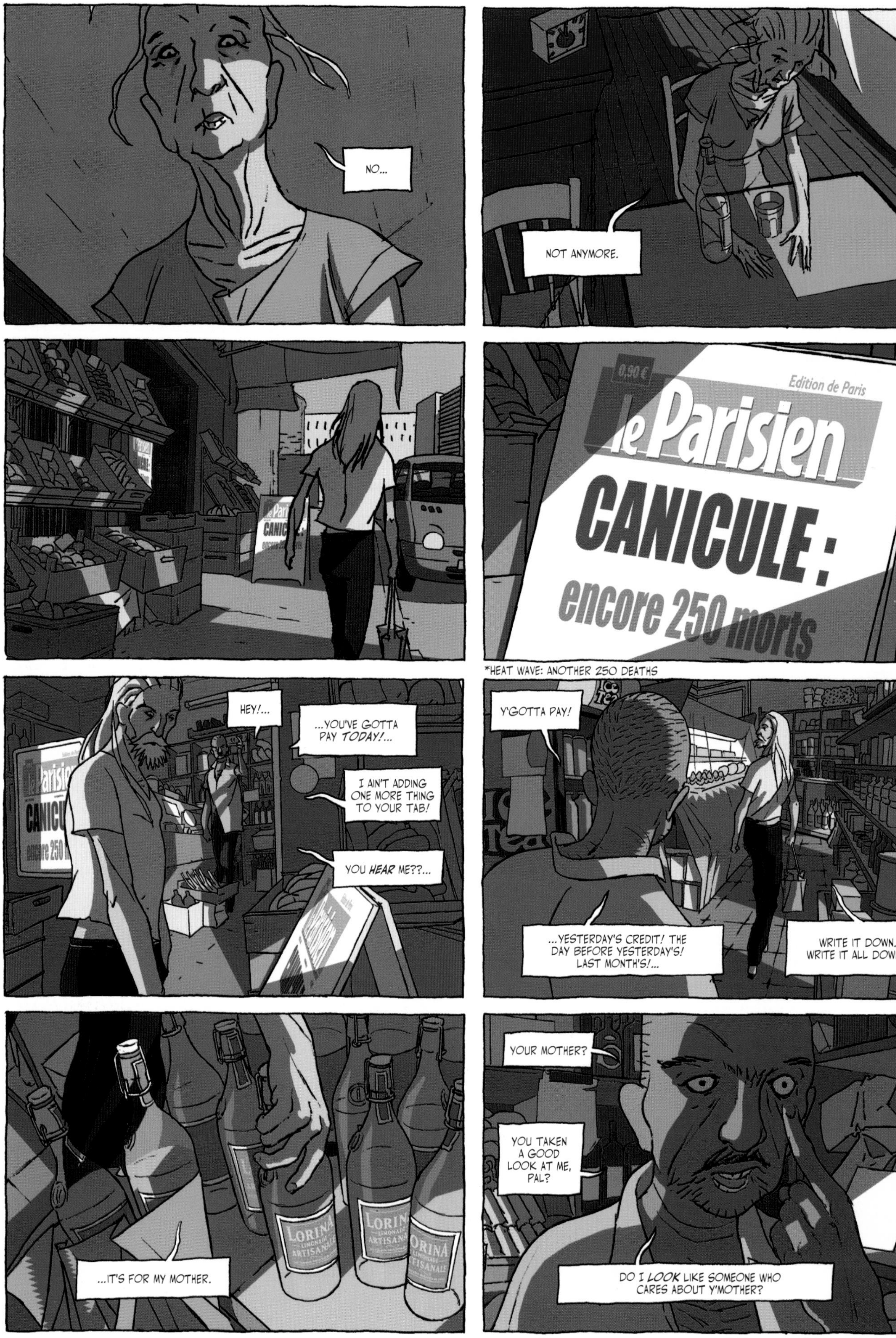
NO...
NOT ANYMORE.
0,90 €
Edition de Paris
le Parisien
CANICULE :
encore 250 morts
*HEAT WAVE: ANOTHER 250 DEATHS
HEY!...
...YOU'VE GOTTA PAY TODAY!...
I AIN'T ADDING ONE MORE THING TO YOUR TAB!
YOU HEAR ME??...
Y'GOTTA PAY!
...YESTERDAY'S CREDIT! THE DAY BEFORE YESTERDAY'S! LAST MONTH'S!...
WRITE IT DOWN. WRITE IT ALL DOWN...
LORINA
LIMONADE
ARTISANALE
...IT'S FOR MY MOTHER.
YOUR MOTHER?
YOU TAKEN A GOOD LOOK AT ME, PAL?
DO I LOOK LIKE SOMEONE WHO CARES ABOUT Y'MOTHER?

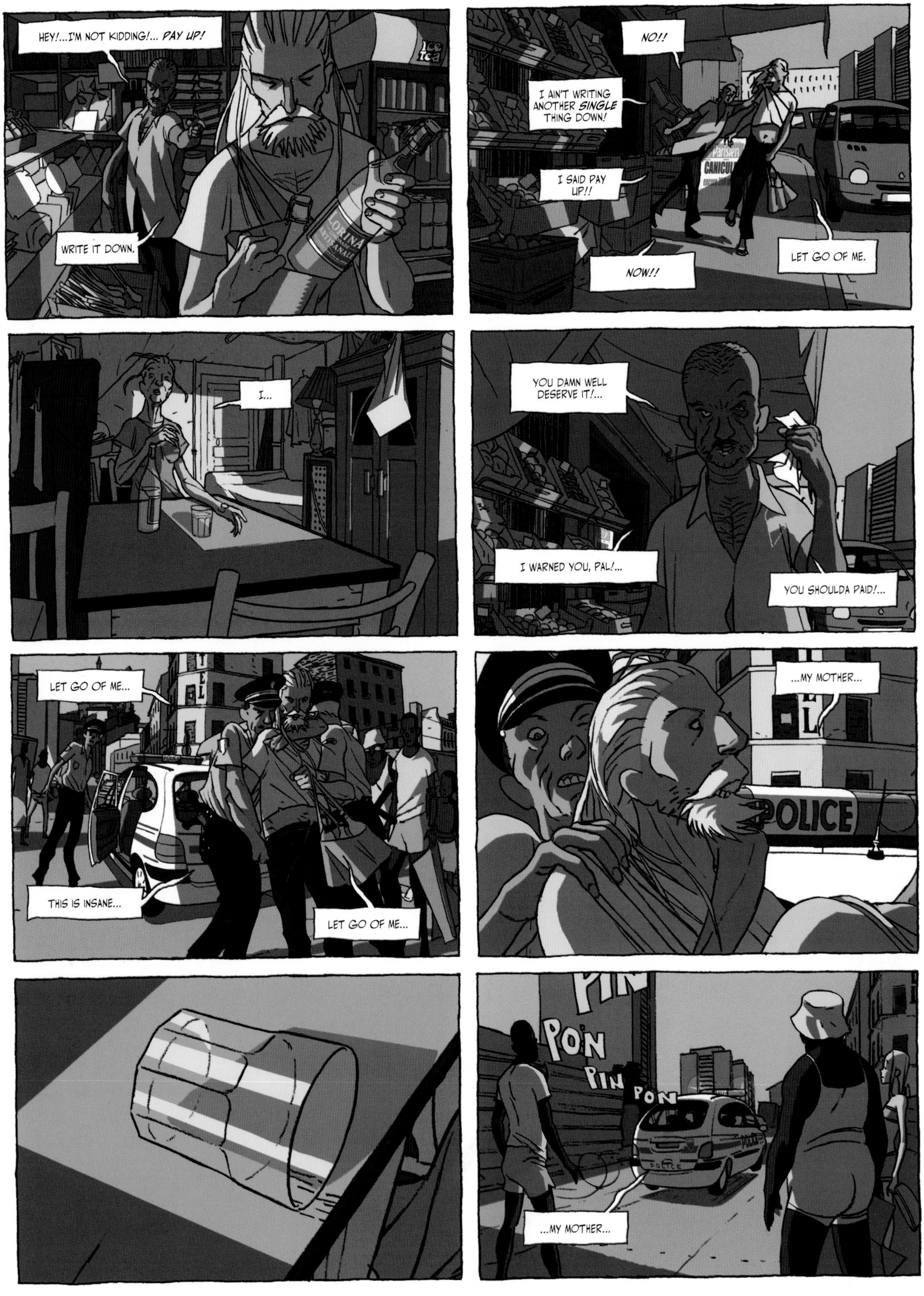
HEY!...I'M NOT KIDDING!... PAY UP!
WRITE IT DOWN.
NO!!
I AIN'T WRITING ANOTHER SINGLE THING DOWN!
I SAID PAY UP!!
NOW!!
LET GO OF ME.
I...
YOU DAMN WELL DESERVE IT!...
I WARNED YOU, PAL!...
YOU SHOULDA PAID!...
LET GO OF ME...
THIS IS INSANE...
LET GO OF ME...
...MY MOTHER...
POLICE
PIN
PON
PIN
PON
...MY MOTHER...

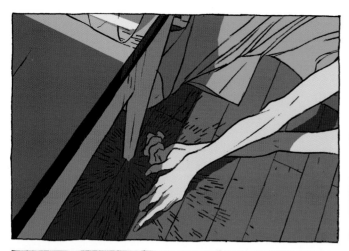

MMMH...

MMM....MMMH...

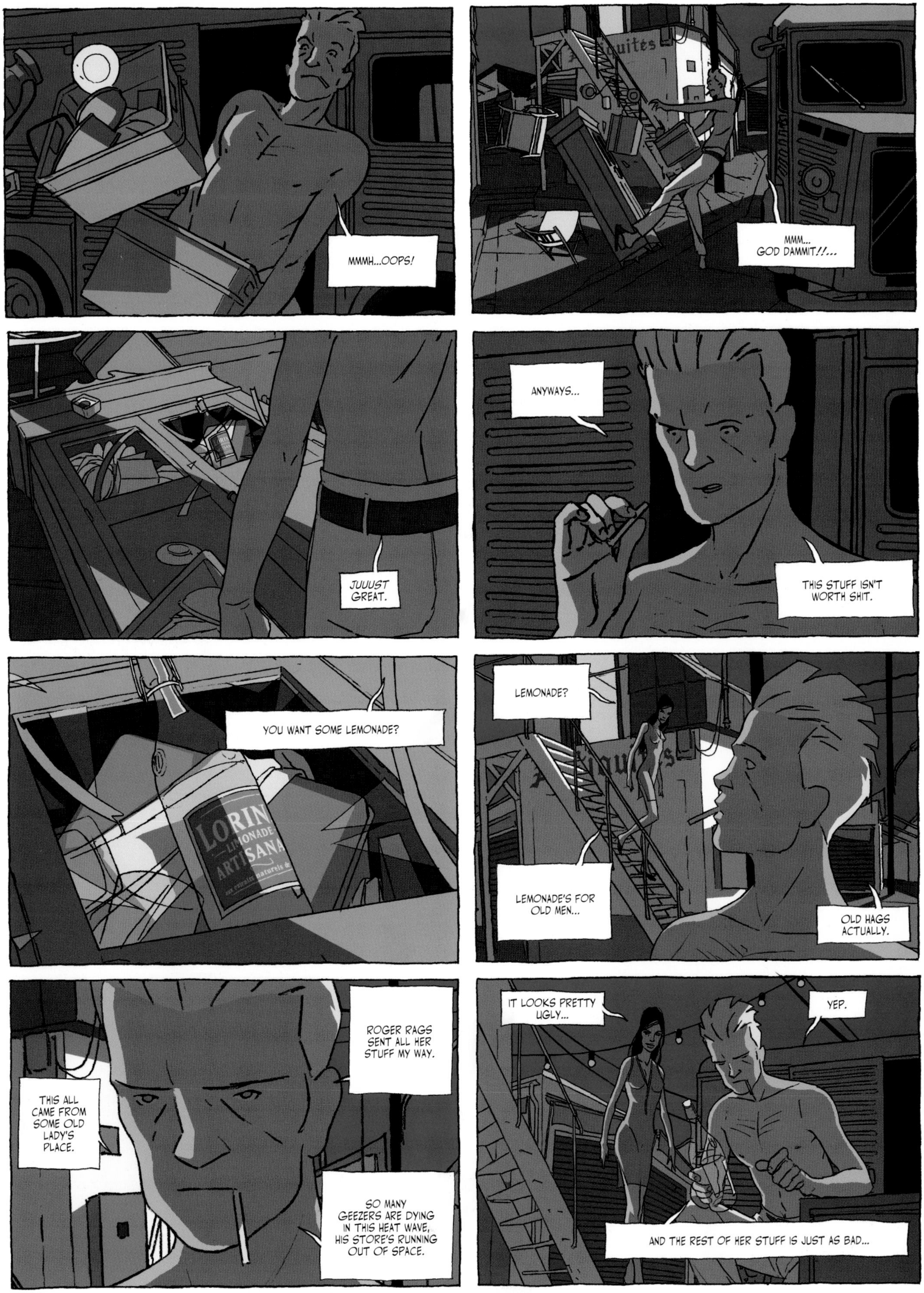
MMMH...OOPS!
MMM...
GOD DAMMIT!!...
JUUUST GREAT.
ANYWAYS...
THIS STUFF ISN'T WORTH SHIT.
YOU WANT SOME LEMONADE?
LORINA LIMONADE ARTISANALE
LEMONADE?
LEMONADE'S FOR OLD MEN...
OLD HAGS ACTUALLY.
THIS ALL CAME FROM SOME OLD LADY'S PLACE.
ROGER RAGS SENT ALL HER STUFF MY WAY.
SO MANY GEEZERS ARE DYING IN THIS HEAT WAVE, HIS STORE'S RUNNING OUT OF SPACE.
IT LOOKS PRETTY UGLY...
YEP.
AND THE REST OF HER STUFF IS JUST AS BAD...

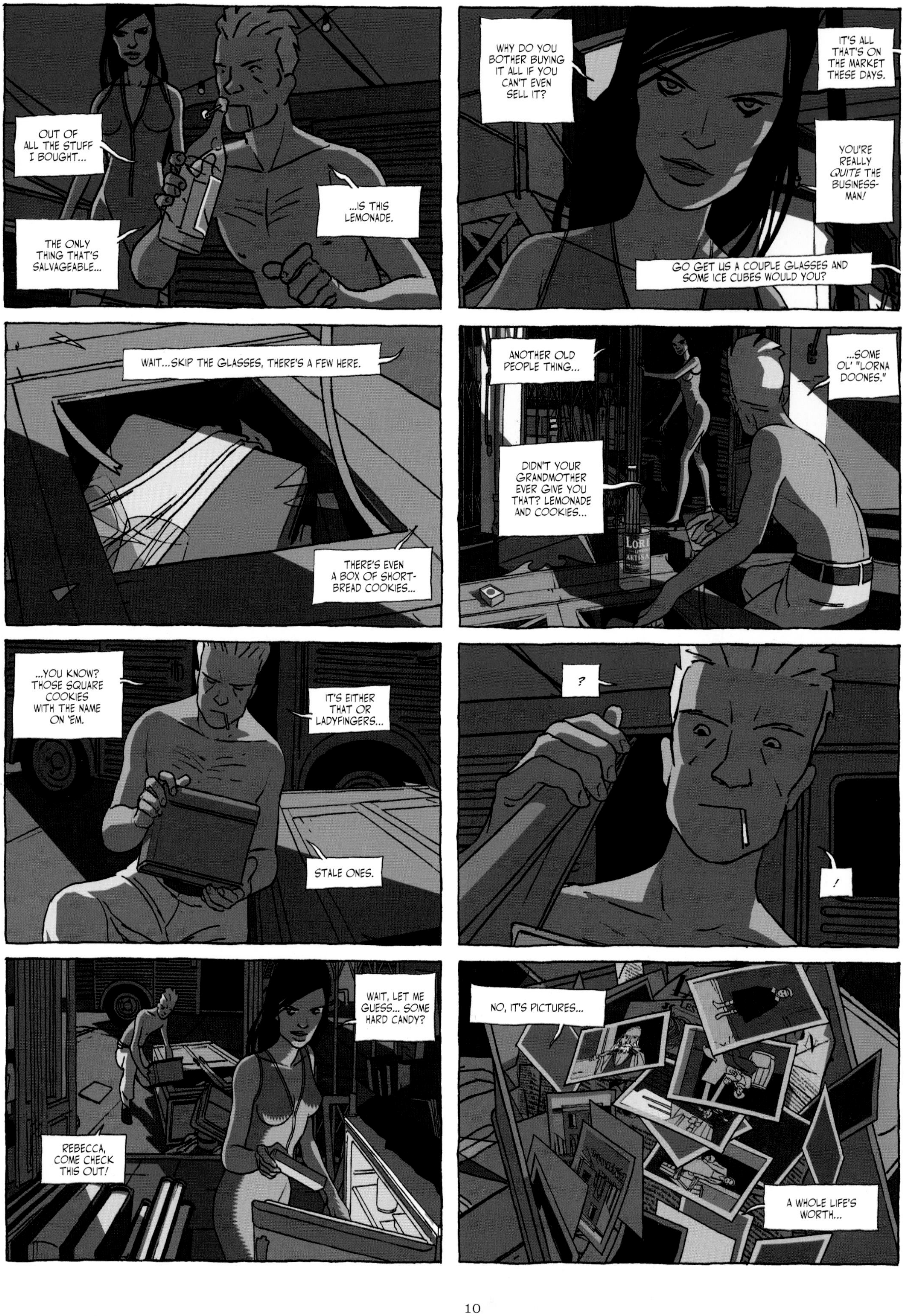
OUT OF ALL THE STUFF I BOUGHT...
THE ONLY THING THAT'S SALVAGEABLE...
...IS THIS LEMONADE.
WHY DO YOU BOTHER BUYING IT ALL IF YOU CAN'T EVEN SELL IT?
IT'S ALL THAT'S ON THE MARKET THESE DAYS.
YOU'RE REALLY *QUITE* THE BUSINESS-MAN!
GO GET US A COUPLE GLASSES AND SOME ICE CUBES WOULD YOU?
WAIT...SKIP THE GLASSES, THERE'S A FEW HERE.
THERE'S EVEN A BOX OF SHORT-BREAD COOKIES...
ANOTHER OLD PEOPLE THING...
...SOME OL' "LORNA DOONES."
DIDN'T YOUR GRANDMOTHER EVER GIVE YOU THAT? LEMONADE AND COOKIES...
...YOU KNOW? THOSE SQUARE COOKIES WITH THE NAME ON 'EM.
IT'S EITHER THAT OR LADYFINGERS...
STALE ONES.
?
!
WAIT, LET ME GUESS... SOME HARD CANDY?
REBECCA, COME CHECK THIS OUT!
NO, IT'S PICTURES...
A WHOLE LIFE'S WORTH...

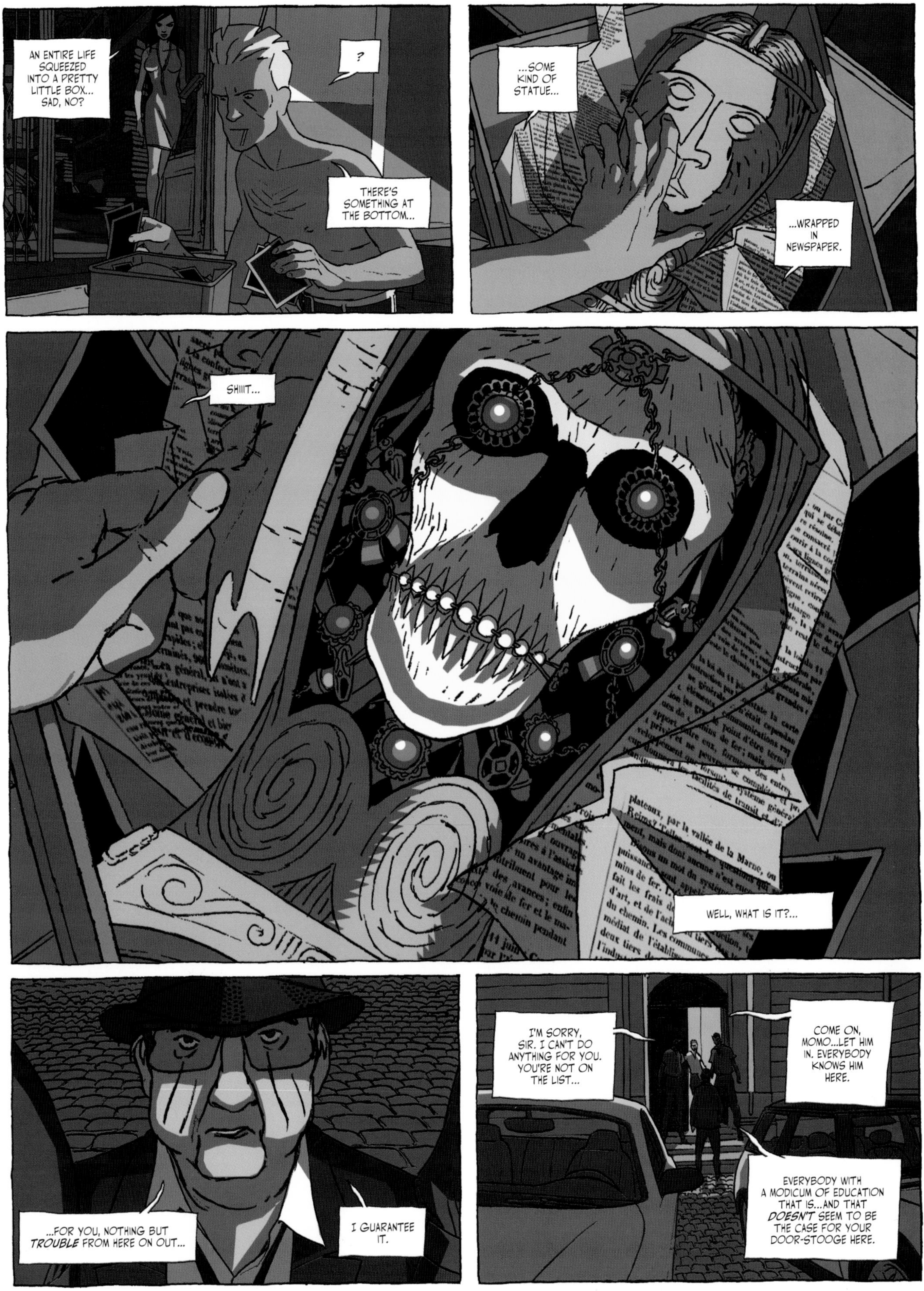
AN ENTIRE LIFE SQUEEZED INTO A PRETTY LITTLE BOX... SAD, NO?
?
THERE'S SOMETHING AT THE BOTTOM...
...SOME KIND OF STATUE...
...WRAPPED IN NEWSPAPER.
SHIIIT...
WELL, WHAT IS IT?...
...FOR YOU, NOTHING BUT *TROUBLE* FROM HERE ON OUT...
I GUARANTEE IT.
I'M SORRY, SIR. I CAN'T DO ANYTHING FOR YOU. YOU'RE NOT ON THE LIST...
COME ON, MOMO...LET HIM IN. EVERYBODY KNOWS HIM HERE.
EVERYBODY WITH A MODICUM OF EDUCATION THAT IS...AND THAT *DOESN'T* SEEM TO BE THE CASE FOR YOUR DOOR-STOOGE HERE.

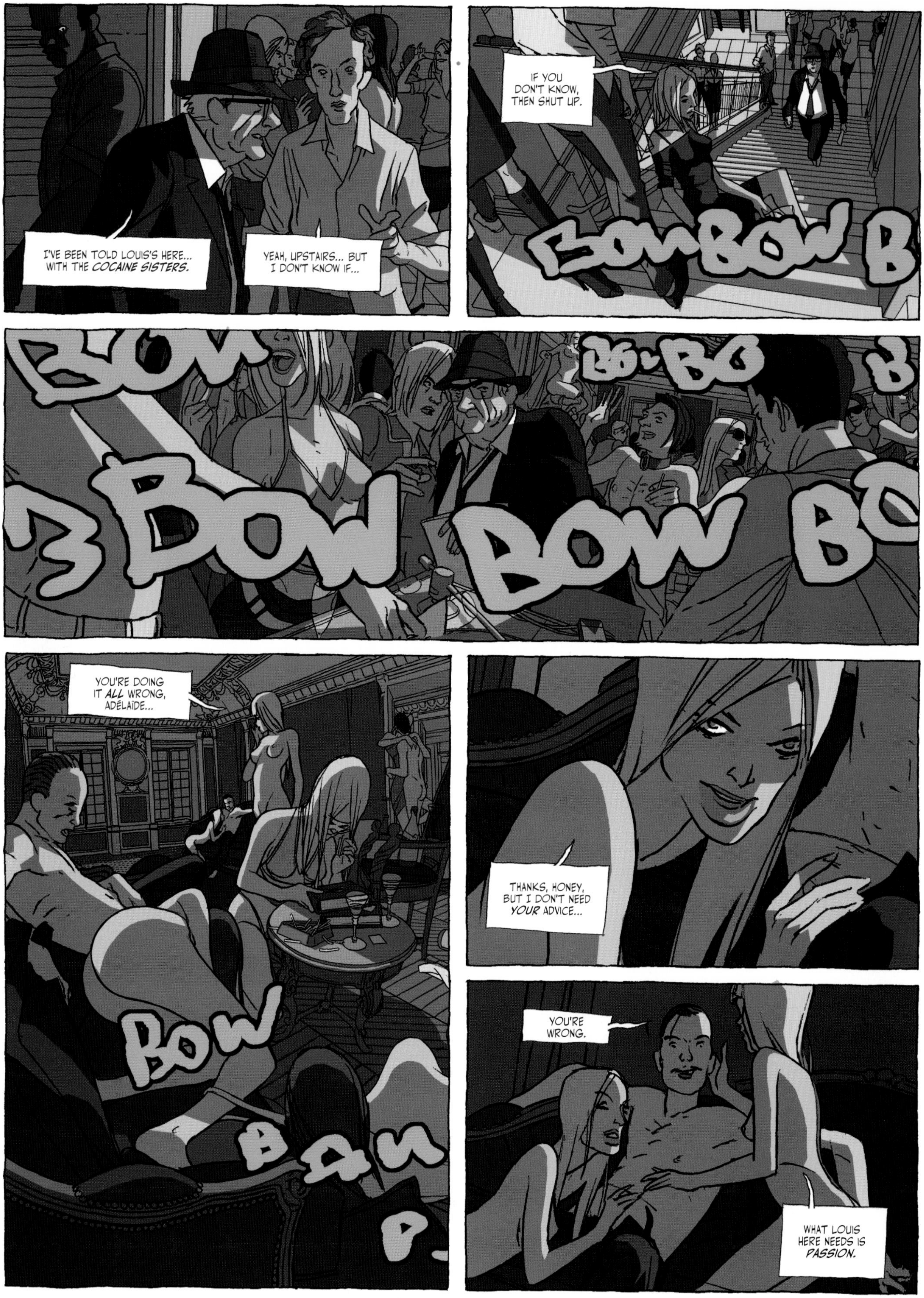
I'VE BEEN TOLD LOUIS'S HERE... WITH THE *COCAINE SISTERS.*
YEAH, UPSTAIRS... BUT I DON'T KNOW IF...
IF YOU DON'T KNOW, THEN SHUT UP.
BOWBOW B
BOW
BOW
BOW BOW BO
YOU'RE DOING IT *ALL* WRONG, ADÉLAÏDE...
BOW
THANKS, HONEY, BUT I DON'T NEED *YOUR* ADVICE...
YOU'RE WRONG.
WHAT LOUIS HERE NEEDS IS *PASSION.*

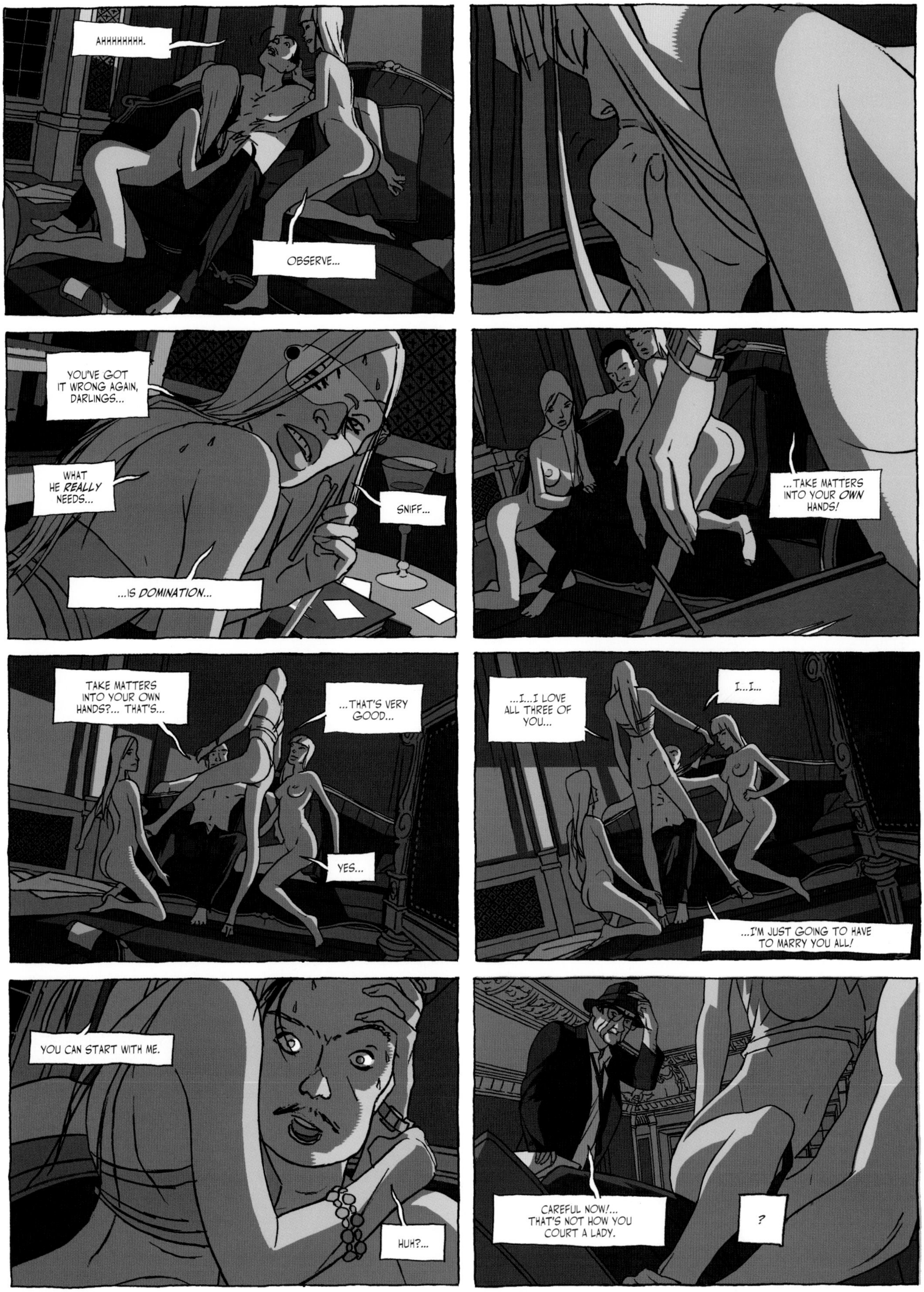
AHHHHHHHH.
OBSERVE...
YOU'VE GOT IT WRONG AGAIN, DARLINGS...
WHAT HE *REALLY* NEEDS...
SNIFF...
...IS *DOMINATION*...
...TAKE MATTERS INTO YOUR *OWN* HANDS!
TAKE MATTERS INTO YOUR OWN HANDS?... THAT'S...
...THAT'S VERY GOOD...
YES...
...I...I LOVE ALL THREE OF YOU...
I...I...
...I'M JUST GOING TO HAVE TO MARRY YOU ALL!
YOU CAN START WITH ME.
HUH?...
CAREFUL NOW!... THAT'S NOT HOW YOU COURT A LADY.
?

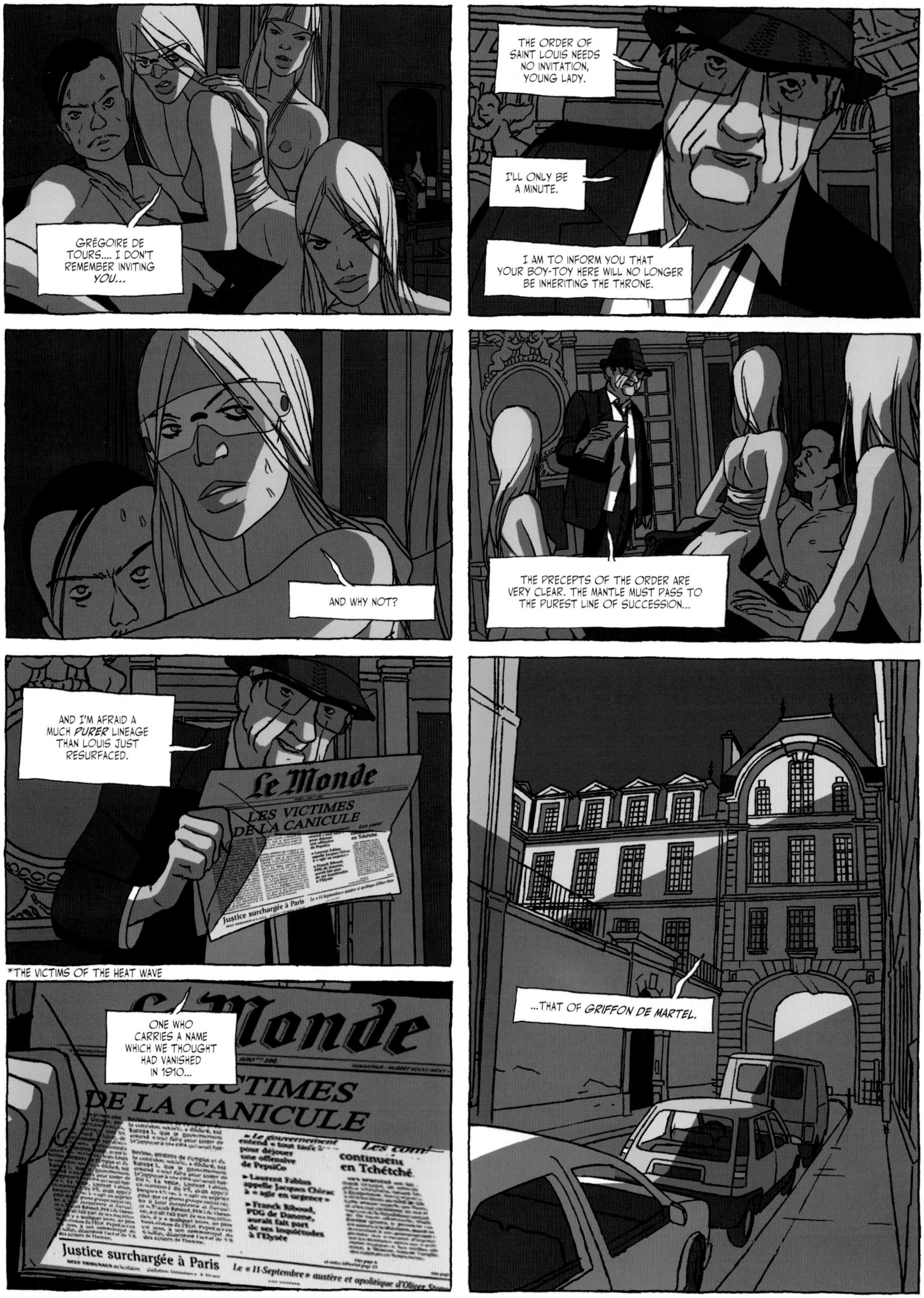
GRÉGOIRE DE TOURS.... I DON'T REMEMBER INVITING *YOU*...
THE ORDER OF SAINT LOUIS NEEDS NO INVITATION, YOUNG LADY.
I'LL ONLY BE A MINUTE.
I AM TO INFORM YOU THAT YOUR BOY-TOY HERE WILL NO LONGER BE INHERITING THE THRONE.
AND WHY NOT?
THE PRECEPTS OF THE ORDER ARE VERY CLEAR. THE MANTLE MUST PASS TO THE PUREST LINE OF SUCCESSION...
AND I'M AFRAID A MUCH *PURER* LINEAGE THAN LOUIS JUST RESURFACED.
Le Monde
LES VICTIMES DE LA CANICULE
Justice surchargée à Paris
...THAT OF *GRIFFON DE MARTEL*.
ONE WHO CARRIES A NAME WHICH WE THOUGHT HAD VANISHED IN 1910...
Le Monde
LES VICTIMES DE LA CANICULE
Le gouvernement
pour déjouer une offensive de PepsiCo
Les com
continuent en Tchétché
Laurent Fabius appelle Jacques Chirac à « agir en urgence »
Franck Riboud, PDG de Danone,
Justice surchargée à Paris
Le « 11-Septembre » austère et apolitique d'Oliver Stone

*THE VICTIMS OF THE HEAT WAVE

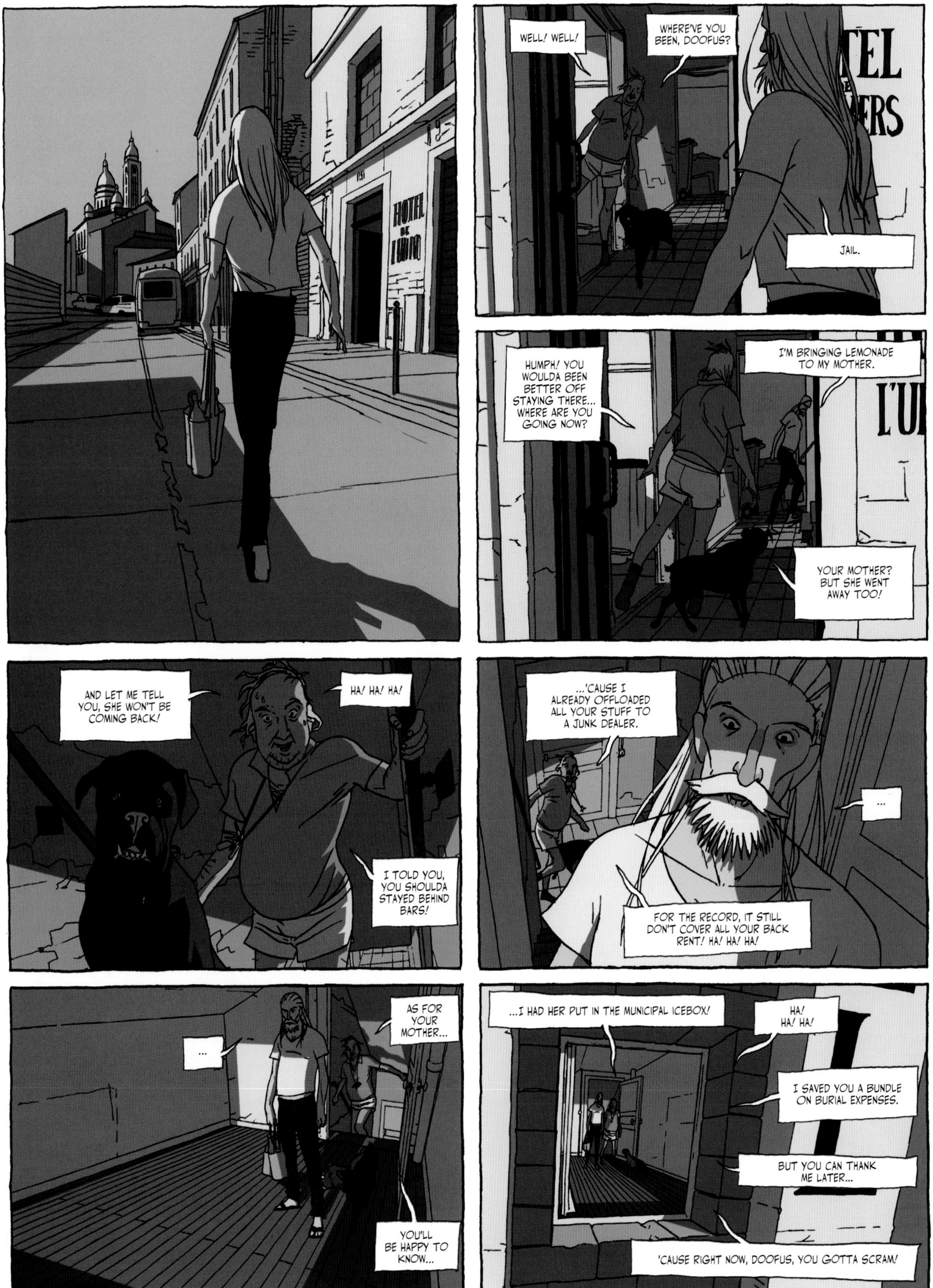
HOTEL DE L'UNION
WELL! WELL!
WHERE'VE YOU BEEN, DOOFUS?
JAIL.
HUMPH! YOU WOULDA BEEN BETTER OFF STAYING THERE... WHERE ARE YOU GOING NOW?
I'M BRINGING LEMONADE TO MY MOTHER.
YOUR MOTHER? BUT SHE WENT AWAY TOO!
AND LET ME TELL YOU, SHE WON'T BE COMING BACK!
HA! HA! HA!
I TOLD YOU, YOU SHOULDA STAYED BEHIND BARS!
...'CAUSE I ALREADY OFFLOADED ALL YOUR STUFF TO A JUNK DEALER.
...
FOR THE RECORD, IT STILL DON'T COVER ALL YOUR BACK RENT! HA! HA! HA!
...
AS FOR YOUR MOTHER...
YOU'LL BE HAPPY TO KNOW...
...I HAD HER PUT IN THE MUNICIPAL ICEBOX!
HA! HA! HA!
I SAVED YOU A BUNDLE ON BURIAL EXPENSES.
BUT YOU CAN THANK ME LATER...
'CAUSE RIGHT NOW, DOOFUS, YOU GOTTA SCRAM!

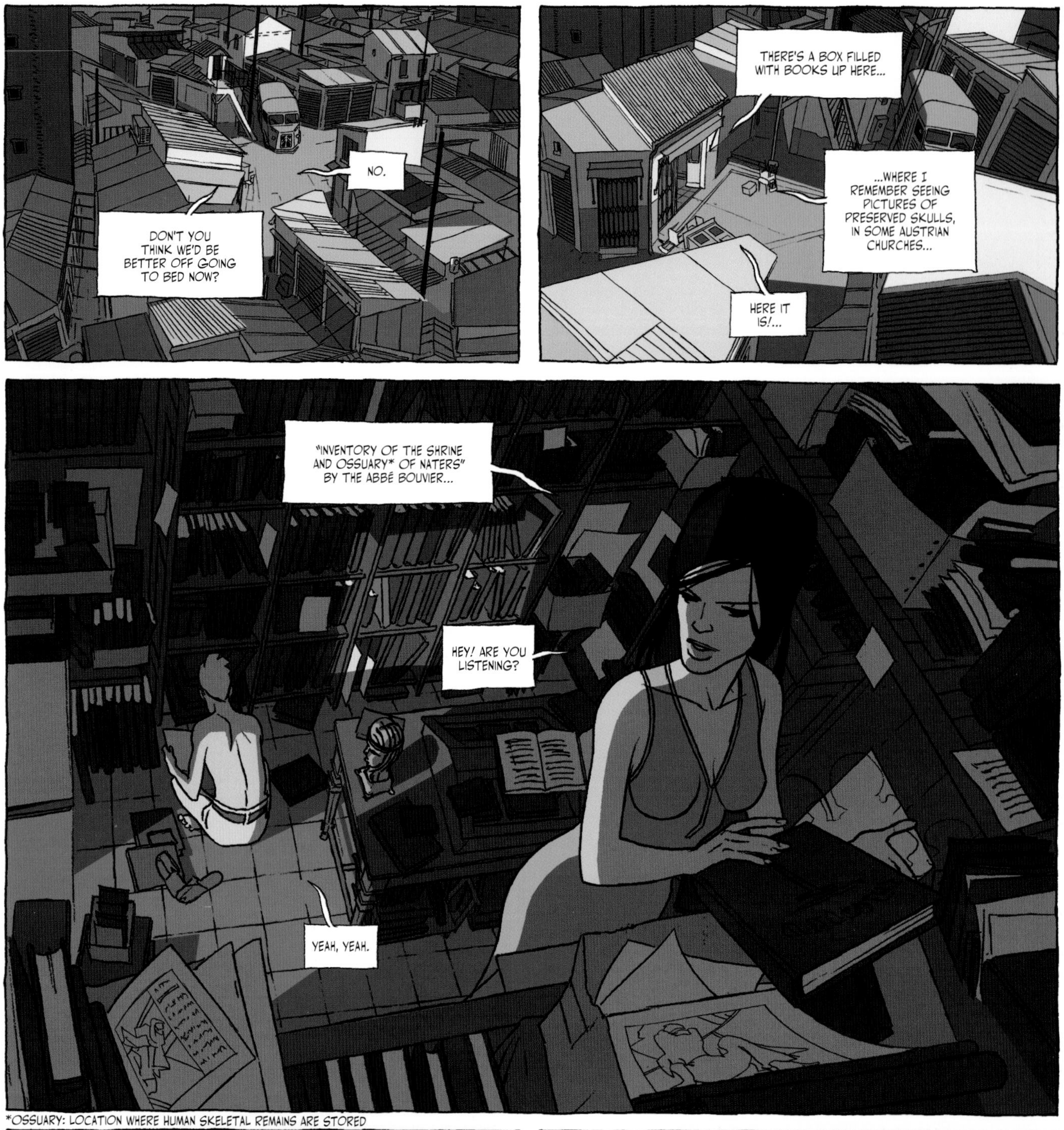
DON'T YOU THINK WE'D BE BETTER OFF GOING TO BED NOW?
NO.
THERE'S A BOX FILLED WITH BOOKS UP HERE...
...WHERE I REMEMBER SEEING PICTURES OF PRESERVED SKULLS, IN SOME AUSTRIAN CHURCHES...
HERE IT IS!...
"INVENTORY OF THE SHRINE AND OSSUARY* OF NATERS" BY THE ABBÉ BOUVIER...
HEY! ARE YOU LISTENING?
YEAH, YEAH.

*OSSUARY: LOCATION WHERE HUMAN SKELETAL REMAINS ARE STORED

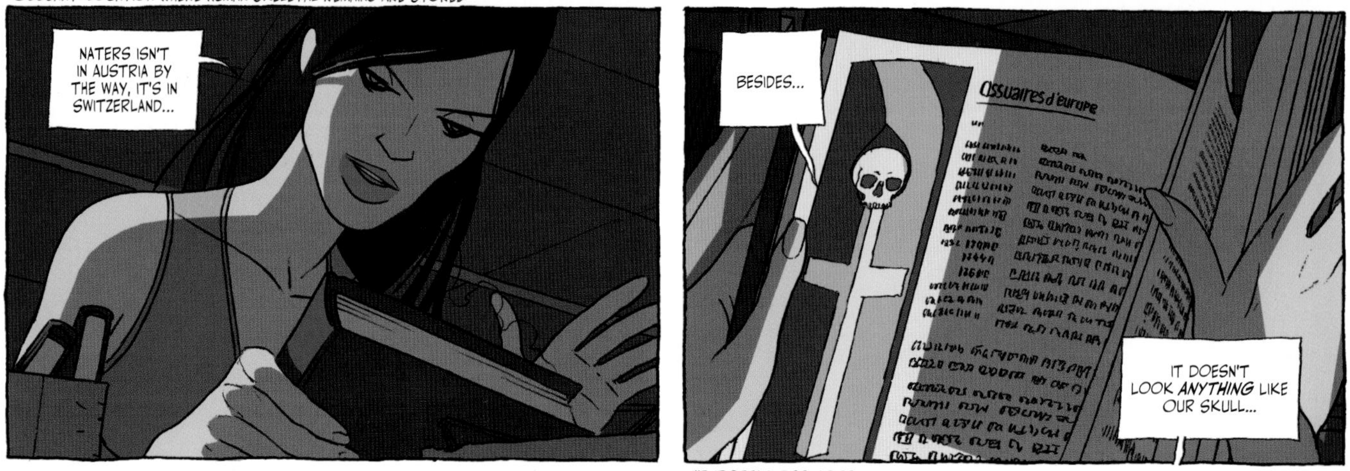
NATERS ISN'T IN AUSTRIA BY THE WAY, IT'S IN SWITZERLAND...
BESIDES...
Ossuaires d'europe
IT DOESN'T LOOK *ANYTHING* LIKE OUR SKULL...

*EUROPEAN OSSUARIES

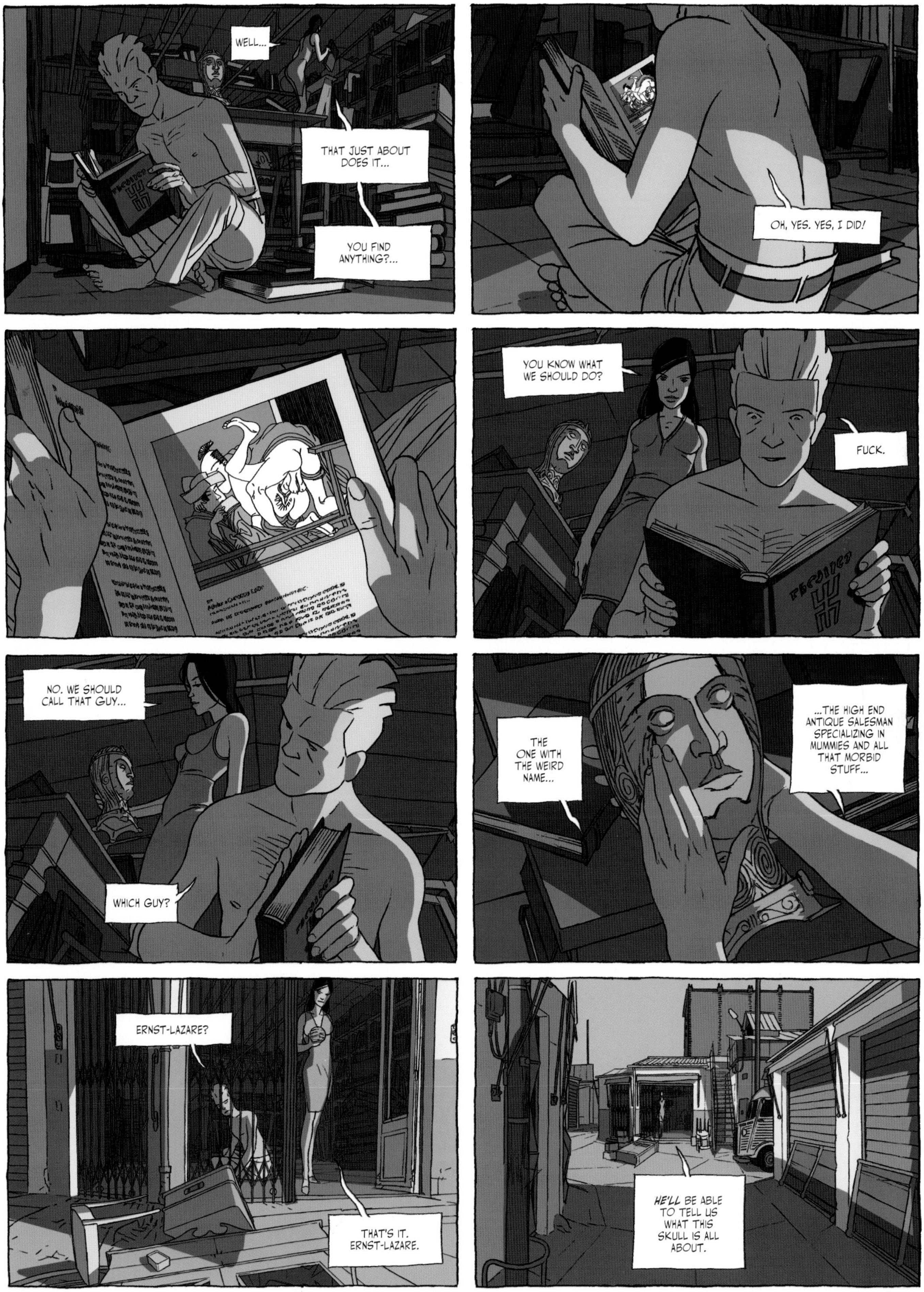
WELL...
THAT JUST ABOUT DOES IT...
YOU FIND ANYTHING?...
OH, YES. YES, I DID!
YOU KNOW WHAT WE SHOULD DO?
FUCK.
NO. WE SHOULD CALL THAT GUY...
WHICH GUY?
THE ONE WITH THE WEIRD NAME...
...THE HIGH END ANTIQUE SALESMAN SPECIALIZING IN MUMMIES AND ALL THAT MORBID STUFF...
ERNST-LAZARE?
THAT'S IT. ERNST-LAZARE.
HE'LL BE ABLE TO TELL US WHAT THIS SKULL IS ALL ABOUT.

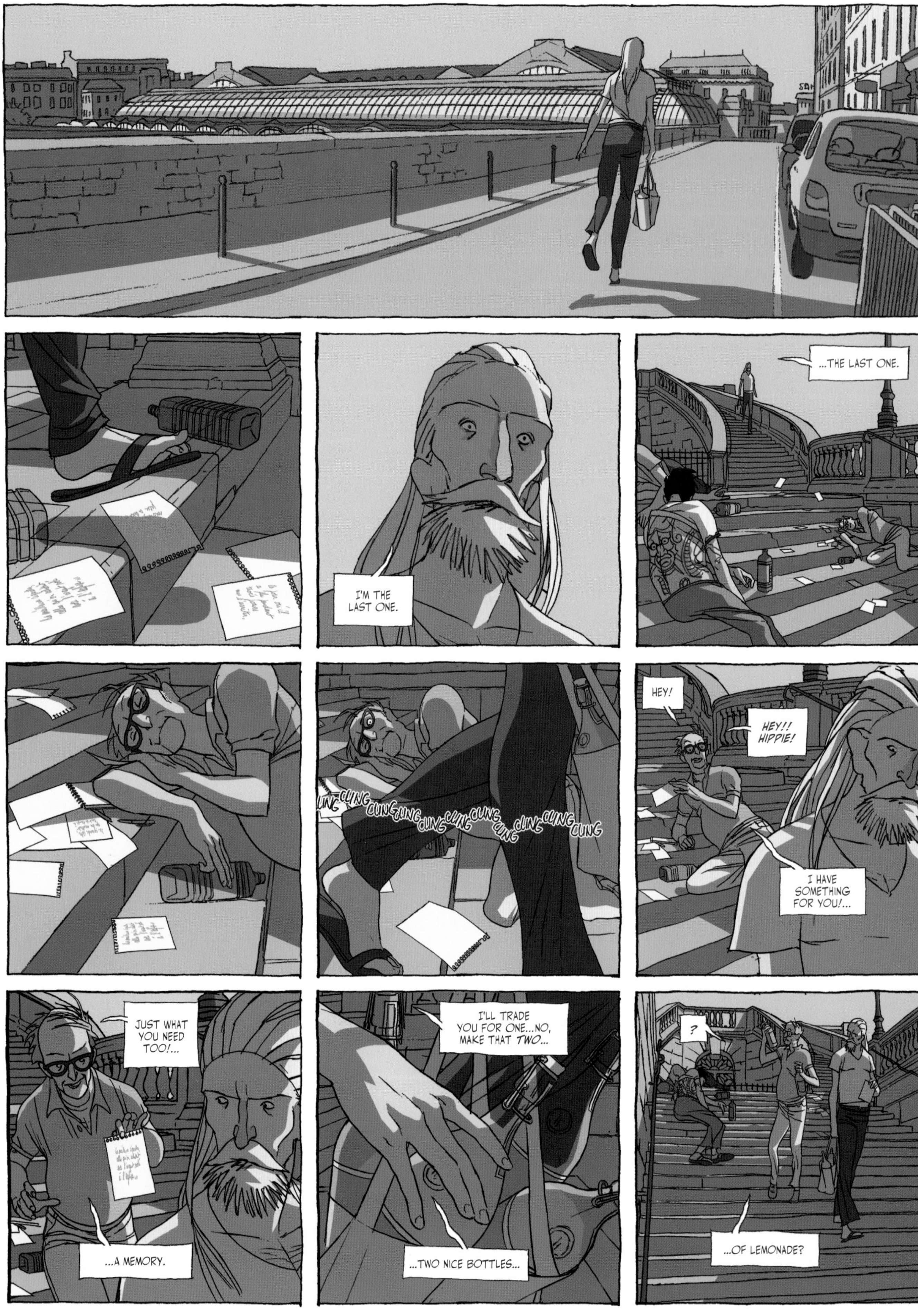
I'M THE LAST ONE.
...THE LAST ONE.
CLING CLING CLING CLING CLING CLING CLING CLING CLING CLING CLING CLING
HEY!
HEY!! HIPPIE!
I HAVE SOMETHING FOR YOU!...
JUST WHAT YOU NEED TOO!...
...A MEMORY.
I'LL TRADE YOU FOR ONE...NO, MAKE THAT TWO...
...TWO NICE BOTTLES...
?
...OF LEMONADE?

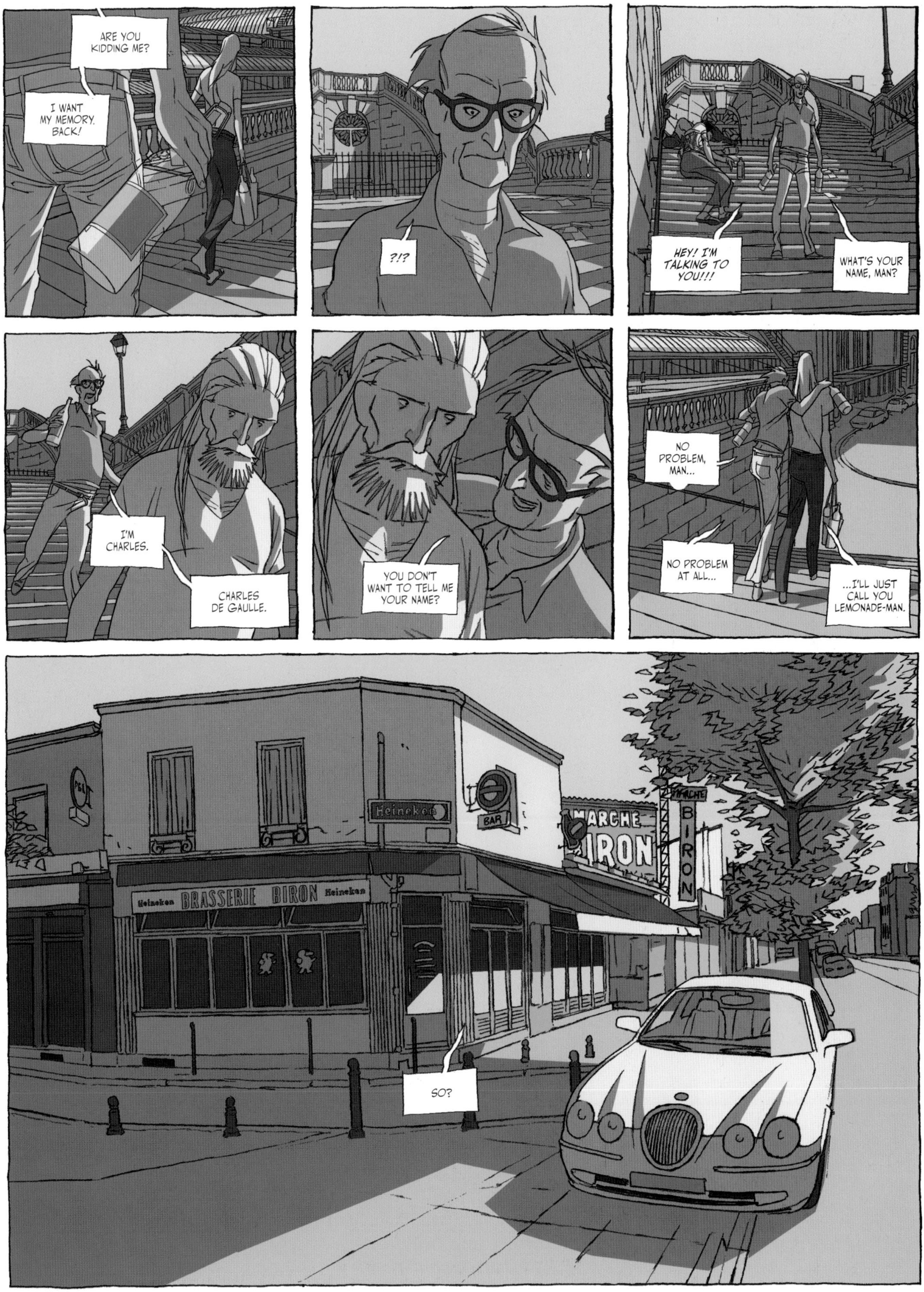
ARE YOU KIDDING ME?
I WANT MY MEMORY. BACK!
?!?
HEY! I'M TALKING TO YOU!!!
WHAT'S YOUR NAME, MAN?
I'M CHARLES.
CHARLES DE GAULLE.
YOU DON'T WANT TO TELL ME YOUR NAME?
NO PROBLEM, MAN...
NO PROBLEM AT ALL...
...I'LL JUST CALL YOU LEMONADE-MAN.
Heineken
BAR
MARCHE BIRON
BIRON
Heineken BRASSERIE BIRON Heineken
SO?

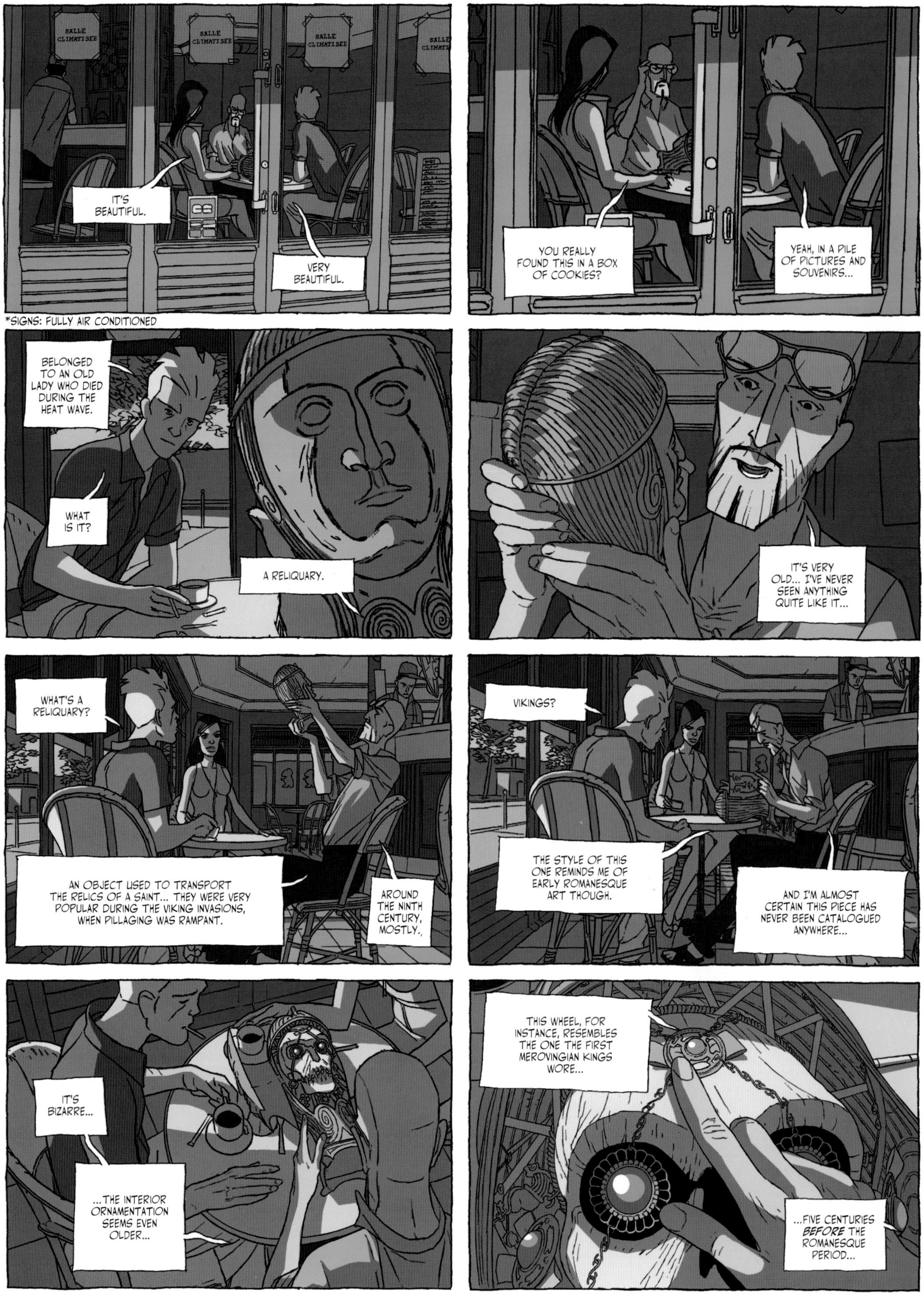
SALLE CLIMATISEE
SALLE CLIMATISEE
SALLE CLIMATISEE
IT'S BEAUTIFUL.
VERY BEAUTIFUL.
YOU REALLY FOUND THIS IN A BOX OF COOKIES?
YEAH, IN A PILE OF PICTURES AND SOUVENIRS...
*SIGNS: FULLY AIR CONDITIONED
BELONGED TO AN OLD LADY WHO DIED DURING THE HEAT WAVE.
WHAT IS IT?
A RELIQUARY.
IT'S VERY OLD... I'VE NEVER SEEN ANYTHING QUITE LIKE IT...
WHAT'S A RELIQUARY?
AN OBJECT USED TO TRANSPORT THE RELICS OF A SAINT... THEY WERE VERY POPULAR DURING THE VIKING INVASIONS, WHEN PILLAGING WAS RAMPANT.
AROUND THE NINTH CENTURY, MOSTLY.
VIKINGS?
THE STYLE OF THIS ONE REMINDS ME OF EARLY ROMANESQUE ART THOUGH.
AND I'M ALMOST CERTAIN THIS PIECE HAS NEVER BEEN CATALOGUED ANYWHERE...
IT'S BIZARRE...
...THE INTERIOR ORNAMENTATION SEEMS EVEN OLDER...
THIS WHEEL, FOR INSTANCE, RESEMBLES THE ONE THE FIRST MEROVINGIAN KINGS WORE...
...FIVE CENTURIES *BEFORE* THE ROMANESQUE PERIOD...

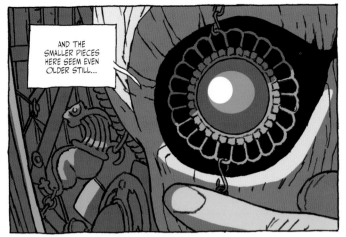

AND THE SMALLER PIECES HERE SEEM EVEN OLDER STILL...

BUT, WHAT'S MOST INTRIGUING...

...IS THE *SHAPE* OF THE SKULL...

I'M NOT SURE...

WHAT ABOUT IT?

...I'LL NEED TO CONDUCT SOME RESEARCH. CAN YOU LEAVE IT WITH ME?

AND HOW DO WE KNOW YOU'RE NOT TRYING TO SWINDLE US?

YOU DON'T.

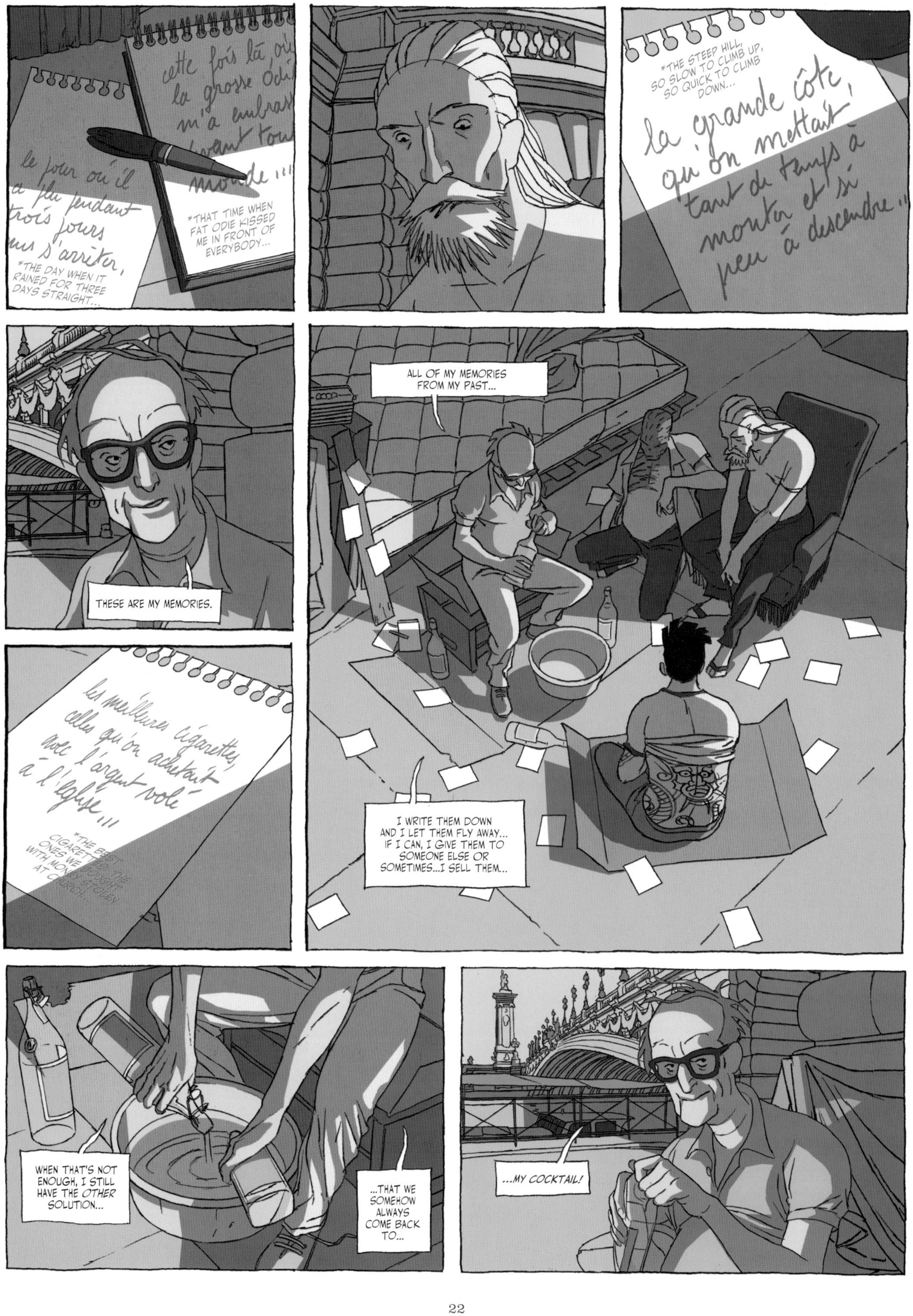
*THAT TIME WHEN FAT ODIE KISSED ME IN FRONT OF EVERYBODY...
*THE DAY WHEN IT RAINED FOR THREE DAYS STRAIGHT...
la grande côte qu'on mettait tant de temps à monter et si peu à descendre...
*THE STEEP HILL, SO SLOW TO CLIMB UP, SO QUICK TO CLIMB DOWN...
THESE ARE MY MEMORIES.
ALL OF MY MEMORIES FROM MY PAST...
I WRITE THEM DOWN AND I LET THEM FLY AWAY... IF I CAN, I GIVE THEM TO SOMEONE ELSE OR SOMETIMES...I SELL THEM...
les meilleures cigarettes, celles qu'on achetait avec l'argent volé à l'église...
*THE BEST CIGARETTES, THE ONES WE BOUGHT WITH MONEY STOLEN AT CHURCH...
WHEN THAT'S NOT ENOUGH, I STILL HAVE THE *OTHER* SOLUTION...
...THAT WE SOMEHOW ALWAYS COME BACK TO...
...MY COCKTAIL!

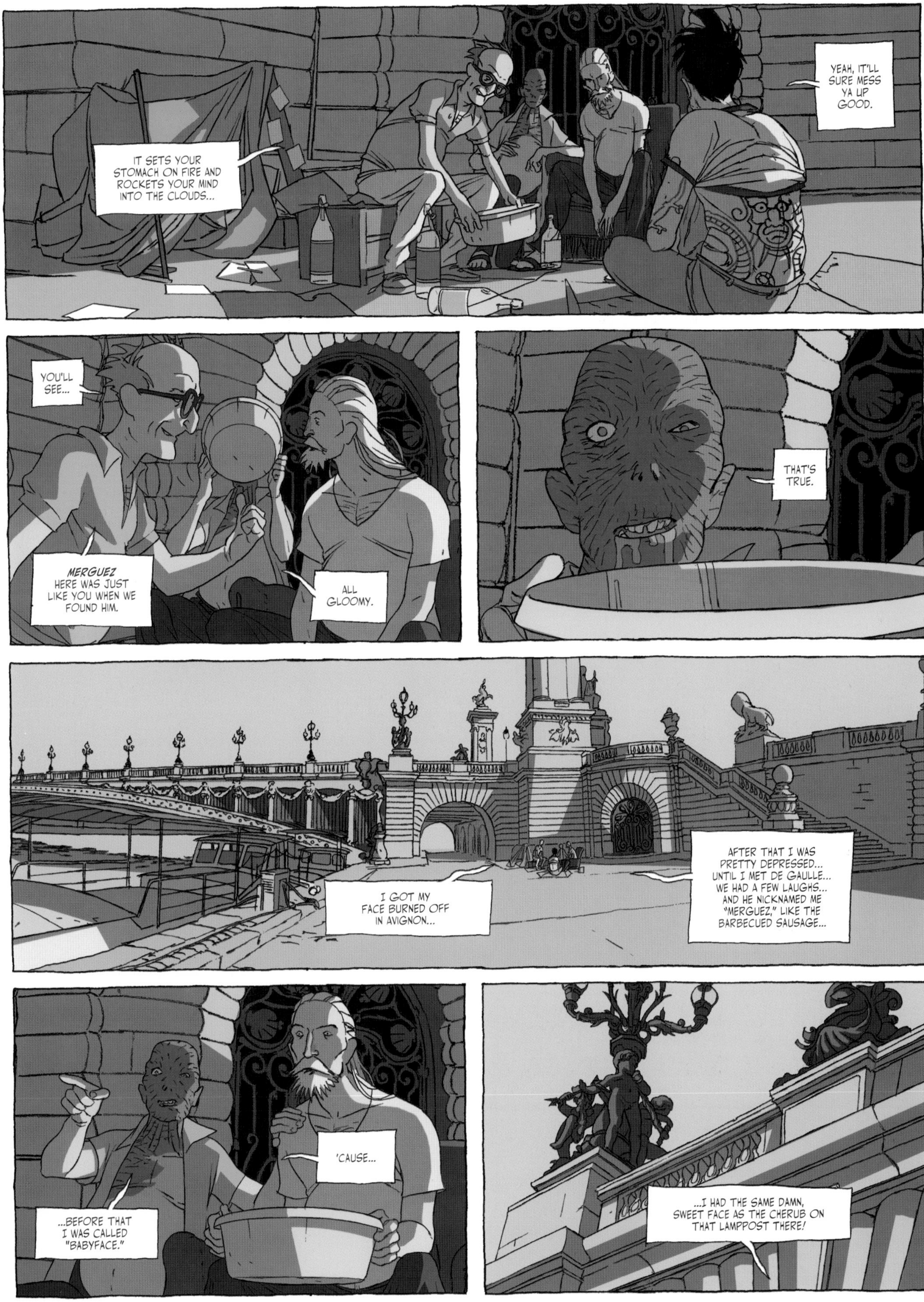
IT SETS YOUR STOMACH ON FIRE AND ROCKETS YOUR MIND INTO THE CLOUDS...
YEAH, IT'LL SURE MESS YA UP GOOD.
YOU'LL SEE...
MERGUEZ HERE WAS JUST LIKE YOU WHEN WE FOUND HIM.
ALL GLOOMY.
THAT'S TRUE.
I GOT MY FACE BURNED OFF IN AVIGNON...
AFTER THAT I WAS PRETTY DEPRESSED... UNTIL I MET DE GAULLE... WE HAD A FEW LAUGHS... AND HE NICKNAMED ME "MERGUEZ," LIKE THE BARBECUED SAUSAGE...
'CAUSE...
...BEFORE THAT I WAS CALLED "BABYFACE."
...I HAD THE SAME DAMN, SWEET FACE AS THE CHERUB ON THAT LAMPPOST THERE!

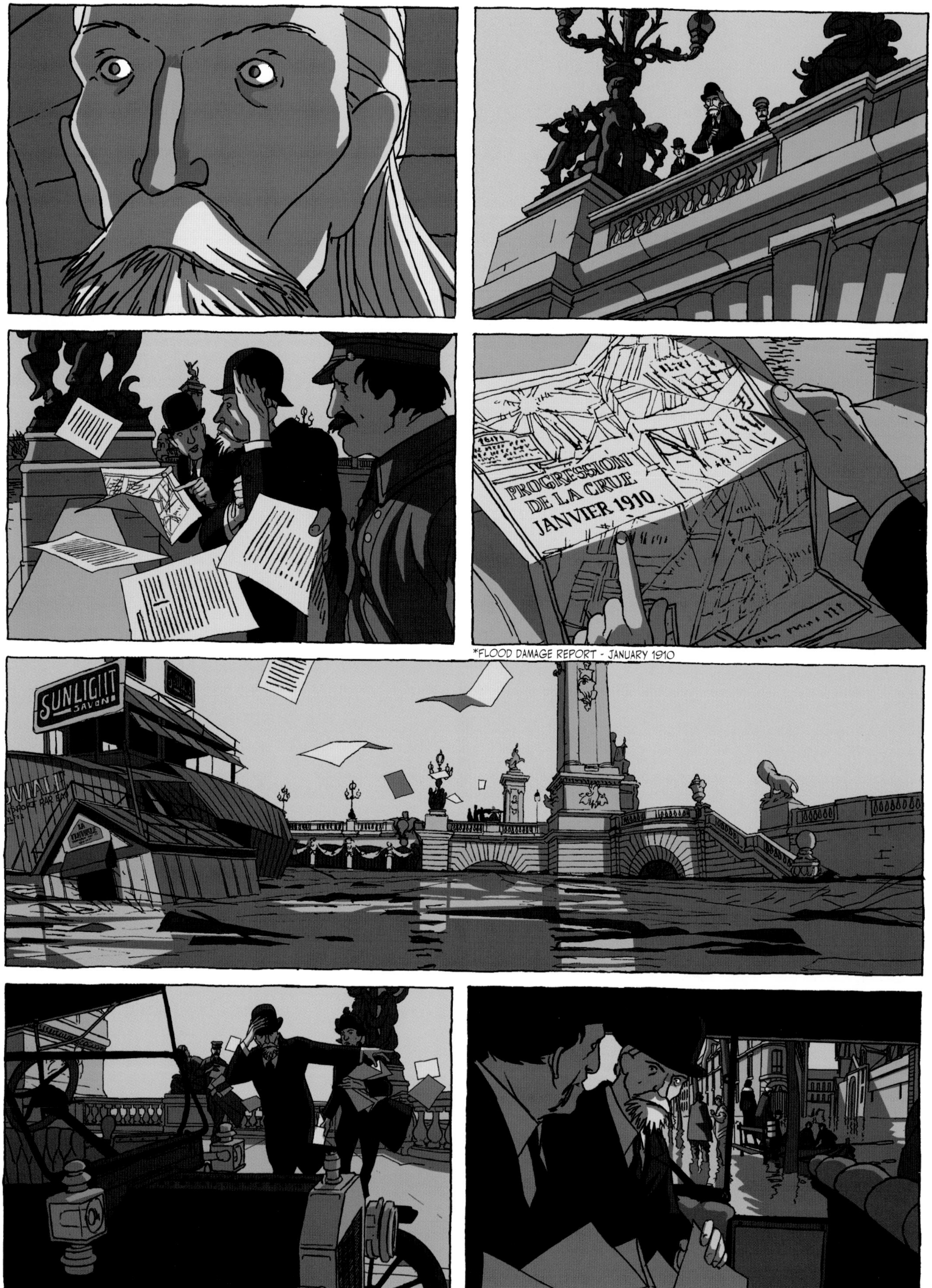
PROGRESSION DE LA CRUE JANVIER 1910
*FLOOD DAMAGE REPORT - JANUARY 1910
SUNLIGHT SAVON

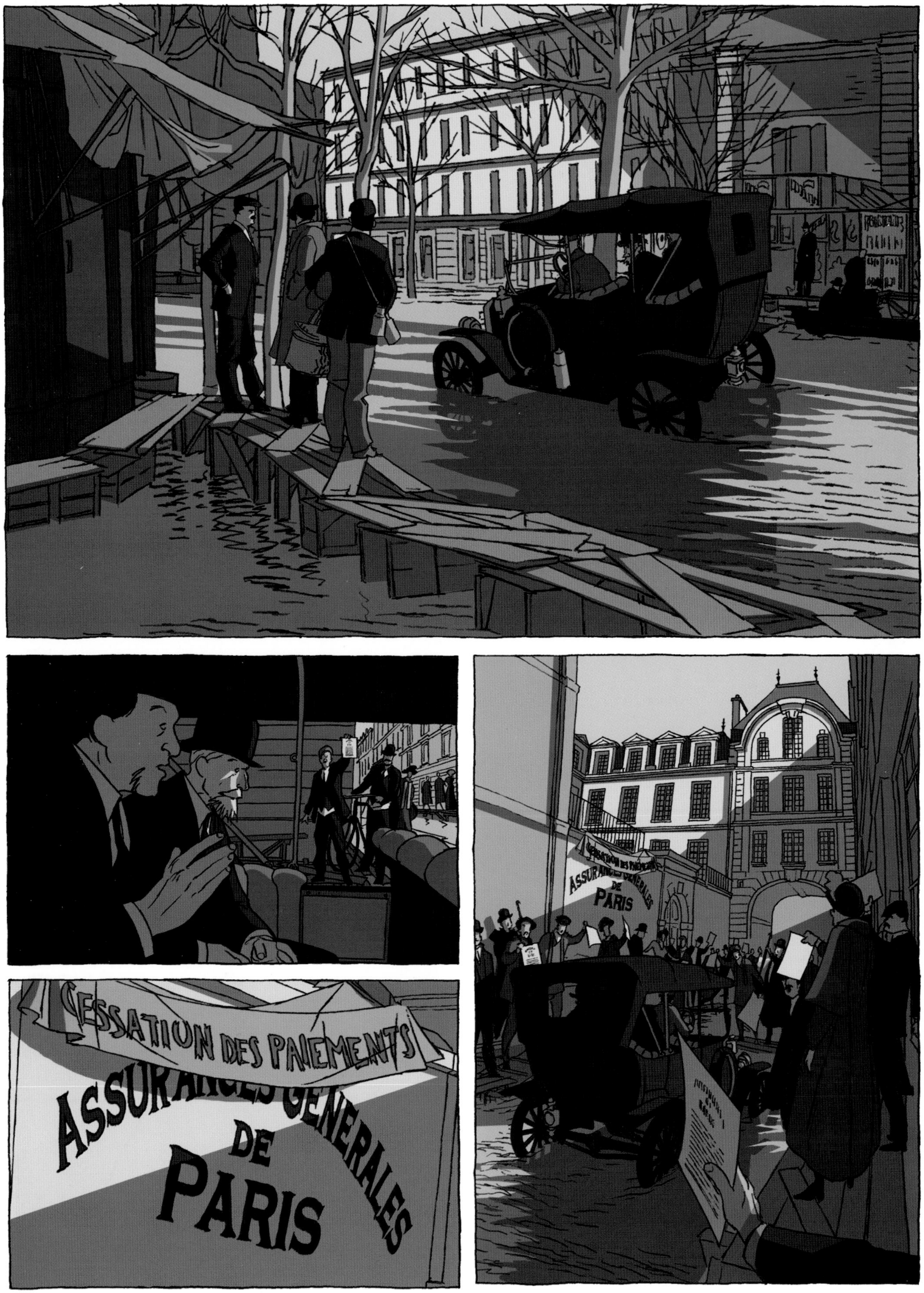
CESSATION DES PAIEMENTS
ASSURANCES GENERALES DE PARIS
CESSATION DES PAIEMENTS
ASSURANCES GENERALES
DE
PARIS

*BANNER: SUSPENSION OF PAYMENT OF BENEFITS / BUSINESS SIGN: GENERAL INSURANCE OF PARIS

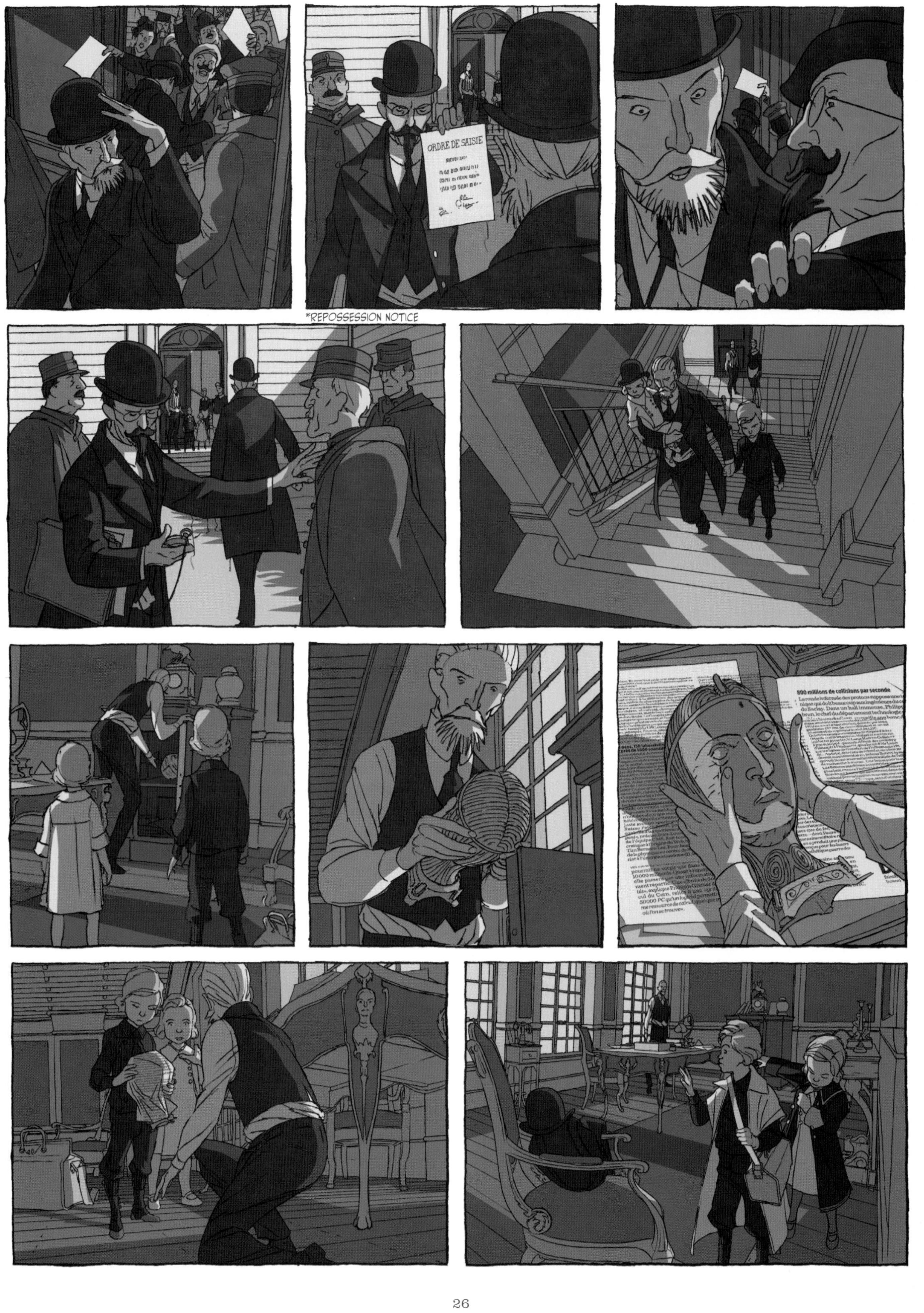
ORDRE DE SAISIE
*REPOSSESSION NOTICE
800 millions de collisions par seconde

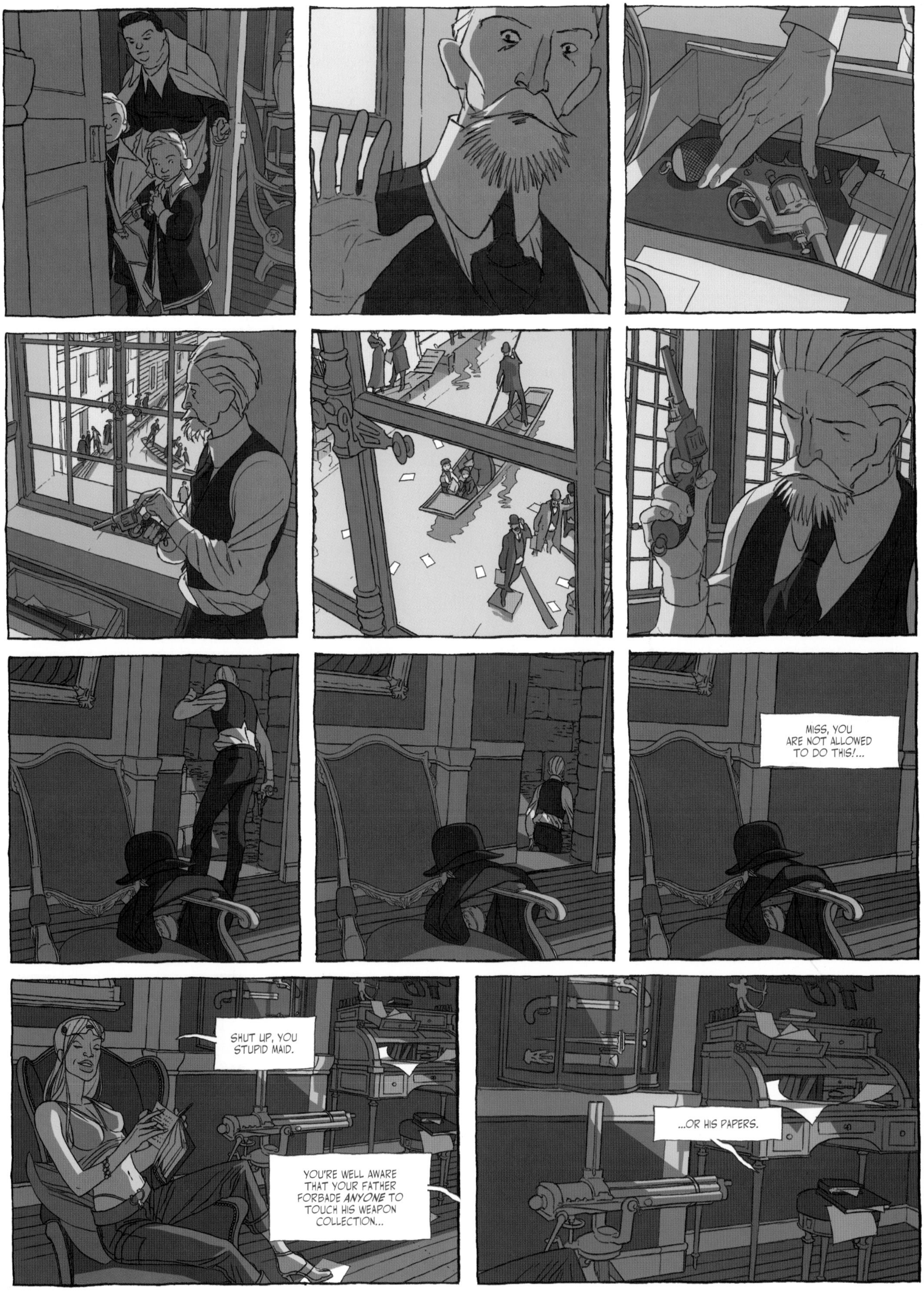
MISS, YOU ARE NOT ALLOWED TO DO THIS!...
SHUT UP, YOU STUPID MAID.
YOU'RE WELL AWARE THAT YOUR FATHER FORBADE *ANYONE* TO TOUCH HIS WEAPON COLLECTION...
...OR HIS PAPERS.

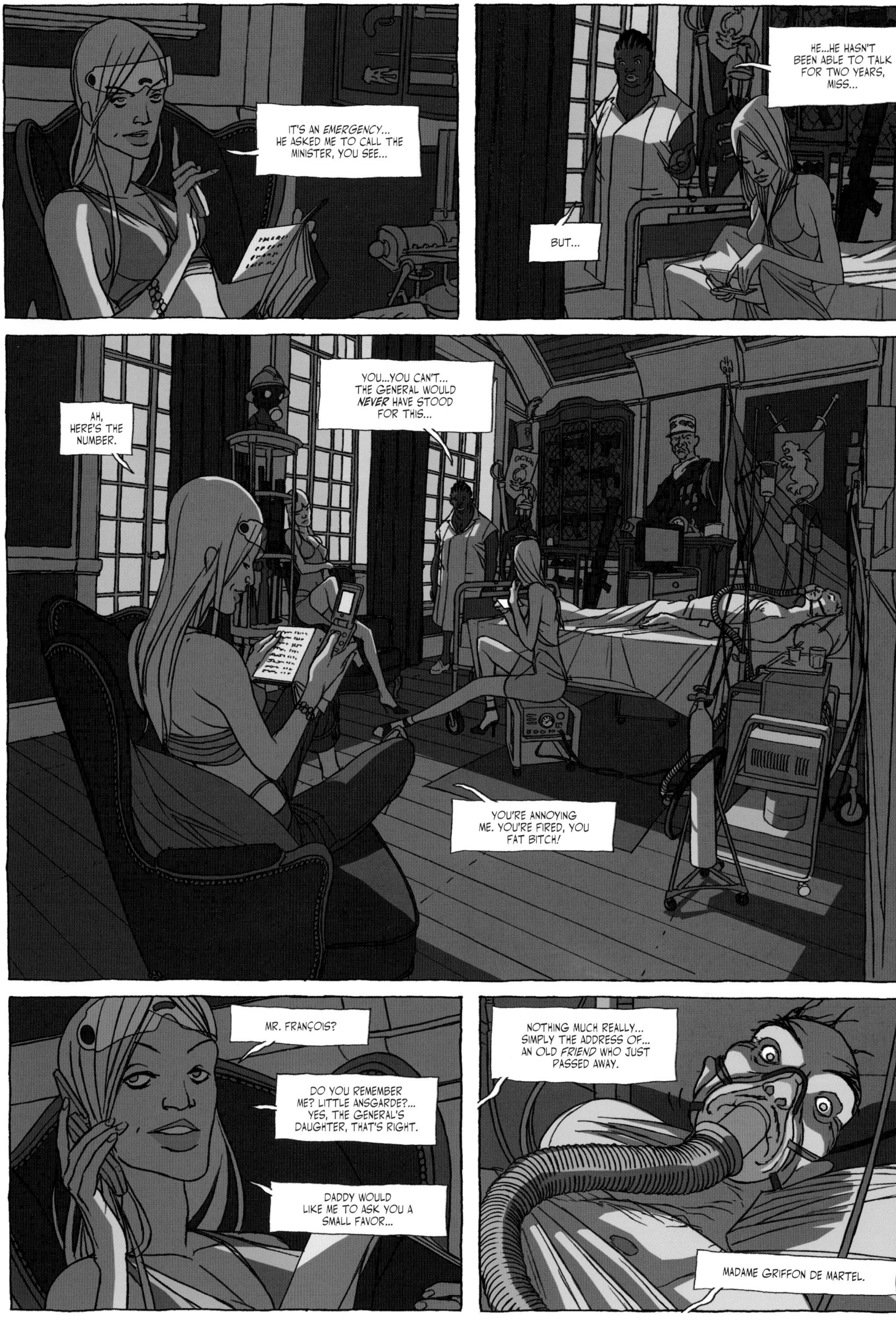
IT'S AN *EMERGENCY*... HE ASKED ME TO CALL THE MINISTER, YOU SEE...
BUT...
HE...HE HASN'T BEEN ABLE TO TALK FOR TWO YEARS, MISS...
AH, HERE'S THE NUMBER.
YOU...YOU CAN'T... THE GENERAL WOULD ***NEVER*** HAVE STOOD FOR THIS...
YOU'RE ANNOYING ME. YOU'RE FIRED, YOU FAT BITCH!
MR. FRANÇOIS?
DO YOU REMEMBER ME? LITTLE ANSGARDE?... YES, THE GENERAL'S DAUGHTER, THAT'S RIGHT.
DADDY WOULD LIKE ME TO ASK YOU A SMALL FAVOR...
NOTHING MUCH REALLY... SIMPLY THE ADDRESS OF... AN OLD *FRIEND* WHO JUST PASSED AWAY.
MADAME GRIFFON DE MARTEL.

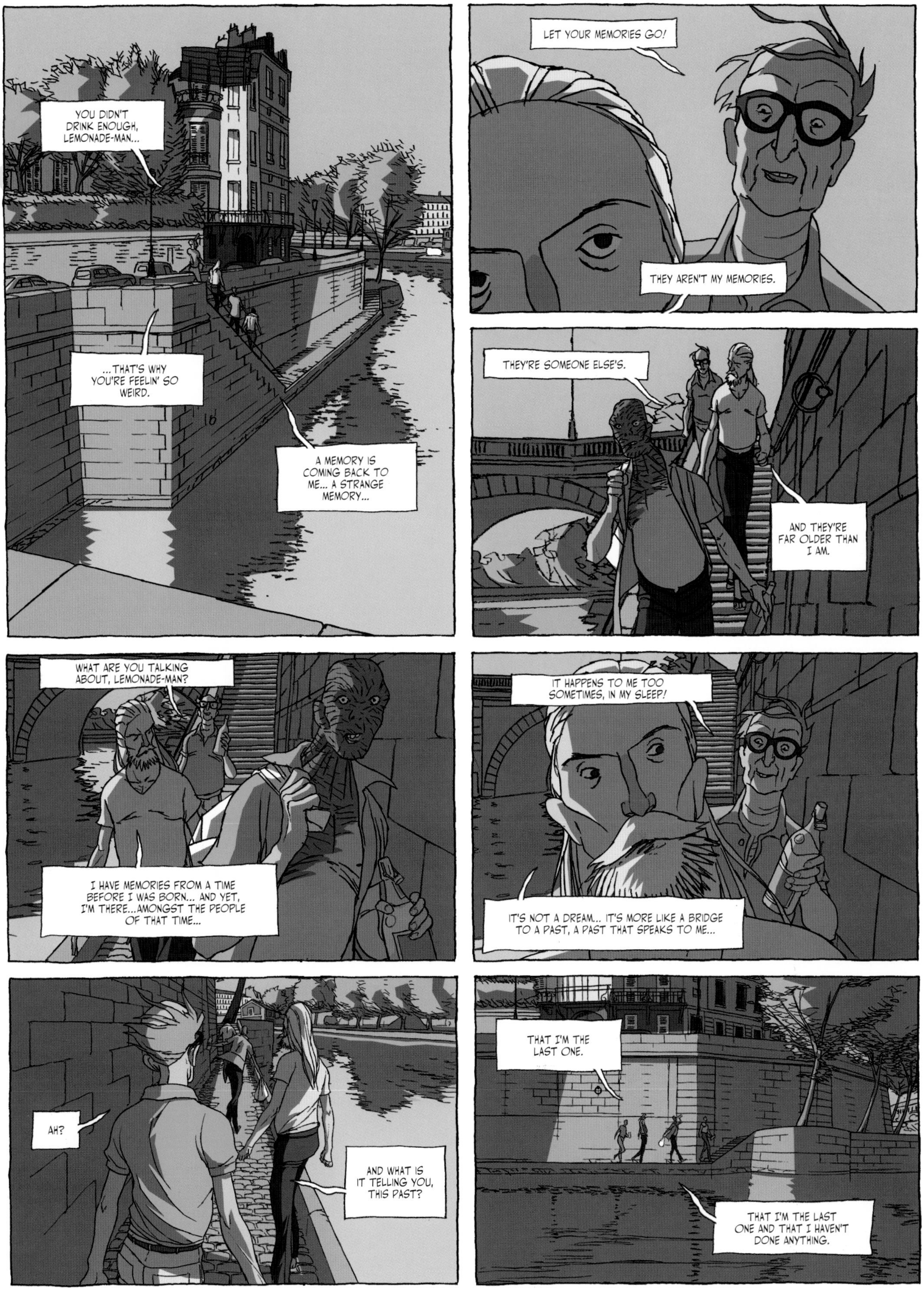
YOU DIDN'T DRINK ENOUGH, LEMONADE-MAN...
...THAT'S WHY YOU'RE FEELIN' SO WEIRD.
A MEMORY IS COMING BACK TO ME... A STRANGE MEMORY...
LET YOUR MEMORIES GO!
THEY AREN'T MY MEMORIES.
THEY'RE SOMEONE ELSE'S.
AND THEY'RE FAR OLDER THAN I AM.
WHAT ARE YOU TALKING ABOUT, LEMONADE-MAN?
I HAVE MEMORIES FROM A TIME BEFORE I WAS BORN... AND YET, I'M THERE...AMONGST THE PEOPLE OF THAT TIME...
IT HAPPENS TO ME TOO SOMETIMES, IN MY SLEEP!
IT'S NOT A DREAM... IT'S MORE LIKE A BRIDGE TO A PAST, A PAST THAT SPEAKS TO ME...
AH?
AND WHAT IS IT TELLING YOU, THIS PAST?
THAT I'M THE LAST ONE.
THAT I'M THE LAST ONE AND THAT I HAVEN'T DONE ANYTHING.

I WONDER IF WE FUCKED UP.

WHAT? BY LEAVING THE RELIQUARY TO ERNST-LAZARE?

I THINK HE'S HONEST.

YEAH. THE GUY MIGHT BE PAWNING IT OFF TO A COLLECTOR AS WE SPEAK.

WHY'S THAT?

WHEN I ASKED HIM "HOW DO WE KNOW YOU'RE NOT TRYING TO SWINDLE US?" HE ANSWERED "YOU DON'T."

SO WHAT?

IT'S AN HONEST ANSWER.

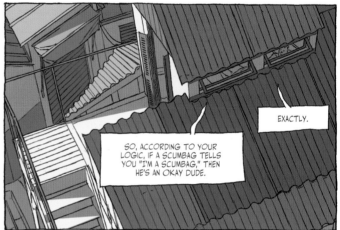

SO, ACCORDING TO YOUR LOGIC, IF A SCUMBAG TELLS YOU "I'M A SCUMBAG," THEN HE'S AN OKAY DUDE.

EXACTLY.

I CALL BULLSHIT.

BOM BOM BOM

WHO'S THAT?

HOW WOULD I KNOW? GO CHECK!

OKAY!...OKAY!

BOM BOM BOM

I'M COMING!

IT'S ABOUT TIME!

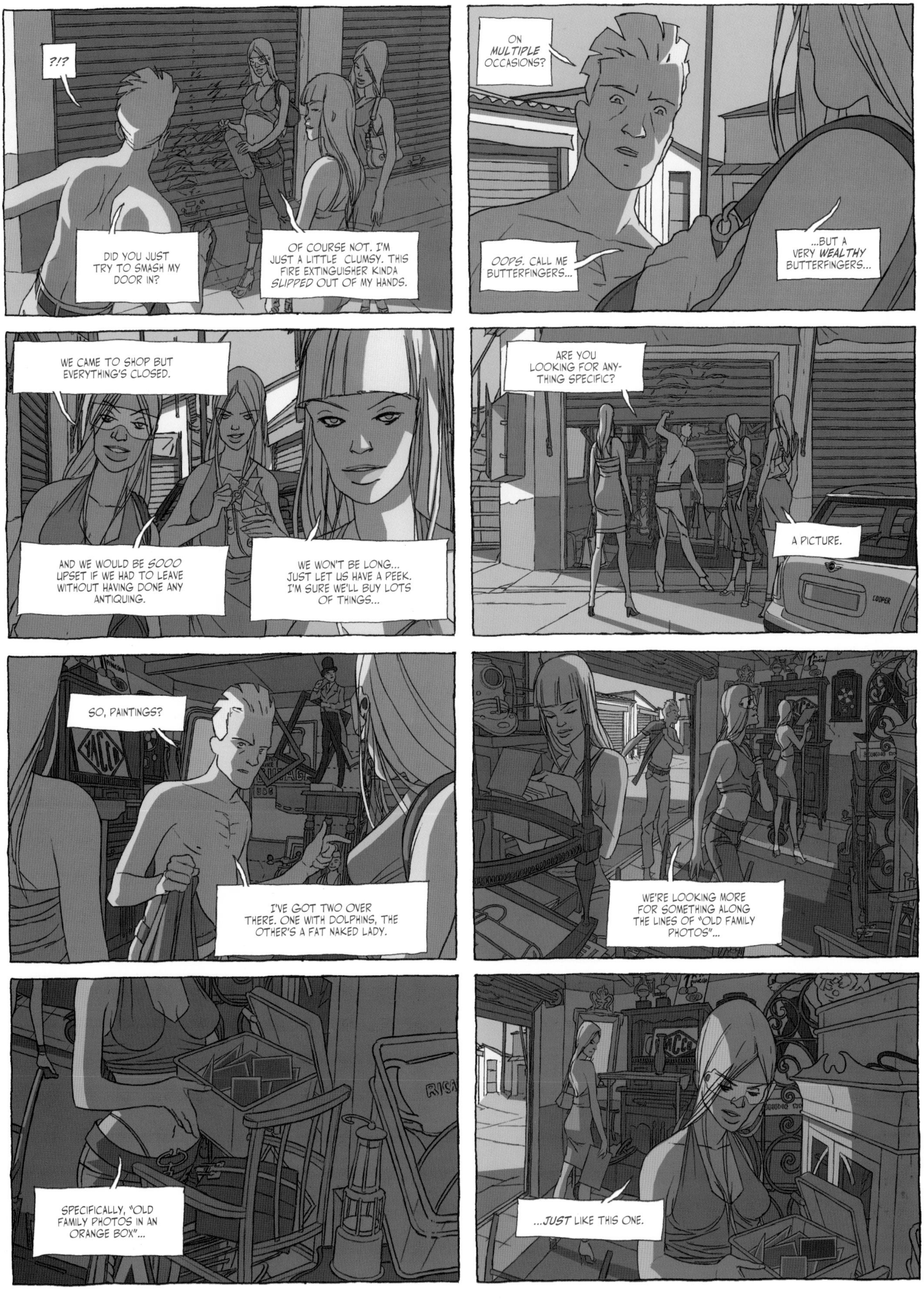
?!?
DID YOU JUST TRY TO SMASH MY DOOR IN?
OF COURSE NOT. I'M JUST A LITTLE CLUMSY. THIS FIRE EXTINGUISHER KINDA SLIPPED OUT OF MY HANDS.
ON MULTIPLE OCCASIONS?
OOPS. CALL ME BUTTERFINGERS...
...BUT A VERY WEALTHY BUTTERFINGERS...
WE CAME TO SHOP BUT EVERYTHING'S CLOSED.
AND WE WOULD BE SOOO UPSET IF WE HAD TO LEAVE WITHOUT HAVING DONE ANY ANTIQUING.
WE WON'T BE LONG... JUST LET US HAVE A PEEK. I'M SURE WE'LL BUY LOTS OF THINGS...
ARE YOU LOOKING FOR ANYTHING SPECIFIC?
A PICTURE.
SO, PAINTINGS?
I'VE GOT TWO OVER THERE. ONE WITH DOLPHINS, THE OTHER'S A FAT NAKED LADY.
WE'RE LOOKING MORE FOR SOMETHING ALONG THE LINES OF "OLD FAMILY PHOTOS"...
SPECIFICALLY, "OLD FAMILY PHOTOS IN AN ORANGE BOX"...
...JUST LIKE THIS ONE.

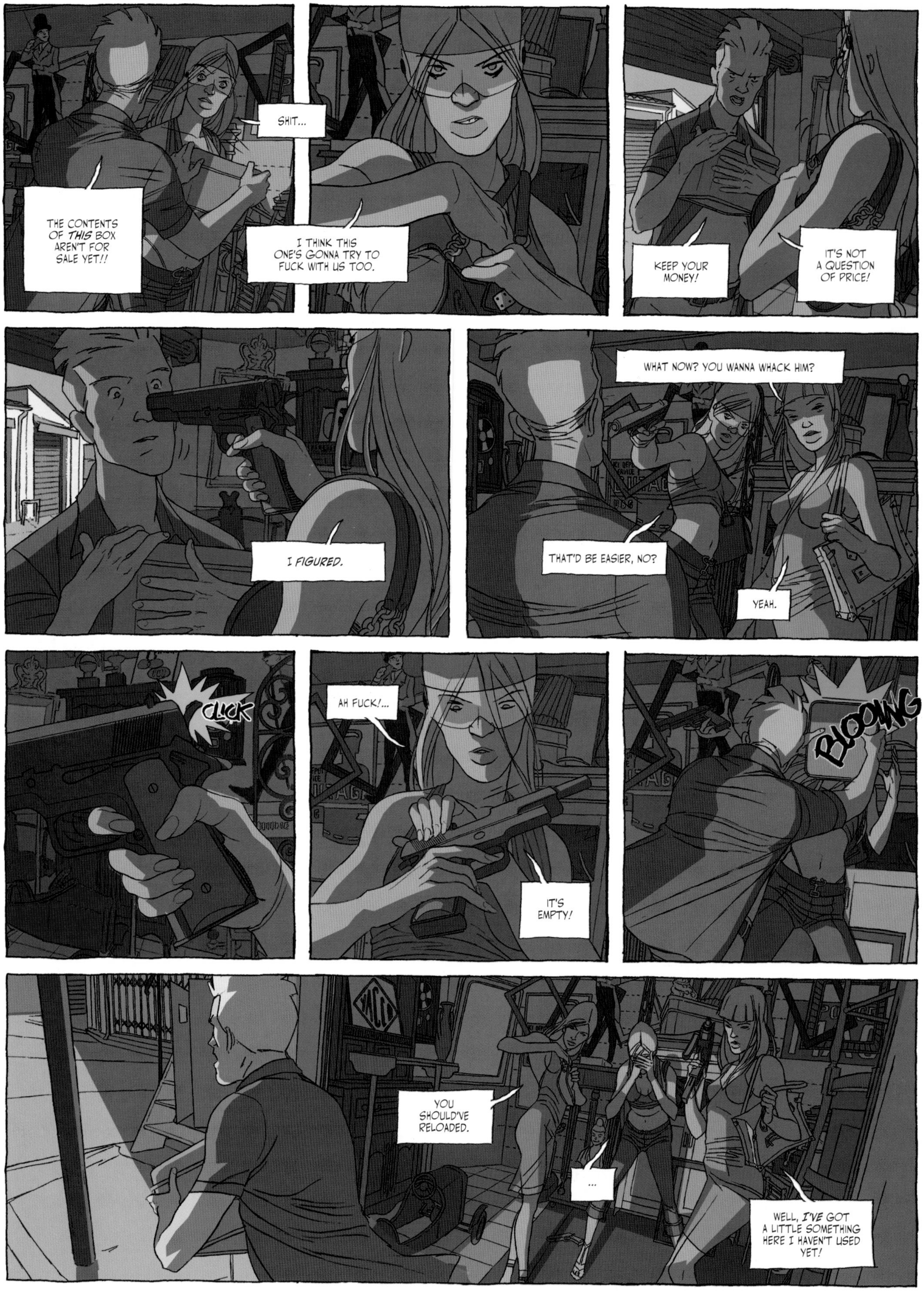
SHIT...
THE CONTENTS OF *THIS* BOX AREN'T FOR SALE YET!!
I THINK THIS ONE'S GONNA TRY TO FUCK WITH US TOO.
KEEP YOUR MONEY!
IT'S NOT A QUESTION OF PRICE!
I *FIGURED.*
WHAT NOW? YOU WANNA WHACK HIM?
THAT'D BE EASIER, NO?
YEAH.
CLICK
AH FUCK!...
IT'S EMPTY!
BLOOWNG
YOU SHOULD'VE RELOADED.
...
WELL, *I'VE* GOT A LITTLE SOMETHING HERE I HAVEN'T USED YET!

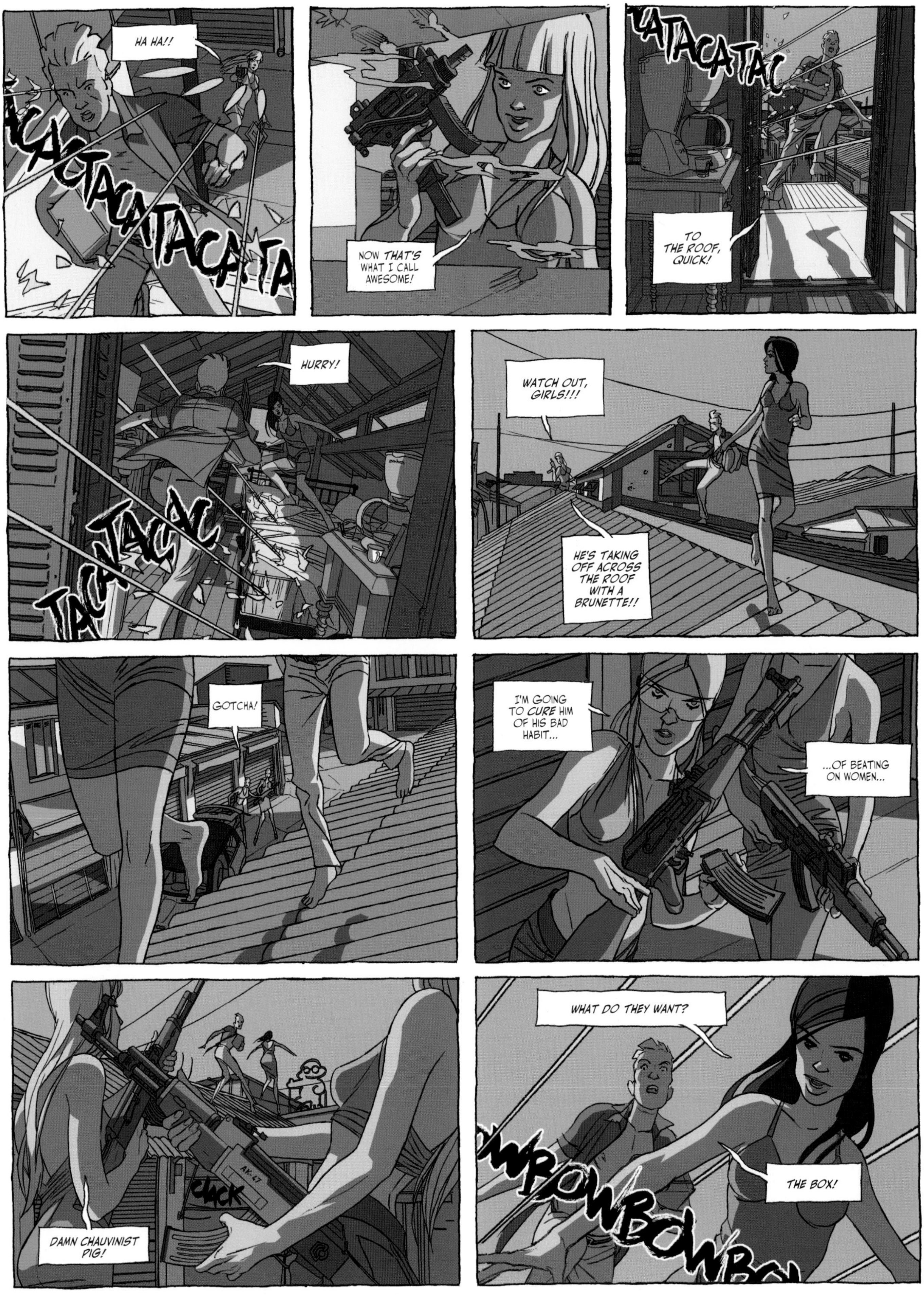
HA HA!!
TACATACATACATACA-TA
NOW THAT'S WHAT I CALL AWESOME!
TATACATAC
TO THE ROOF, QUICK!
HURRY!
TACATACATAC
WATCH OUT, GIRLS!!!
HE'S TAKING OFF ACROSS THE ROOF WITH A BRUNETTE!!
GOTCHA!
I'M GOING TO CURE HIM OF HIS BAD HABIT...
...OF BEATING ON WOMEN...
AK-47
CLACK
DAMN CHAUVINIST PIG!
WHAT DO THEY WANT?
THE BOX!

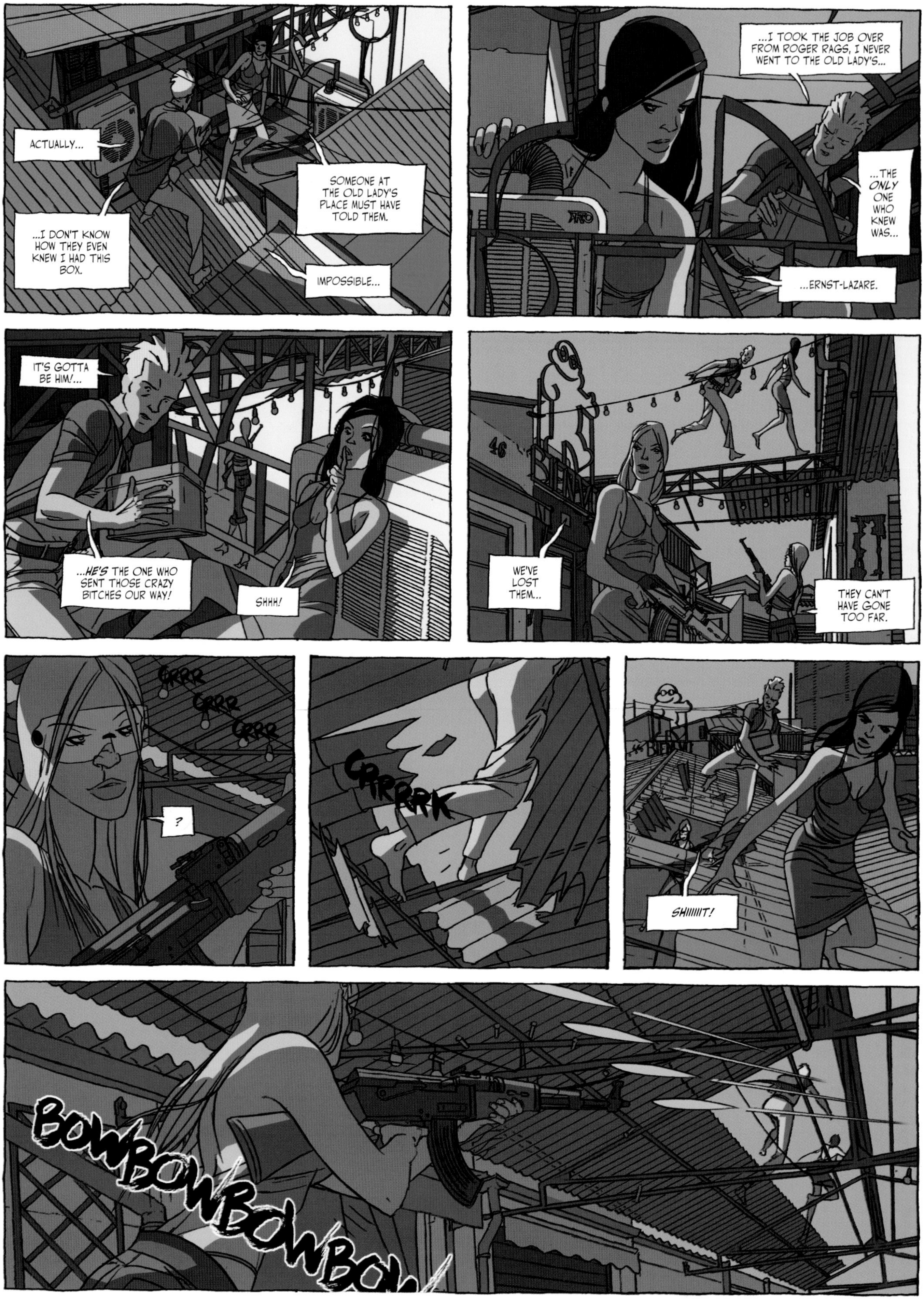
ACTUALLY...
...I DON'T KNOW HOW THEY EVEN KNEW I HAD THIS BOX.
SOMEONE AT THE OLD LADY'S PLACE MUST HAVE TOLD THEM.
IMPOSSIBLE...
...I TOOK THE JOB OVER FROM ROGER RAGS, I NEVER WENT TO THE OLD LADY'S...
...THE ONLY ONE WHO KNEW WAS...
...ERNST-LAZARE.
IT'S GOTTA BE HIM!...
...HE'S THE ONE WHO SENT THOSE CRAZY BITCHES OUR WAY!
SHHH!
WE'VE LOST THEM...
THEY CAN'T HAVE GONE TOO FAR.
GRRR GRRR GRRR
?
CRRRRK
SHIIIIIT!
BOWBOWBOWBOWBOW!

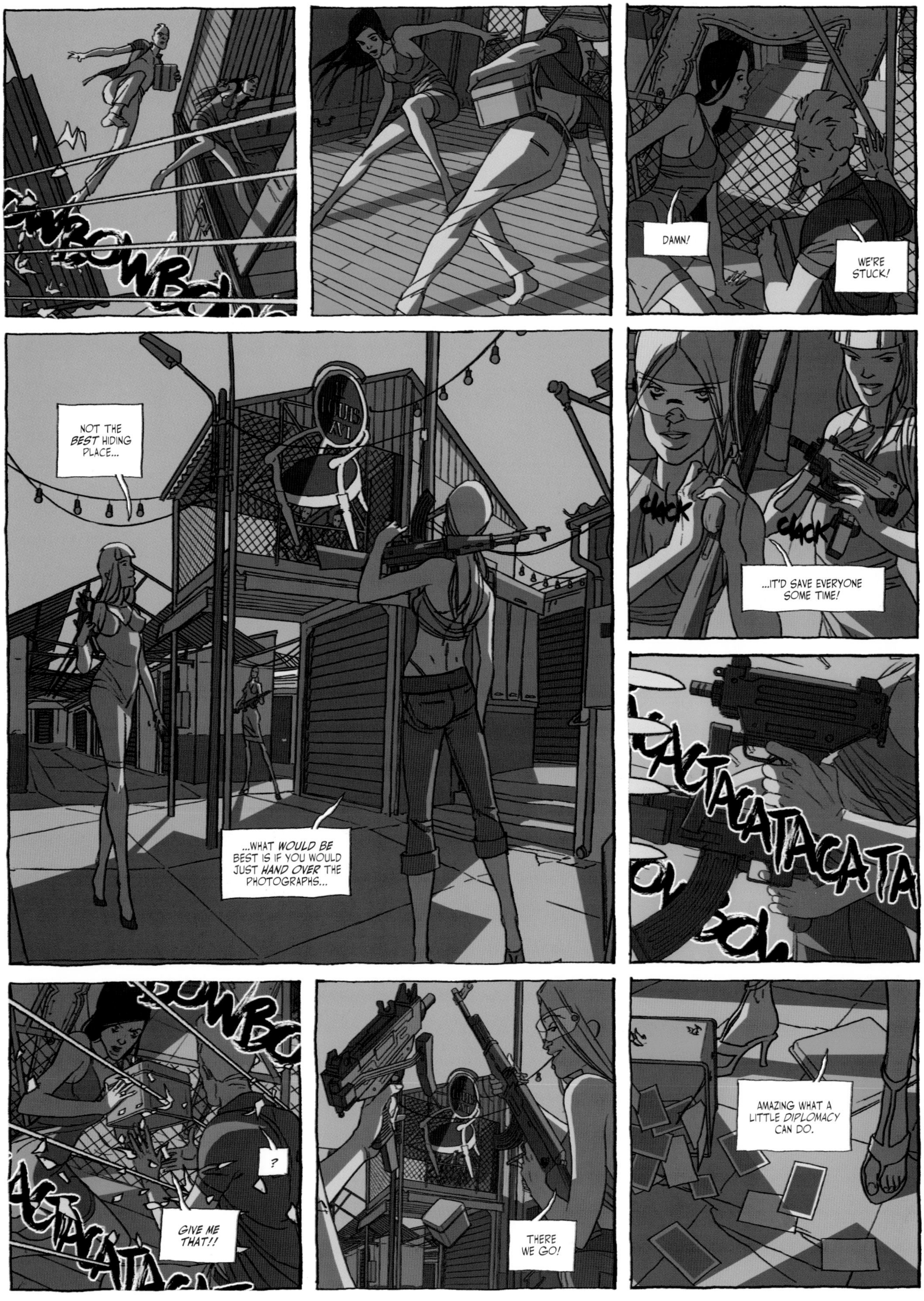
DAMN!
WE'RE STUCK!
NOT THE BEST HIDING PLACE...
...WHAT WOULD BE BEST IS IF YOU WOULD JUST HAND OVER THE PHOTOGRAPHS...
CLACK
CLACK
...IT'D SAVE EVERYONE SOME TIME!
?
GIVE ME THAT!!
THERE WE GO!
AMAZING WHAT A LITTLE DIPLOMACY CAN DO.

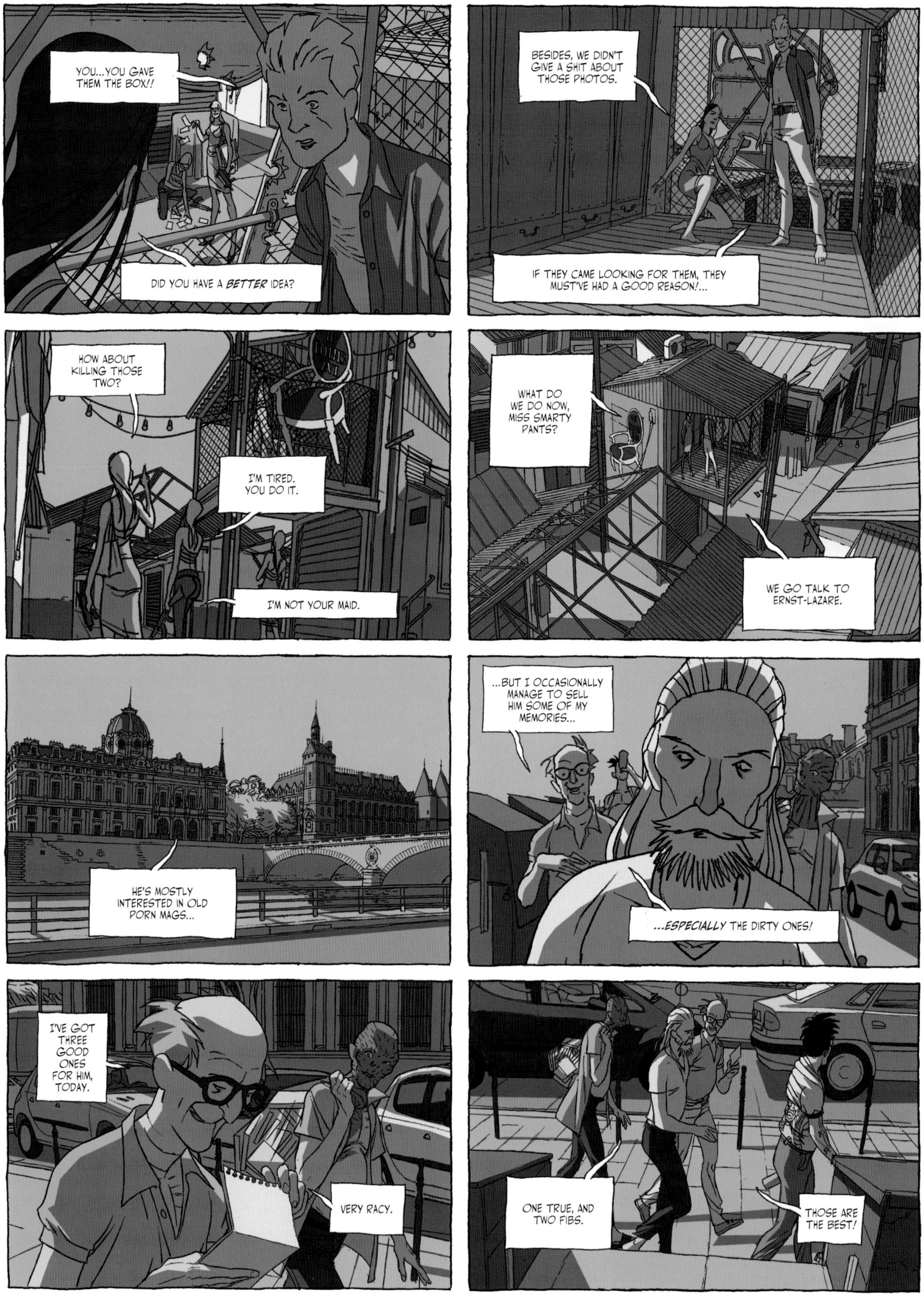
YOU...YOU GAVE THEM THE BOX!!
DID YOU HAVE A *BETTER* IDEA?
BESIDES, WE DIDN'T GIVE A SHIT ABOUT THOSE PHOTOS.
IF THEY CAME LOOKING FOR THEM, THEY MUST'VE HAD A GOOD REASON!...
HOW ABOUT KILLING THOSE TWO?
I'M TIRED. YOU DO IT.
I'M NOT YOUR MAID.
WHAT DO WE DO NOW, MISS SMARTY PANTS?
WE GO TALK TO ERNST-LAZARE.
HE'S MOSTLY INTERESTED IN OLD PORN MAGS...
...BUT I OCCASIONALLY MANAGE TO SELL HIM SOME OF MY MEMORIES...
...*ESPECIALLY* THE DIRTY ONES!
I'VE GOT THREE GOOD ONES FOR HIM, TODAY.
VERY RACY.
ONE TRUE, AND TWO FIBS.
THOSE ARE THE BEST!

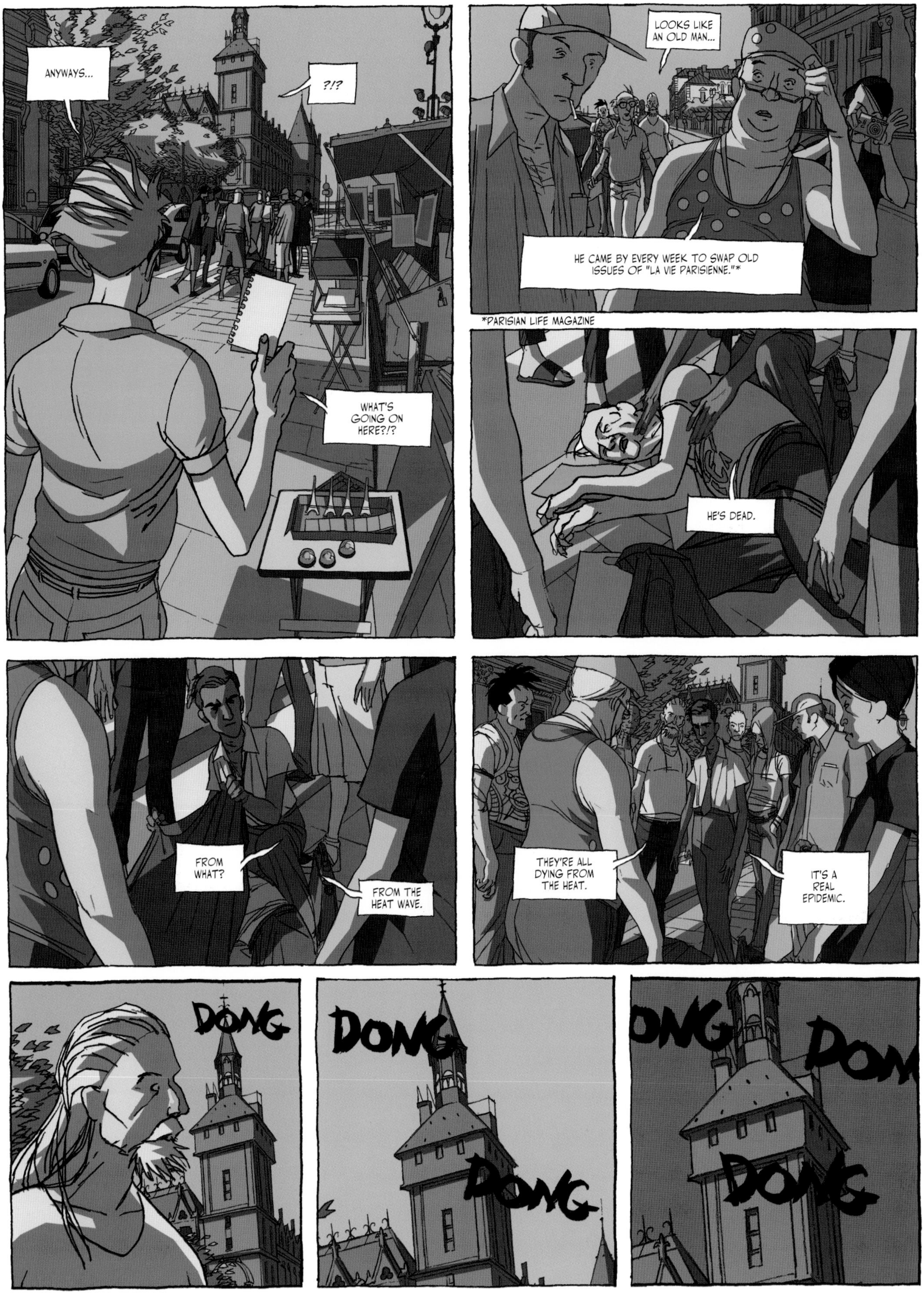
ANYWAYS...
?!?
WHAT'S GOING ON HERE?!?
LOOKS LIKE AN OLD MAN...
HE CAME BY EVERY WEEK TO SWAP OLD ISSUES OF "LA VIE PARISIENNE."*
HE'S DEAD.
FROM WHAT?
FROM THE HEAT WAVE.
THEY'RE ALL DYING FROM THE HEAT.
IT'S A REAL EPIDEMIC.
DONG
DONG
DONG
ONG
DOM
DONG

*PARISIAN LIFE MAGAZINE

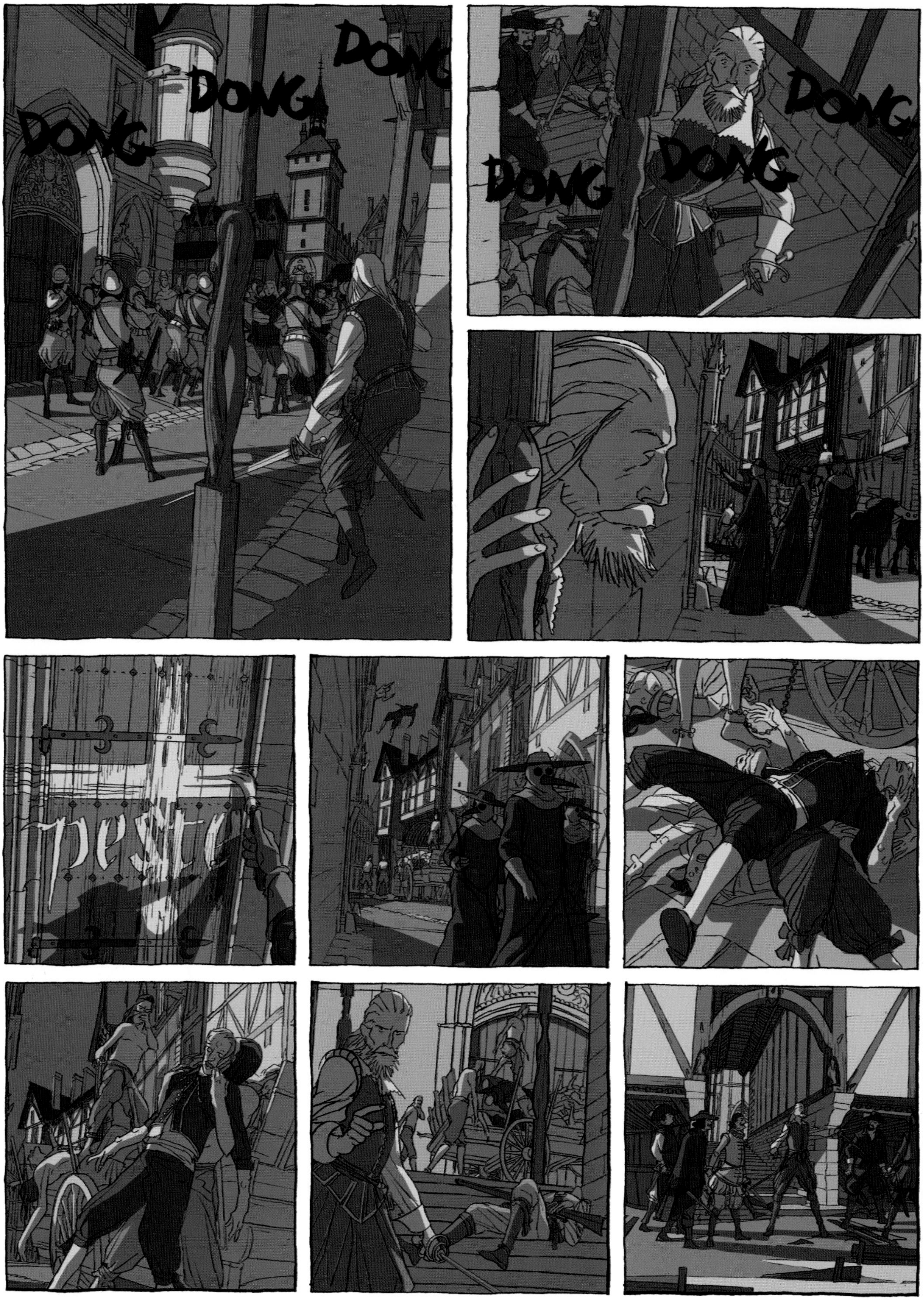
DONG
DONG
DONG
DONG
DONG
DONG
peste

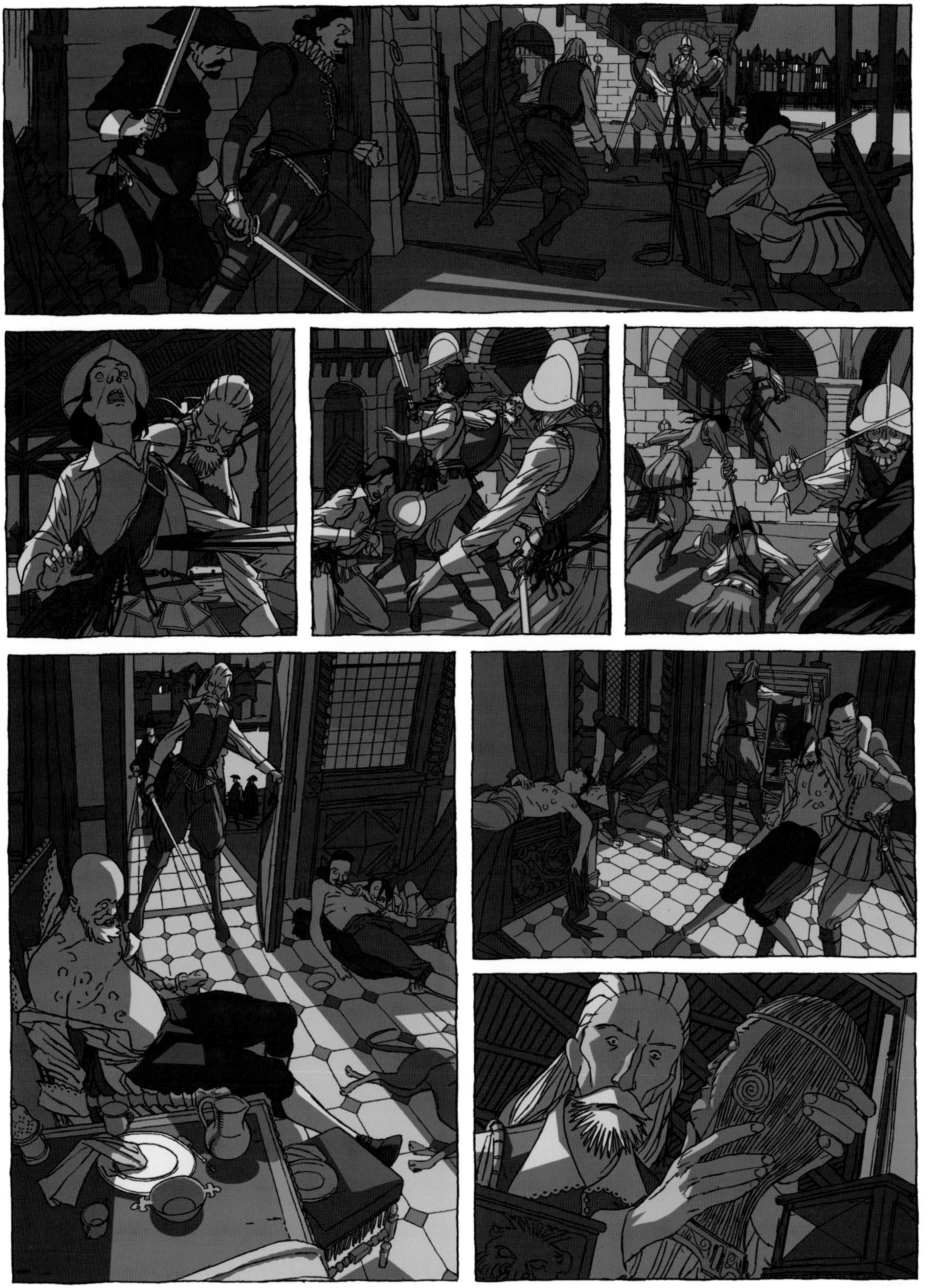

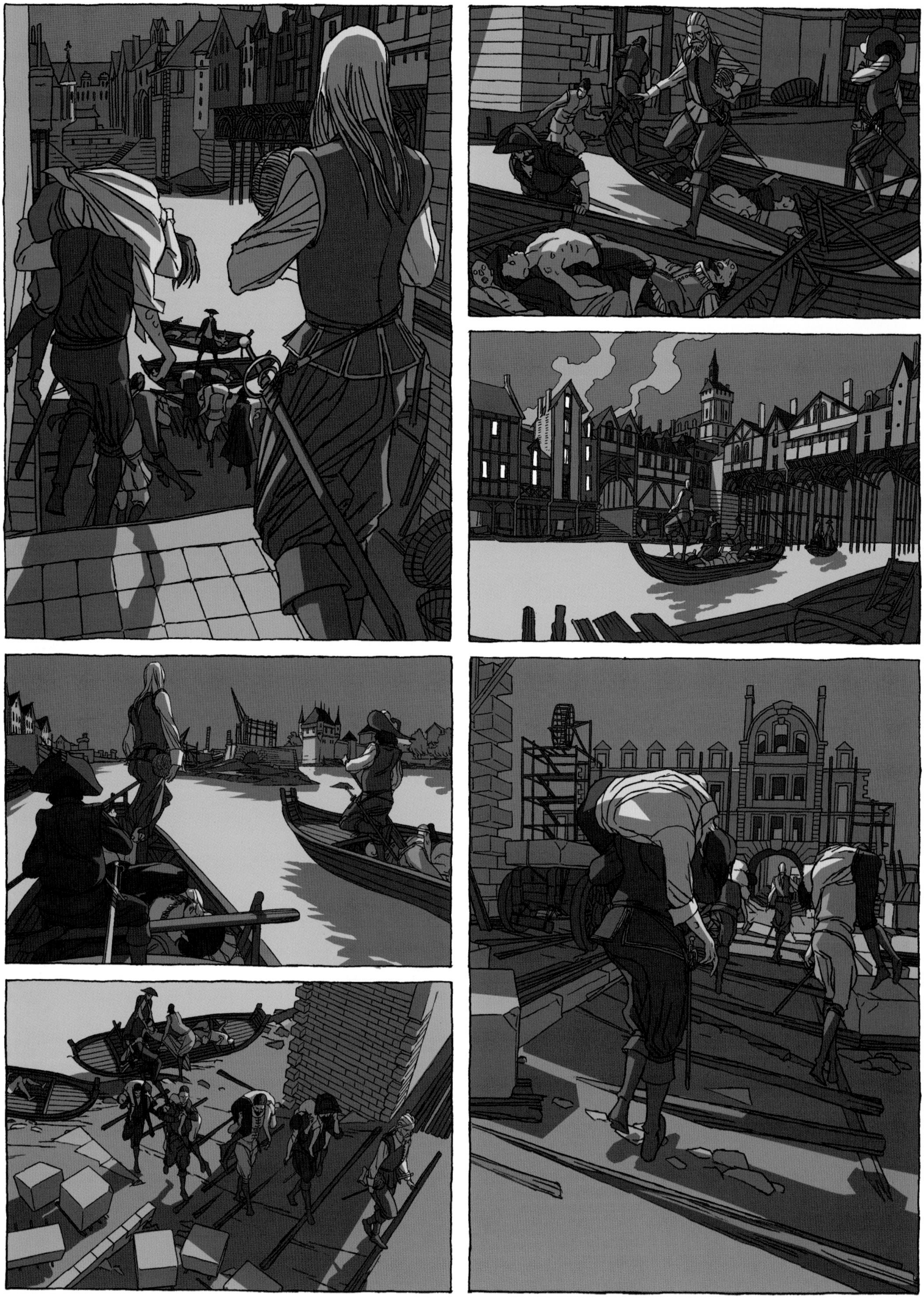

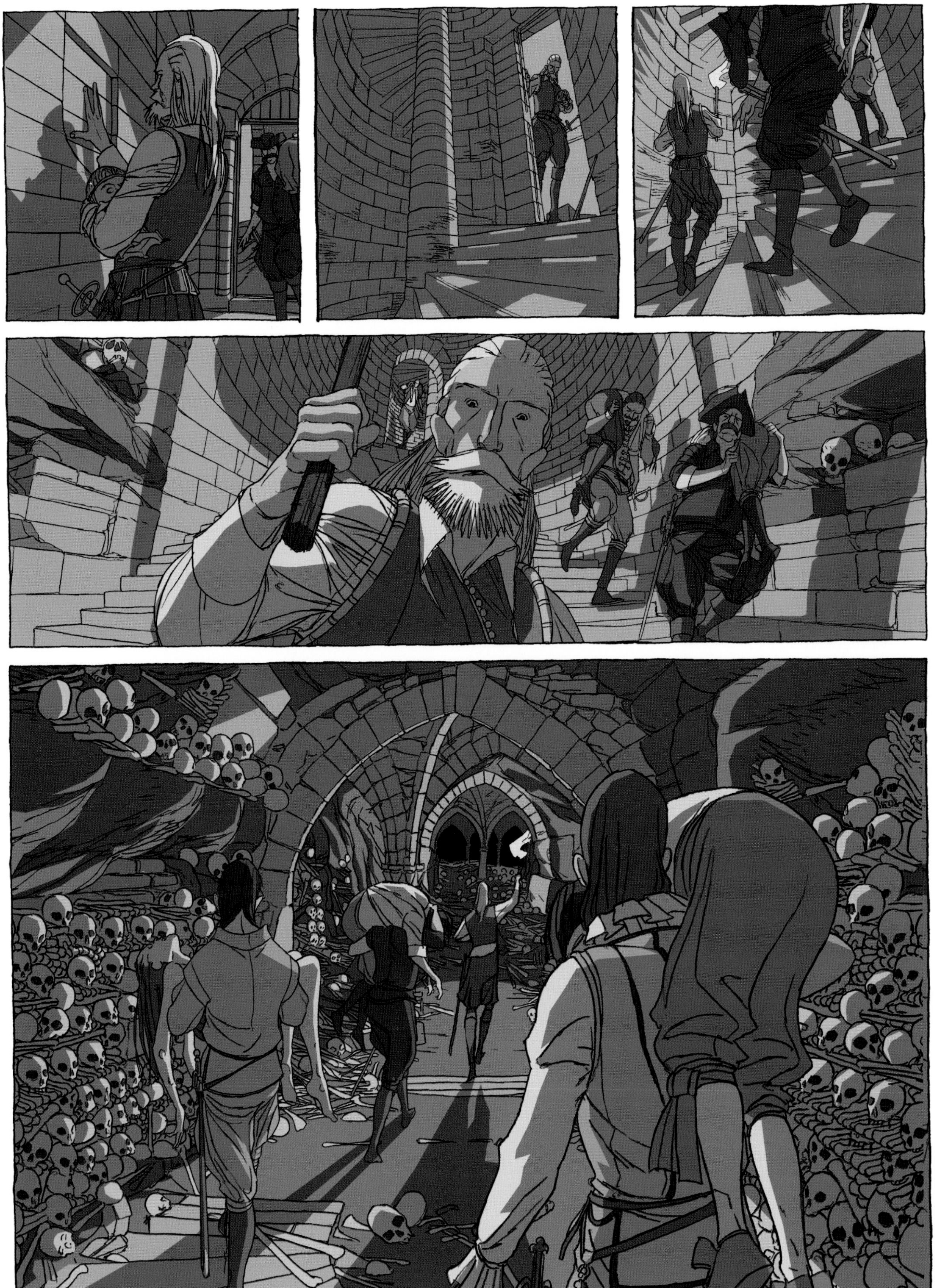

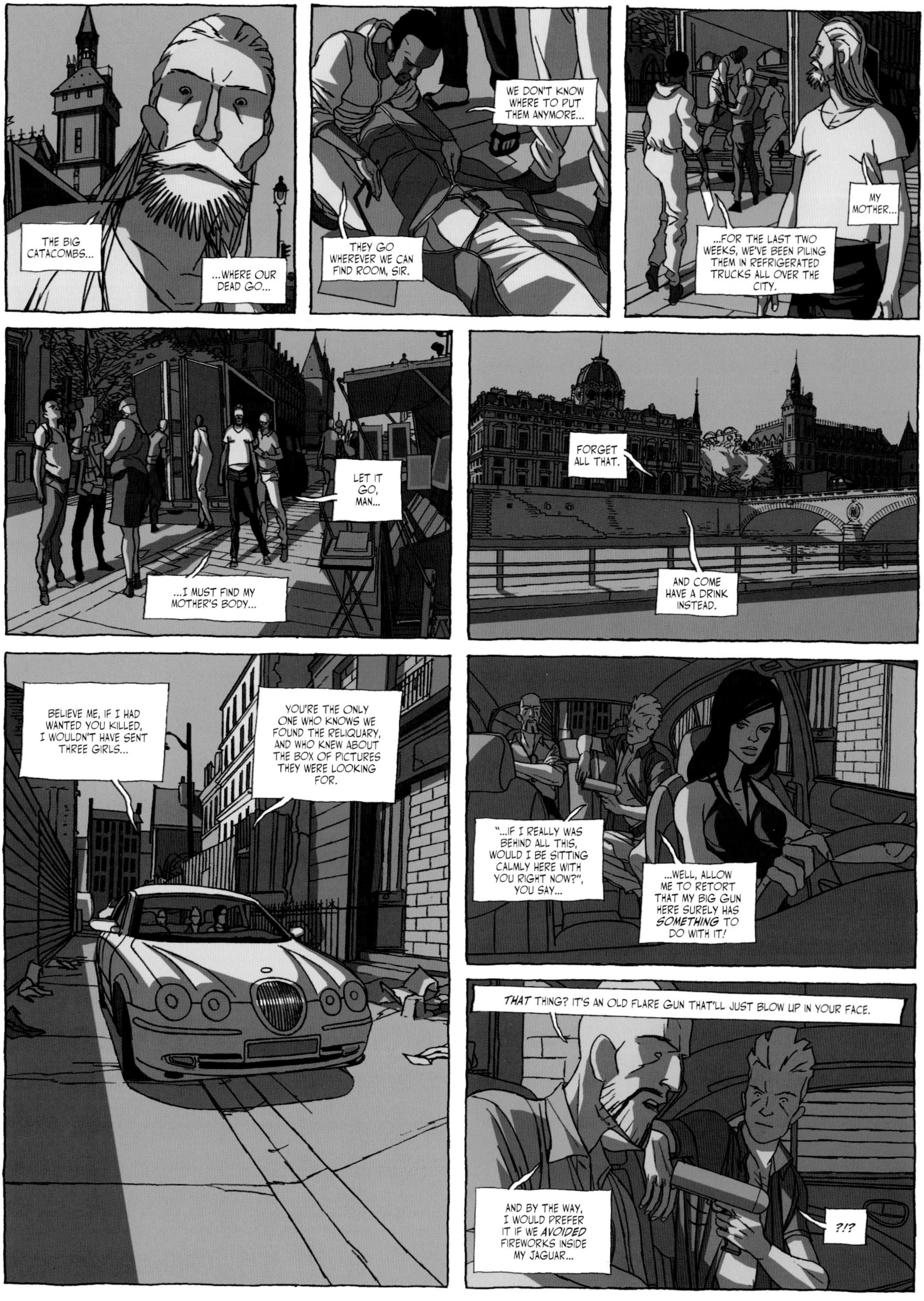

THE BIG CATACOMBS...
...WHERE OUR DEAD GO...
WE DON'T KNOW WHERE TO PUT THEM ANYMORE...
THEY GO WHEREVER WE CAN FIND ROOM, SIR.
...FOR THE LAST TWO WEEKS, WE'VE BEEN PILING THEM IN REFRIGERATED TRUCKS ALL OVER THE CITY.
MY MOTHER...
LET IT GO, MAN...
...I MUST FIND MY MOTHER'S BODY...
FORGET ALL THAT.
AND COME HAVE A DRINK INSTEAD.
BELIEVE ME, IF I HAD WANTED YOU KILLED, I WOULDN'T HAVE SENT THREE GIRLS...
YOU'RE THE ONLY ONE WHO KNOWS WE FOUND THE RELIQUARY, AND WHO KNEW ABOUT THE BOX OF PICTURES THEY WERE LOOKING FOR.
"...IF I REALLY WAS BEHIND ALL THIS, WOULD I BE SITTING CALMLY HERE WITH YOU RIGHT NOW?", YOU SAY...
...WELL, ALLOW ME TO RETORT THAT MY BIG GUN HERE SURELY HAS SOMETHING TO DO WITH IT!
THAT THING? IT'S AN OLD FLARE GUN THAT'LL JUST BLOW UP IN YOUR FACE.
AND BY THE WAY, I WOULD PREFER IT IF WE AVOIDED FIREWORKS INSIDE MY JAGUAR...
?!?

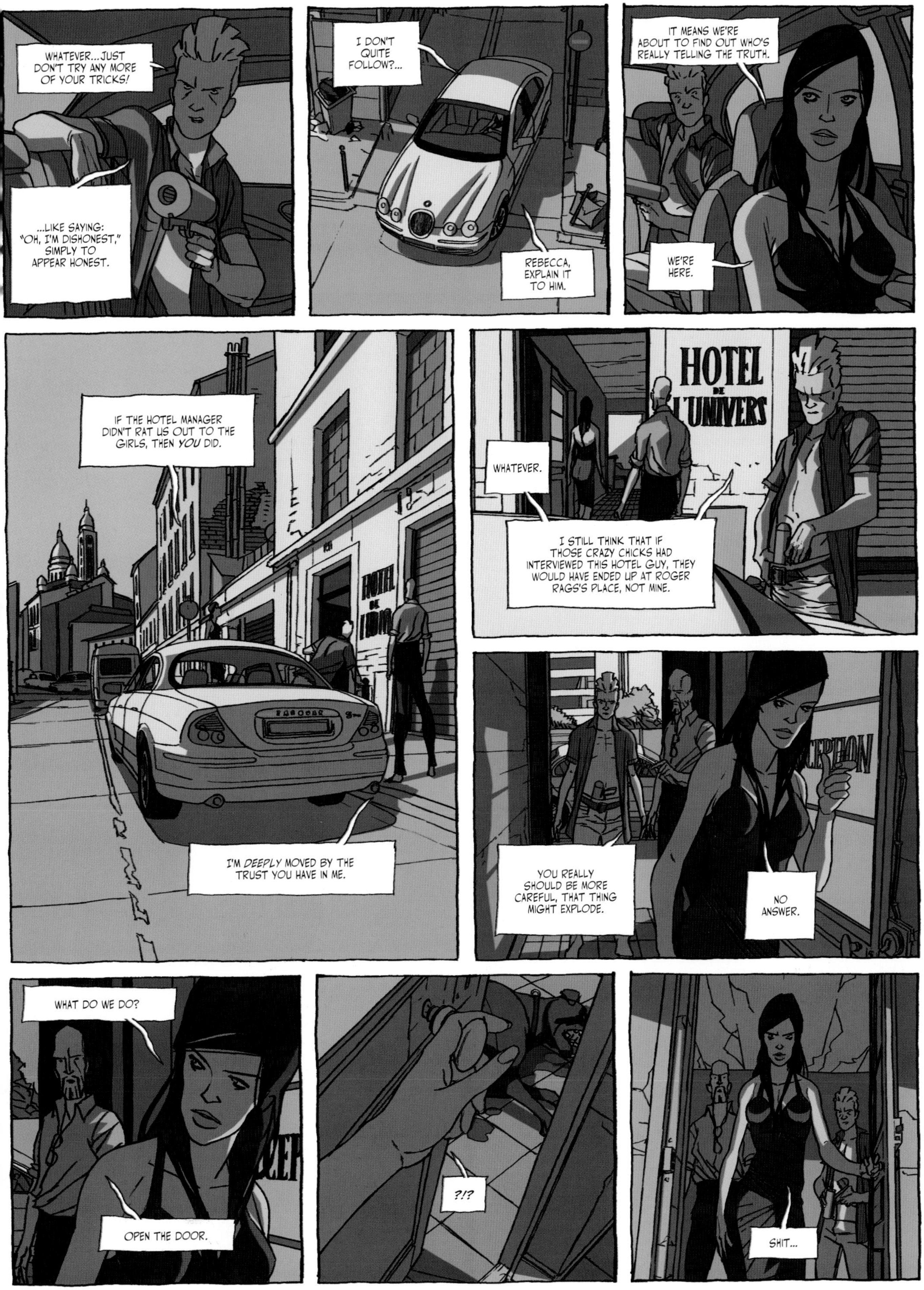
WHATEVER... JUST DON'T TRY ANY MORE OF YOUR TRICKS!
...LIKE SAYING: "OH, I'M DISHONEST," SIMPLY TO APPEAR HONEST.
I DON'T QUITE FOLLOW?...
REBECCA, EXPLAIN IT TO HIM.
IT MEANS WE'RE ABOUT TO FIND OUT WHO'S REALLY TELLING THE TRUTH.
WE'RE HERE.
IF THE HOTEL MANAGER DIDN'T RAT US OUT TO THE GIRLS, THEN YOU DID.
I'M DEEPLY MOVED BY THE TRUST YOU HAVE IN ME.
HOTEL DE L'UNIVERS
WHATEVER.
I STILL THINK THAT IF THOSE CRAZY CHICKS HAD INTERVIEWED THIS HOTEL GUY, THEY WOULD HAVE ENDED UP AT ROGER RAGS'S PLACE, NOT MINE.
YOU REALLY SHOULD BE MORE CAREFUL, THAT THING MIGHT EXPLODE.
NO ANSWER.
WHAT DO WE DO?
OPEN THE DOOR.
?!?
SHIT...

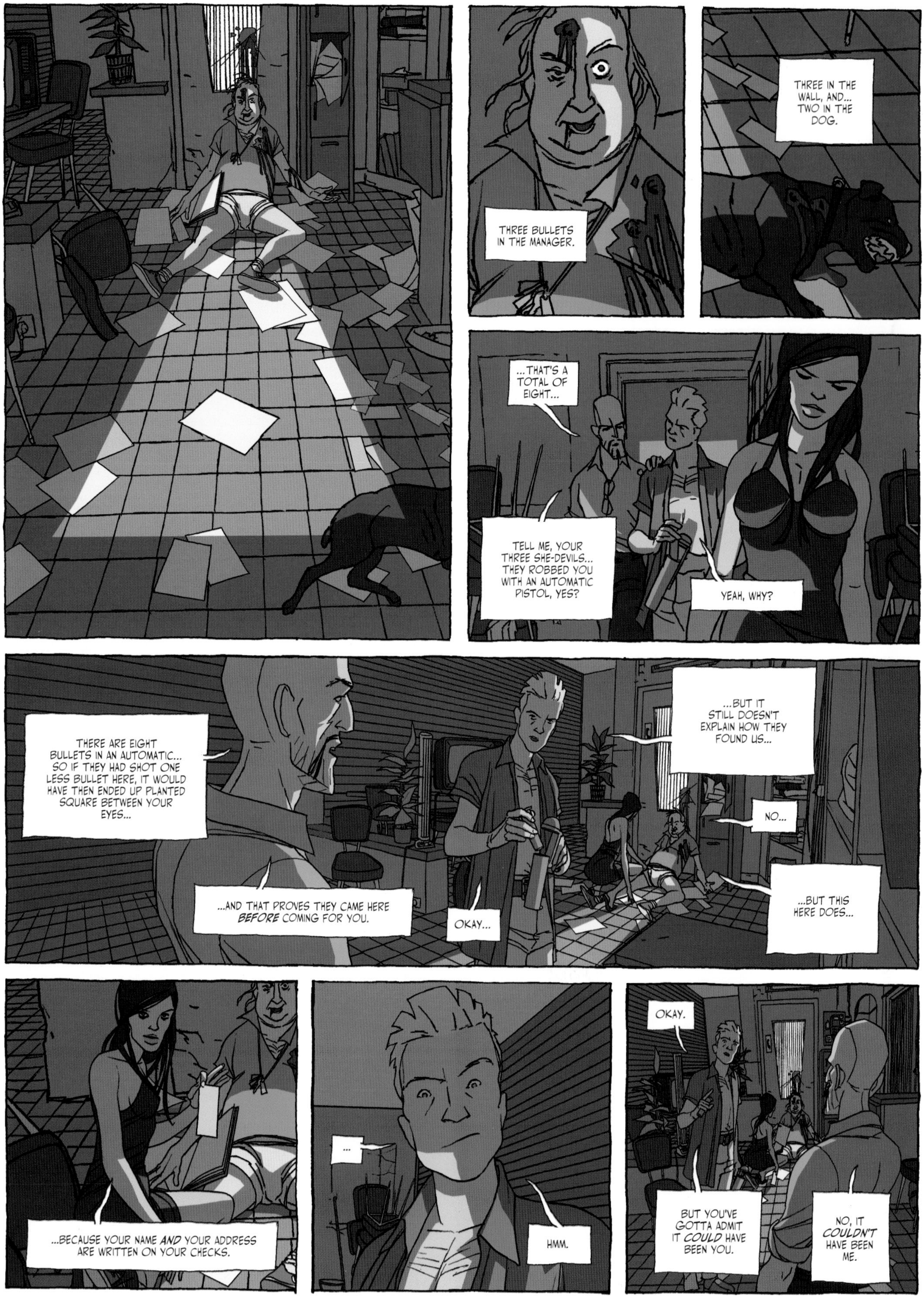
THREE BULLETS IN THE MANAGER.
THREE IN THE WALL, AND... TWO IN THE DOG.
...THAT'S A TOTAL OF EIGHT...
TELL ME, YOUR THREE SHE-DEVILS... THEY ROBBED YOU WITH AN AUTOMATIC PISTOL, YES?
YEAH, WHY?
THERE ARE EIGHT BULLETS IN AN AUTOMATIC... SO IF THEY HAD SHOT ONE LESS BULLET HERE, IT WOULD HAVE THEN ENDED UP PLANTED SQUARE BETWEEN YOUR EYES...
...AND THAT PROVES THEY CAME HERE *BEFORE* COMING FOR YOU.
OKAY...
...BUT IT STILL DOESN'T EXPLAIN HOW THEY FOUND US...
NO...
...BUT THIS HERE DOES...
...BECAUSE YOUR NAME *AND* YOUR ADDRESS ARE WRITTEN ON YOUR CHECKS.
...
HMM.
OKAY.
BUT YOU'VE GOTTA ADMIT IT *COULD* HAVE BEEN YOU.
NO, IT *COULDN'T* HAVE BEEN ME.

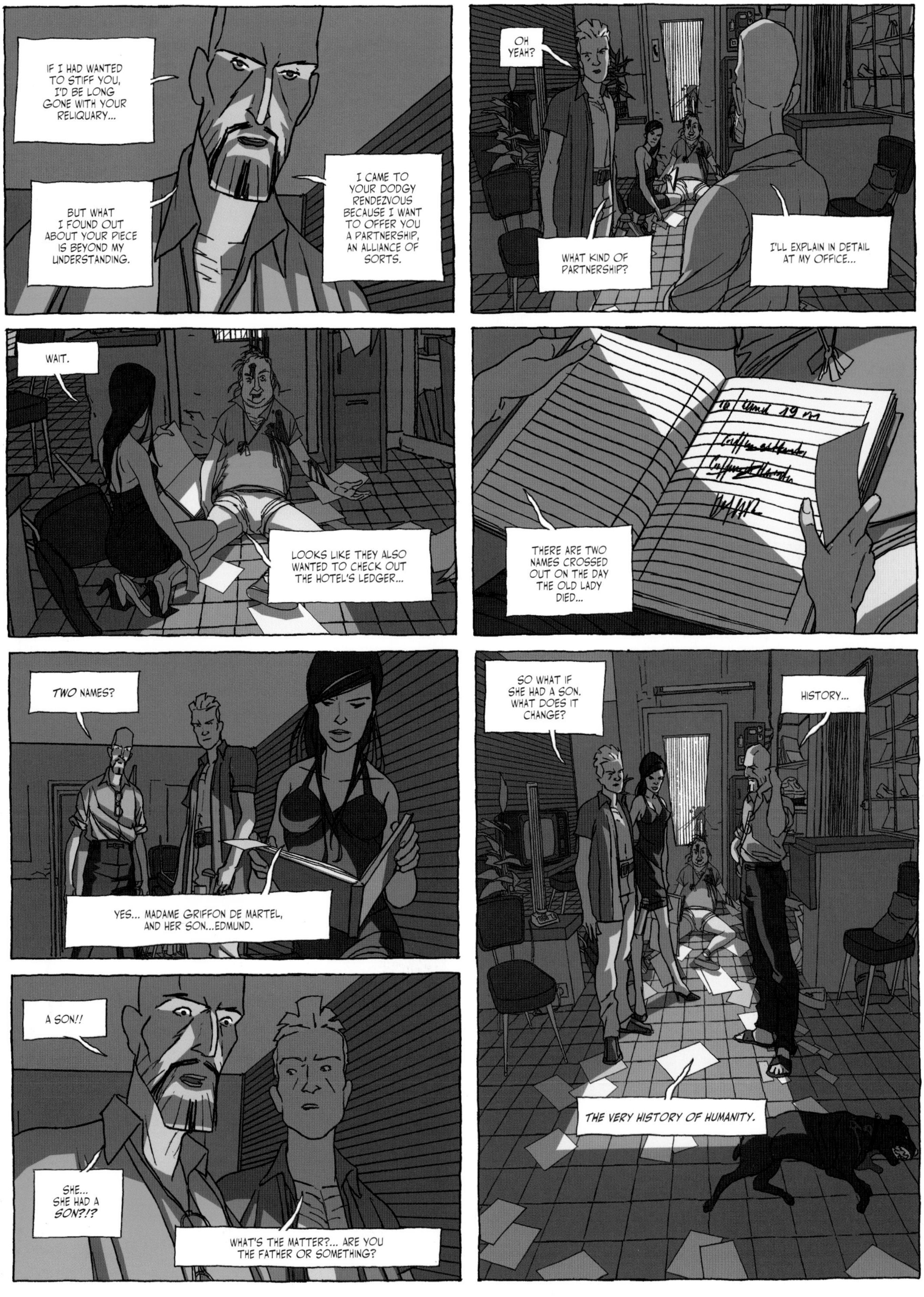
IF I HAD WANTED TO STIFF YOU, I'D BE LONG GONE WITH YOUR RELIQUARY...
BUT WHAT I FOUND OUT ABOUT YOUR PIECE IS BEYOND MY UNDERSTANDING.
I CAME TO YOUR DODGY RENDEZVOUS BECAUSE I WANT TO OFFER YOU A PARTNERSHIP, AN ALLIANCE OF SORTS.
OH YEAH?
WHAT KIND OF PARTNERSHIP?
I'LL EXPLAIN IN DETAIL AT MY OFFICE...
WAIT.
LOOKS LIKE THEY ALSO WANTED TO CHECK OUT THE HOTEL'S LEDGER...
THERE ARE TWO NAMES CROSSED OUT ON THE DAY THE OLD LADY DIED...
TWO NAMES?
YES... MADAME GRIFFON DE MARTEL, AND HER SON...EDMUND.
A SON!!
SHE... SHE HAD A *SON?!?*
WHAT'S THE MATTER?... ARE YOU THE FATHER OR SOMETHING?
SO WHAT IF SHE HAD A SON. WHAT DOES IT CHANGE?
HISTORY...
THE VERY HISTORY OF HUMANITY.

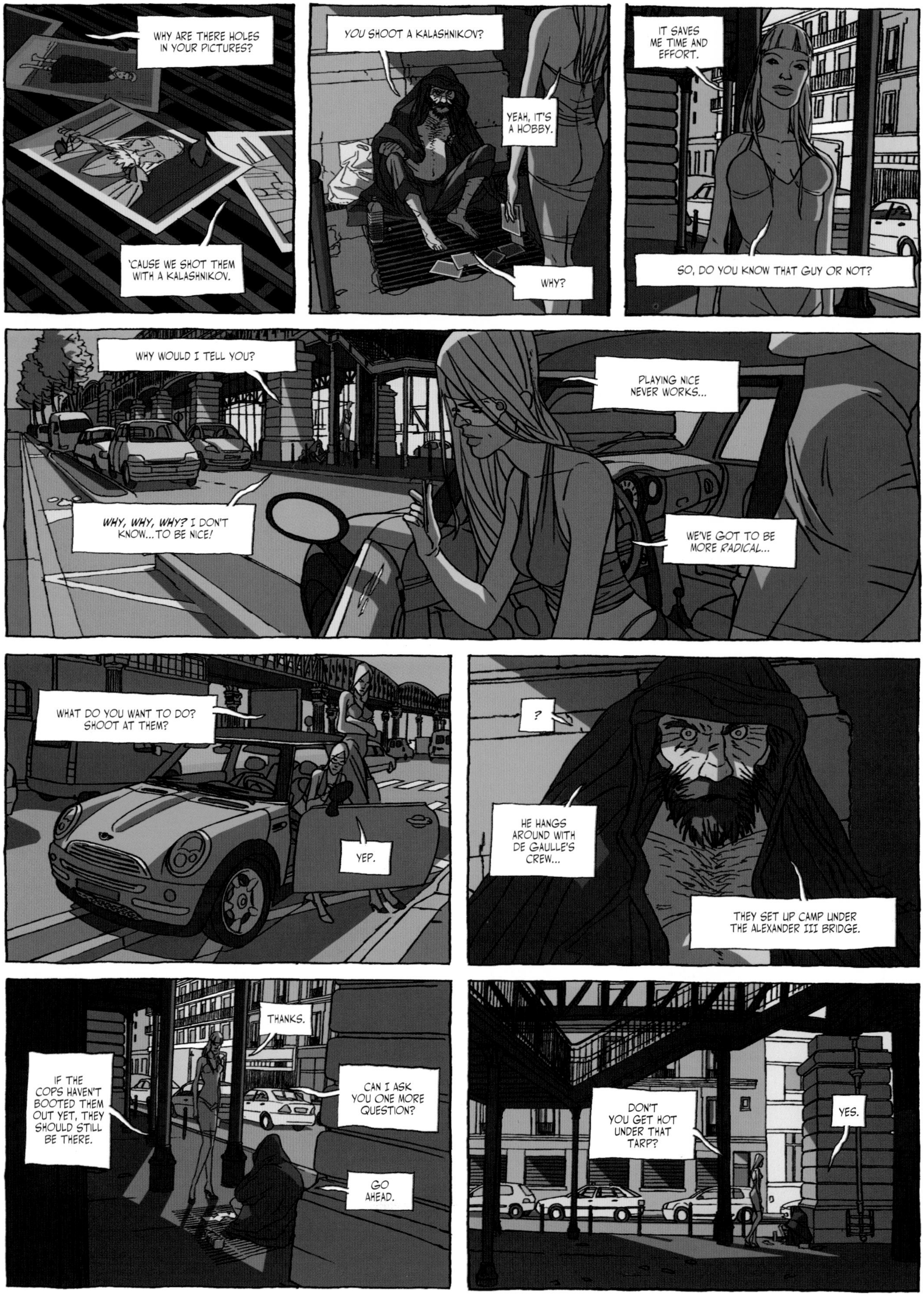
WHY ARE THERE HOLES IN YOUR PICTURES?
'CAUSE WE SHOT THEM WITH A KALASHNIKOV.
YOU SHOOT A KALASHNIKOV?
YEAH, IT'S A HOBBY.
WHY?
IT SAVES ME TIME AND EFFORT.
SO, DO YOU KNOW THAT GUY OR NOT?
WHY WOULD I TELL YOU?
WHY, WHY, WHY? I DON'T KNOW...TO BE NICE!
PLAYING NICE NEVER WORKS...
WE'VE GOT TO BE MORE RADICAL...
WHAT DO YOU WANT TO DO? SHOOT AT THEM?
YEP.
?
HE HANGS AROUND WITH DE GAULLE'S CREW...
THEY SET UP CAMP UNDER THE ALEXANDER III BRIDGE.
IF THE COPS HAVEN'T BOOTED THEM OUT YET, THEY SHOULD STILL BE THERE.
THANKS.
CAN I ASK YOU ONE MORE QUESTION?
GO AHEAD.
DON'T YOU GET HOT UNDER THAT TARP?
YES.

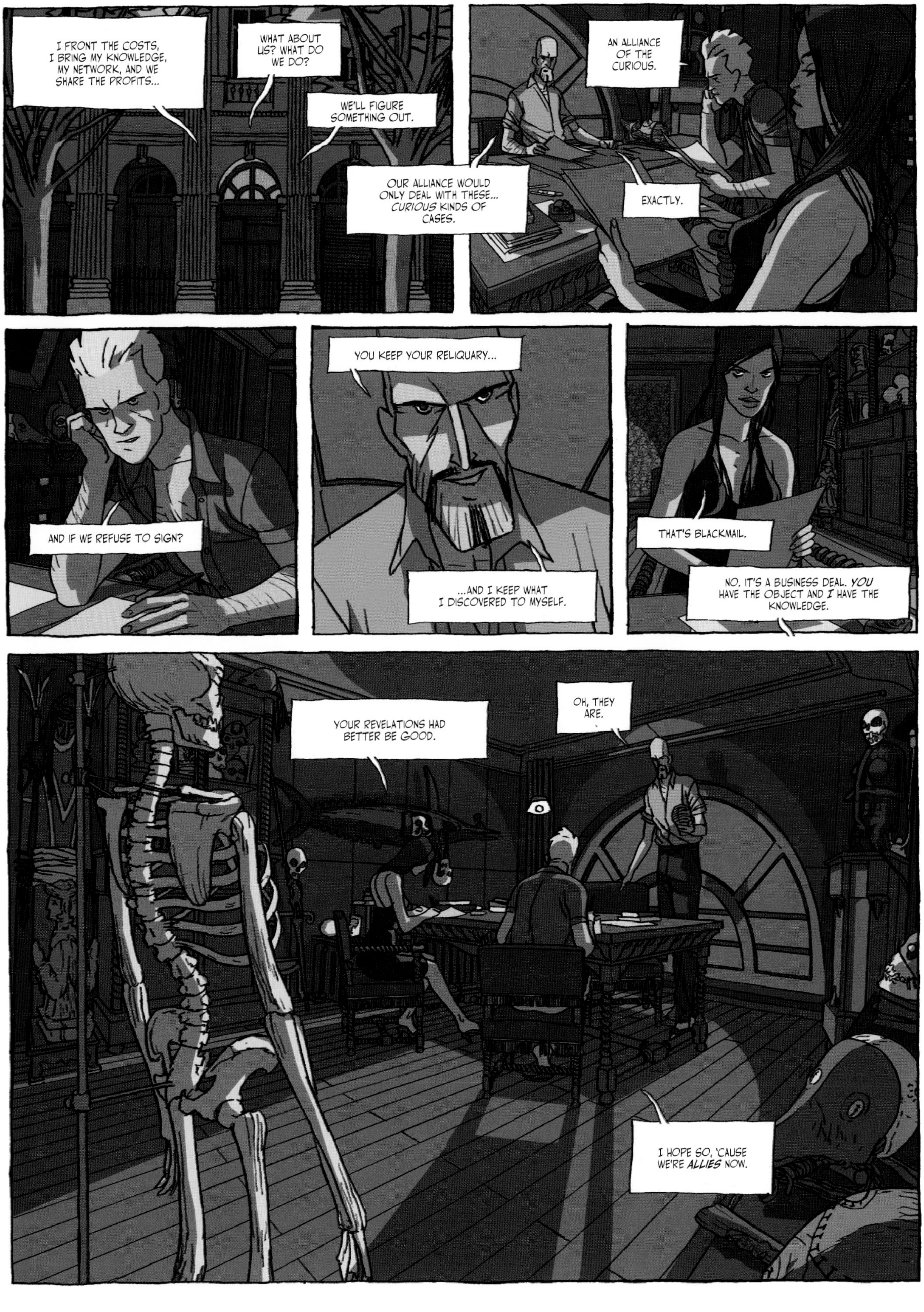
I FRONT THE COSTS, I BRING MY KNOWLEDGE, MY NETWORK, AND WE SHARE THE PROFITS...
WHAT ABOUT US? WHAT DO WE DO?
WE'LL FIGURE SOMETHING OUT.
AN ALLIANCE OF THE CURIOUS.
OUR ALLIANCE WOULD ONLY DEAL WITH THESE... *CURIOUS* KINDS OF CASES.
EXACTLY.
AND IF WE REFUSE TO SIGN?
YOU KEEP YOUR RELIQUARY...
...AND I KEEP WHAT I DISCOVERED TO MYSELF.
THAT'S BLACKMAIL.
NO. IT'S A BUSINESS DEAL. ***YOU*** HAVE THE OBJECT AND ***I*** HAVE THE KNOWLEDGE.
YOUR REVELATIONS HAD BETTER BE GOOD.
OH, THEY ARE.
I HOPE SO, 'CAUSE WE'RE ***ALLIES*** NOW.

THE FIRST MYSTERY IS THE RELIQUARY ITSELF.

YOU SEE, THESE OBJECTS HAVE ALWAYS BELONGED TO A MONASTERY, A DIOCESE, OR A PARISH... THE KIND OF PLACE WHERE EVERYTHING IS CAREFULLY RECORDED.

YET THIS PIECE ISN'T LISTED ANYWHERE.

YOU DIDN'T FIND ANYTHING?

NOTHING AT ALL.

BOY, AM I FEELING *GREAT* ABOUT THIS ALLIANCE SO FAR...

JUST WAIT. THE *REAL* REVELATION CAME FROM HIM...

HE SEEMS QUITE DEAD.

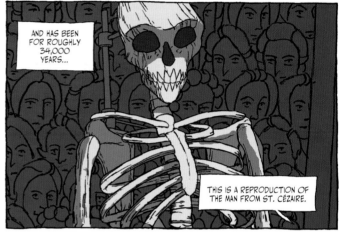

AND HAS BEEN FOR ROUGHLY 34,000 YEARS...

THIS IS A REPRODUCTION OF THE MAN FROM ST. CÉZAIRE.

A *NEANDERTHAL* SKELETON DISCOVERED IN FRANCE IN 1979.

THIS SPECIMEN PROVED THAT THE NEANDERTHALS DIDN'T DISAPPEAR AT THE END OF THE MIDDLE PALEOLITHIC, BUT SURVIVED LONG AFTERWARDS AND COEXISTED WITH ANOTHER HUMAN GROUP -- OUR GROUP, THE HOMOSAPIENS...

NEANDERTHALS AND HOMOSAPIENS, AREN'T THEY THE SAME?

NO. THEY ARE TWO DISTINCT SPECIES OF HOMINIDS.

TWO SPECIES THAT COULDN'T MIX BECAUSE THEY WERE GENETICALLY INCOMPATIBLE.

THEIR MOR-PHOLOGY WAS ALSO QUITE DIFFERENT.

48

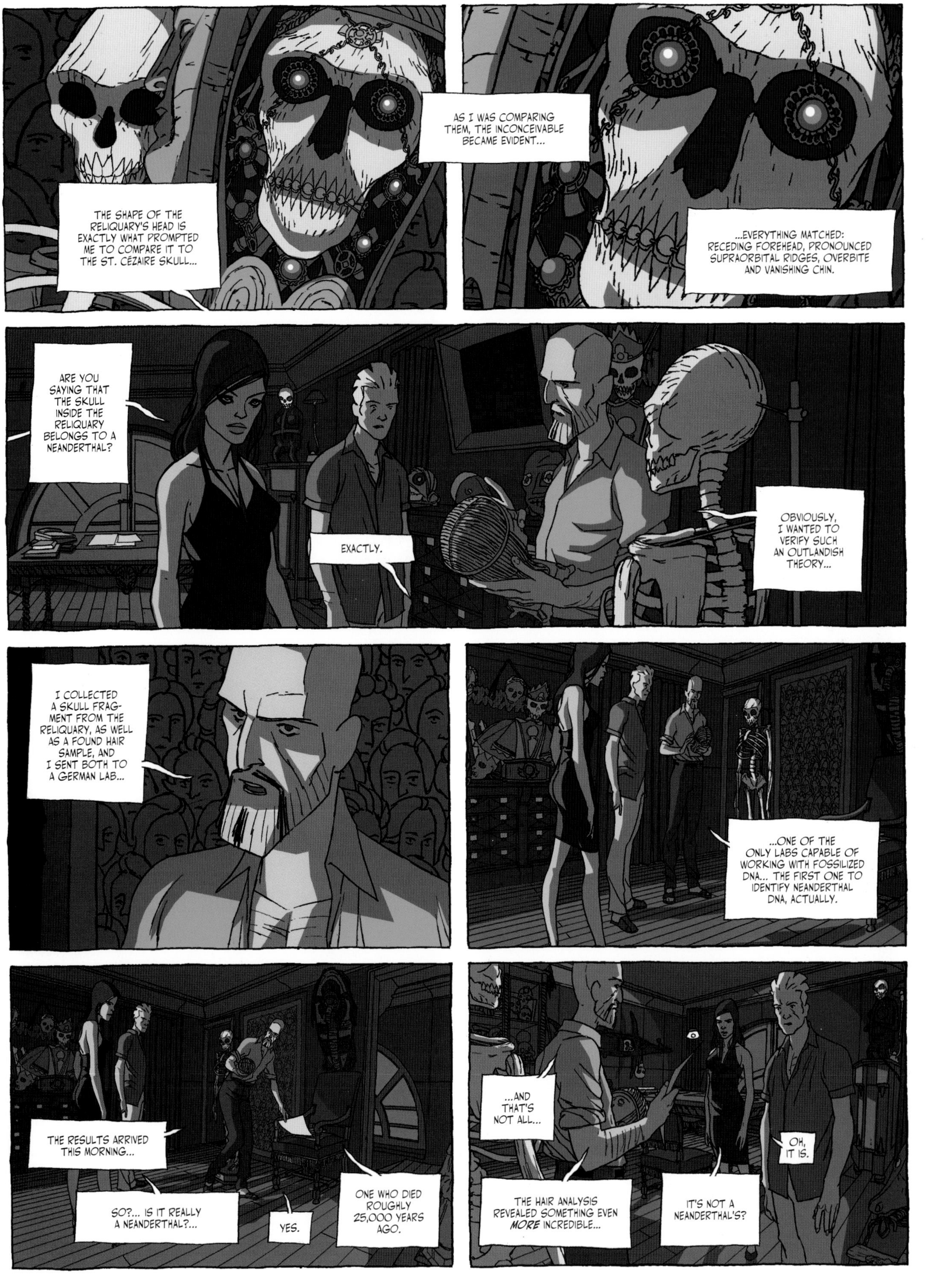
THE SHAPE OF THE RELIQUARY'S HEAD IS EXACTLY WHAT PROMPTED ME TO COMPARE IT TO THE ST. CÉZAIRE SKULL...
AS I WAS COMPARING THEM, THE INCONCEIVABLE BECAME EVIDENT...
...EVERYTHING MATCHED: RECEDING FOREHEAD, PRONOUNCED SUPRAORBITAL RIDGES, OVERBITE AND VANISHING CHIN.
ARE YOU SAYING THAT THE SKULL INSIDE THE RELIQUARY BELONGS TO A NEANDERTHAL?
EXACTLY.
OBVIOUSLY, I WANTED TO VERIFY SUCH AN OUTLANDISH THEORY...
I COLLECTED A SKULL FRAG-MENT FROM THE RELIQUARY, AS WELL AS A FOUND HAIR SAMPLE, AND I SENT BOTH TO A GERMAN LAB...
...ONE OF THE ONLY LABS CAPABLE OF WORKING WITH FOSSILIZED DNA... THE FIRST ONE TO IDENTIFY NEANDERTHAL DNA, ACTUALLY.
THE RESULTS ARRIVED THIS MORNING...
SO?... IS IT REALLY A NEANDERTHAL?...
YES.
ONE WHO DIED ROUGHLY 25,000 YEARS AGO.
...AND THAT'S NOT ALL...
THE HAIR ANALYSIS REVEALED SOMETHING EVEN *MORE* INCREDIBLE...
IT'S NOT A NEANDERTHAL'S?
OH, IT IS.

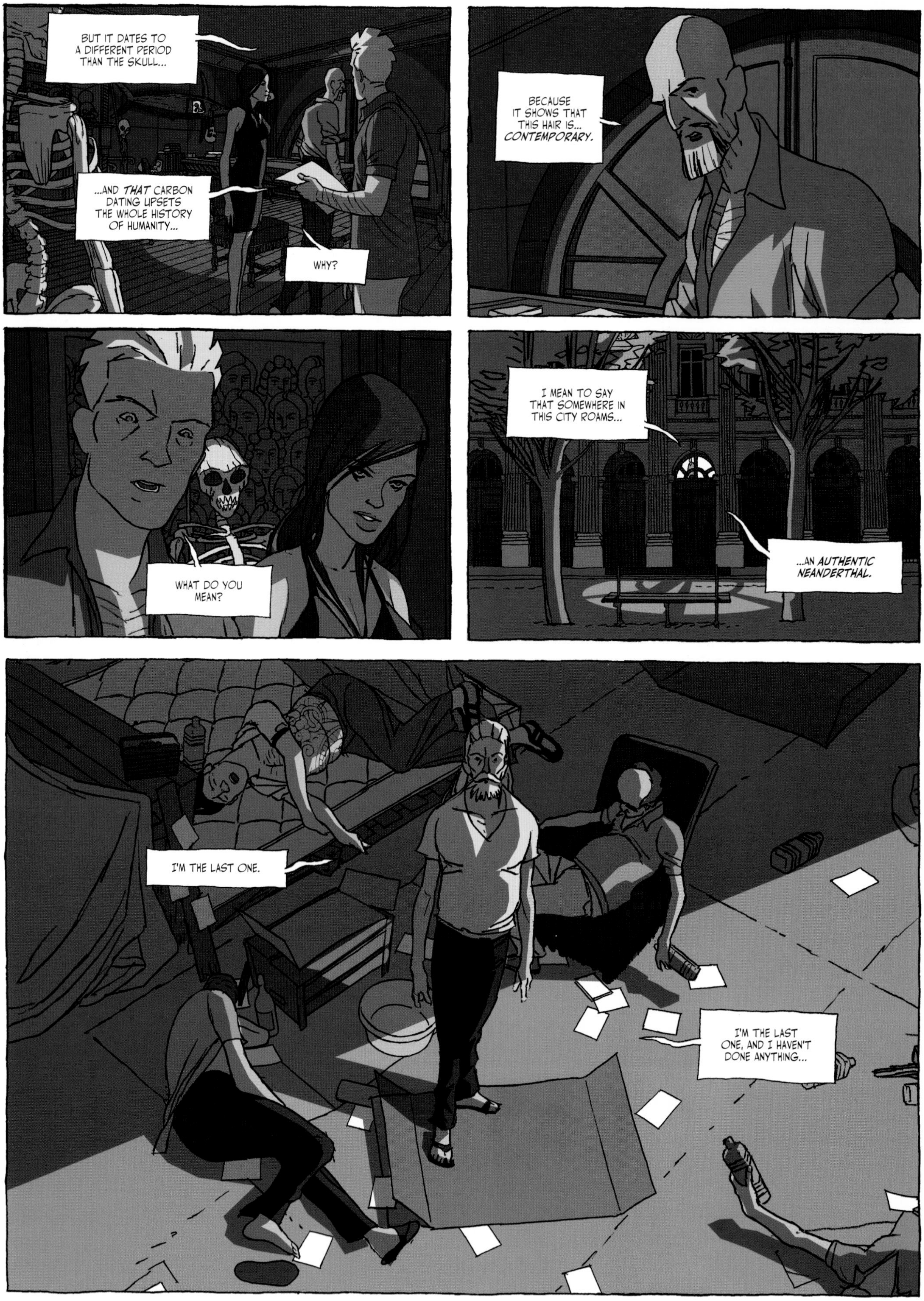
BUT IT DATES TO A DIFFERENT PERIOD THAN THE SKULL...
...AND THAT CARBON DATING UPSETS THE WHOLE HISTORY OF HUMANITY...
WHY?
BECAUSE IT SHOWS THAT THIS HAIR IS... CONTEMPORARY.
WHAT DO YOU MEAN?
I MEAN TO SAY THAT SOMEWHERE IN THIS CITY ROAMS...
...AN AUTHENTIC NEANDERTHAL.
I'M THE LAST ONE.
I'M THE LAST ONE, AND I HAVEN'T DONE ANYTHING...

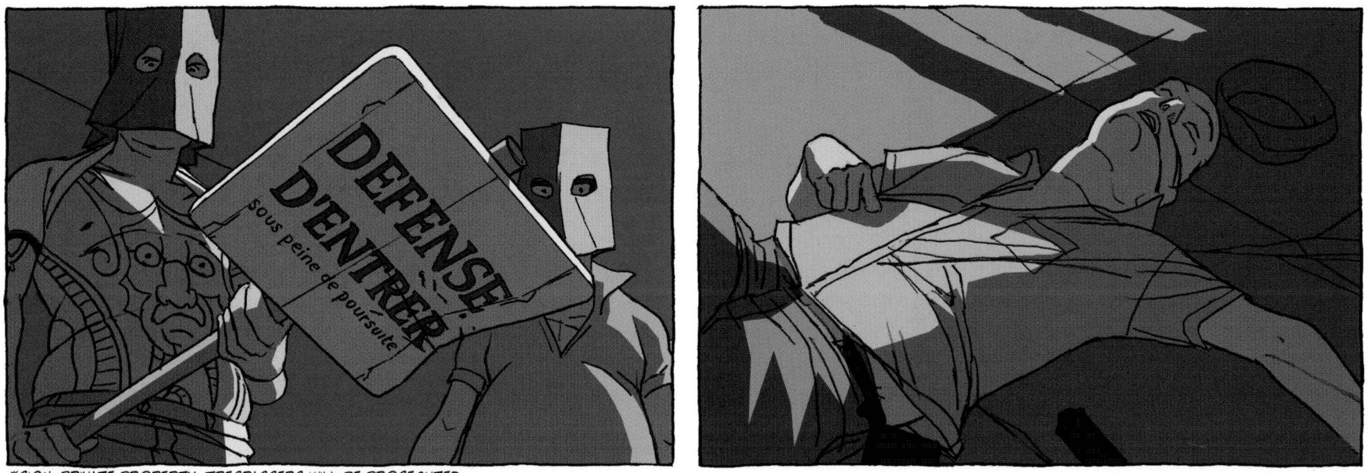
DEFENSE D'ENTRER
sous peine de poursuite

*SIGN: PRIVATE PROPERTY, TRESPASSERS WILL BE PROSECUTED

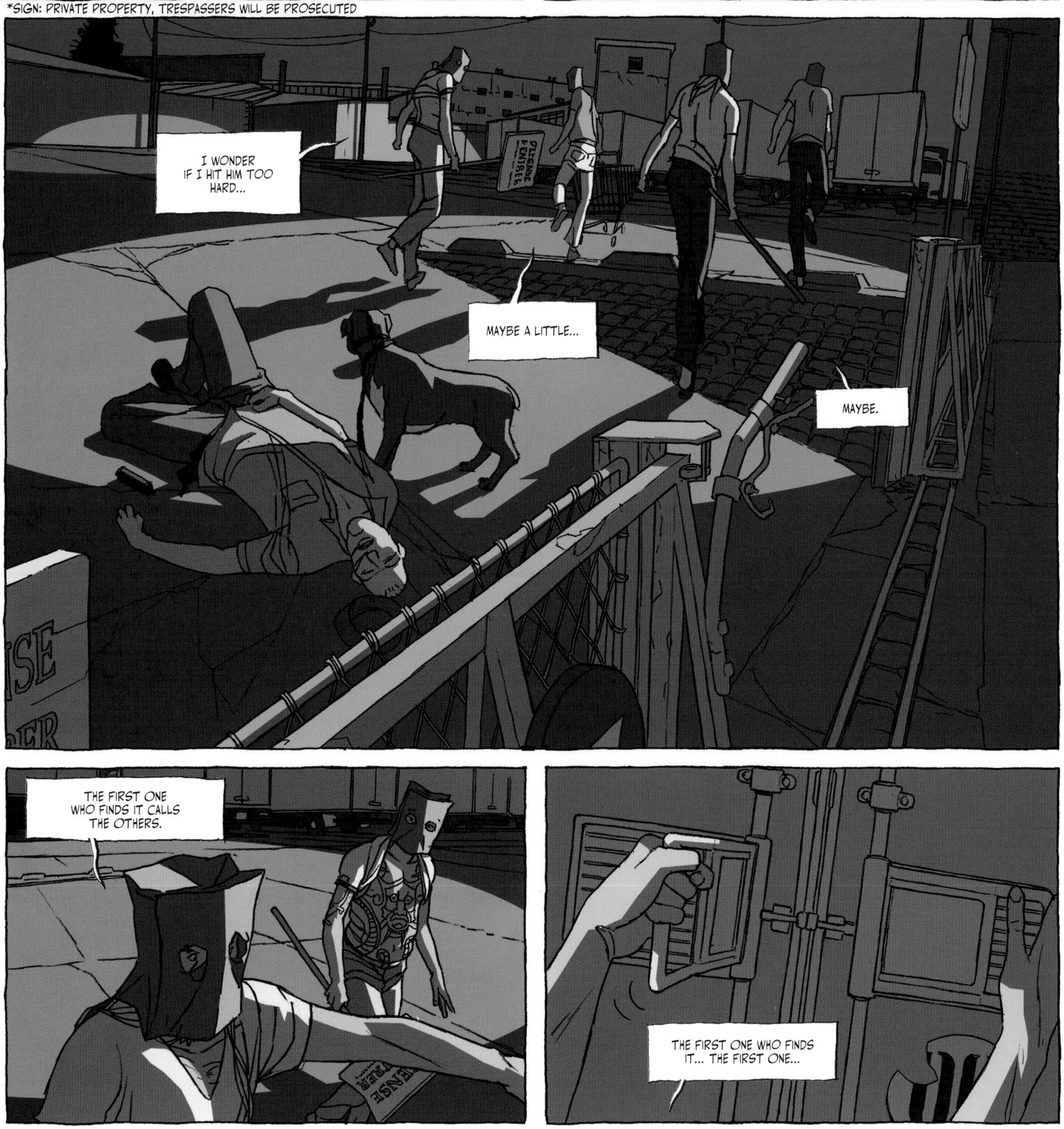
I WONDER IF I HIT HIM TOO HARD...
MAYBE A LITTLE...
MAYBE.
THE FIRST ONE WHO FINDS IT CALLS THE OTHERS.
THE FIRST ONE WHO FINDS IT... THE FIRST ONE...

I, FOR ONE, AM NOT SURE I WANT TO FIND IT.

ALL THESE DEAD BODIES...

...IT GIVES ME THE CREEPS.

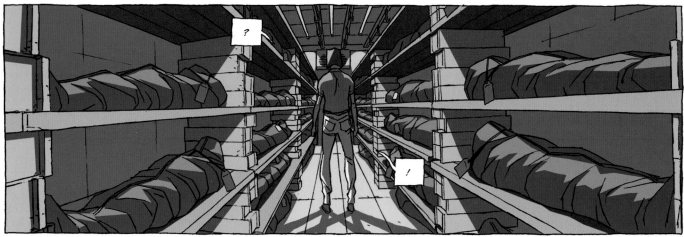

?

!

SHIT...

...IT'S HER.

*NAME: GRIFFON DE MARTEL / DATE: 07.17.07

I GOT HER, GUYS!

I *FOUND* HER!!

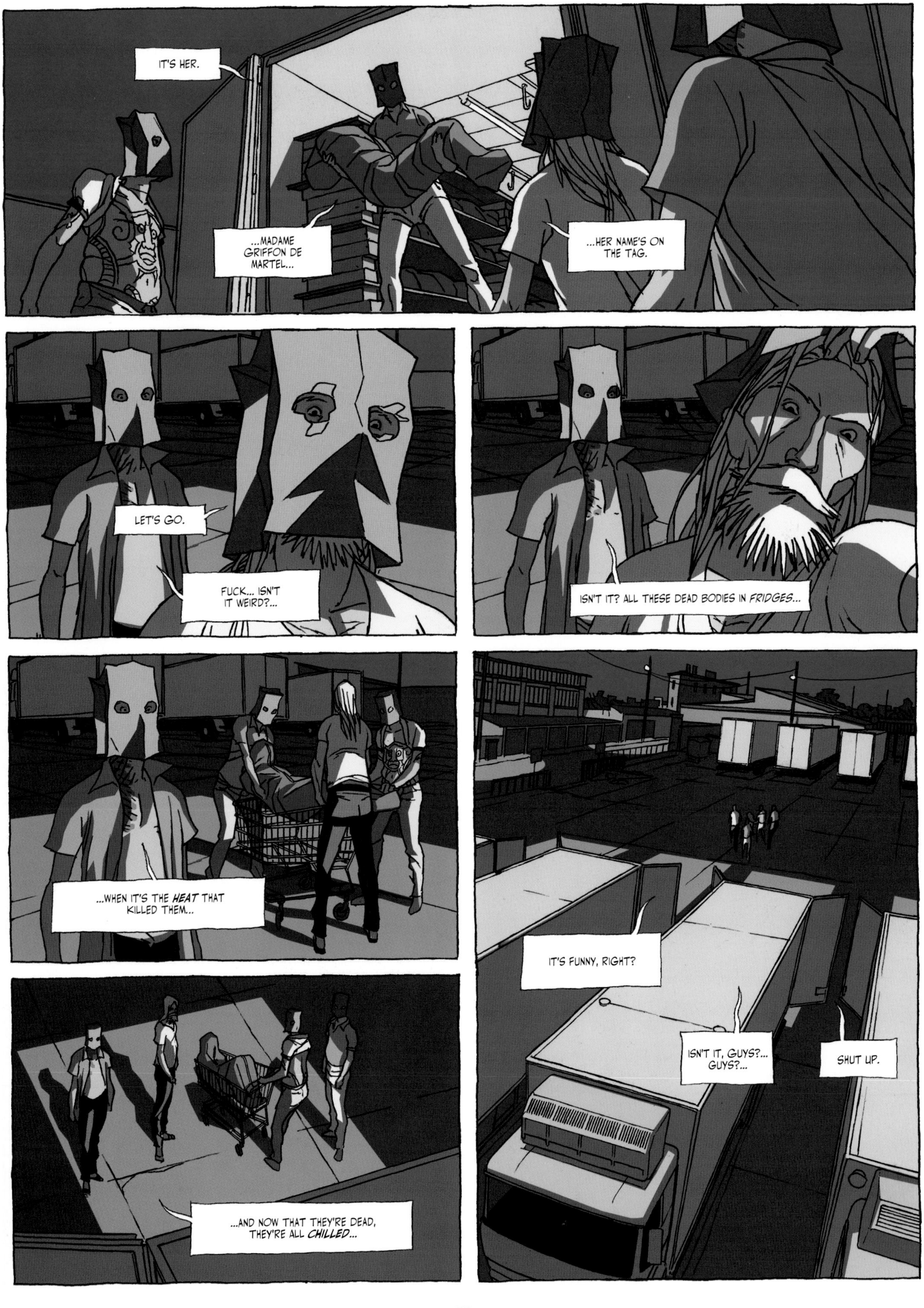
IT'S HER.
...MADAME GRIFFON DE MARTEL...
...HER NAME'S ON THE TAG.
LET'S GO.
FUCK... ISN'T IT WEIRD?...
ISN'T IT? ALL THESE DEAD BODIES IN FRIDGES...
...WHEN IT'S THE HEAT THAT KILLED THEM...
...AND NOW THAT THEY'RE DEAD, THEY'RE ALL CHILLED...
IT'S FUNNY, RIGHT?
ISN'T IT, GUYS?... GUYS?...
SHUT UP.

*BODY OF ONE OF THE VICTIMS OF THE HEAT WAVE, MME GRIFFON DE MARTEL, DISAPPEARS FROM THE MORGUE

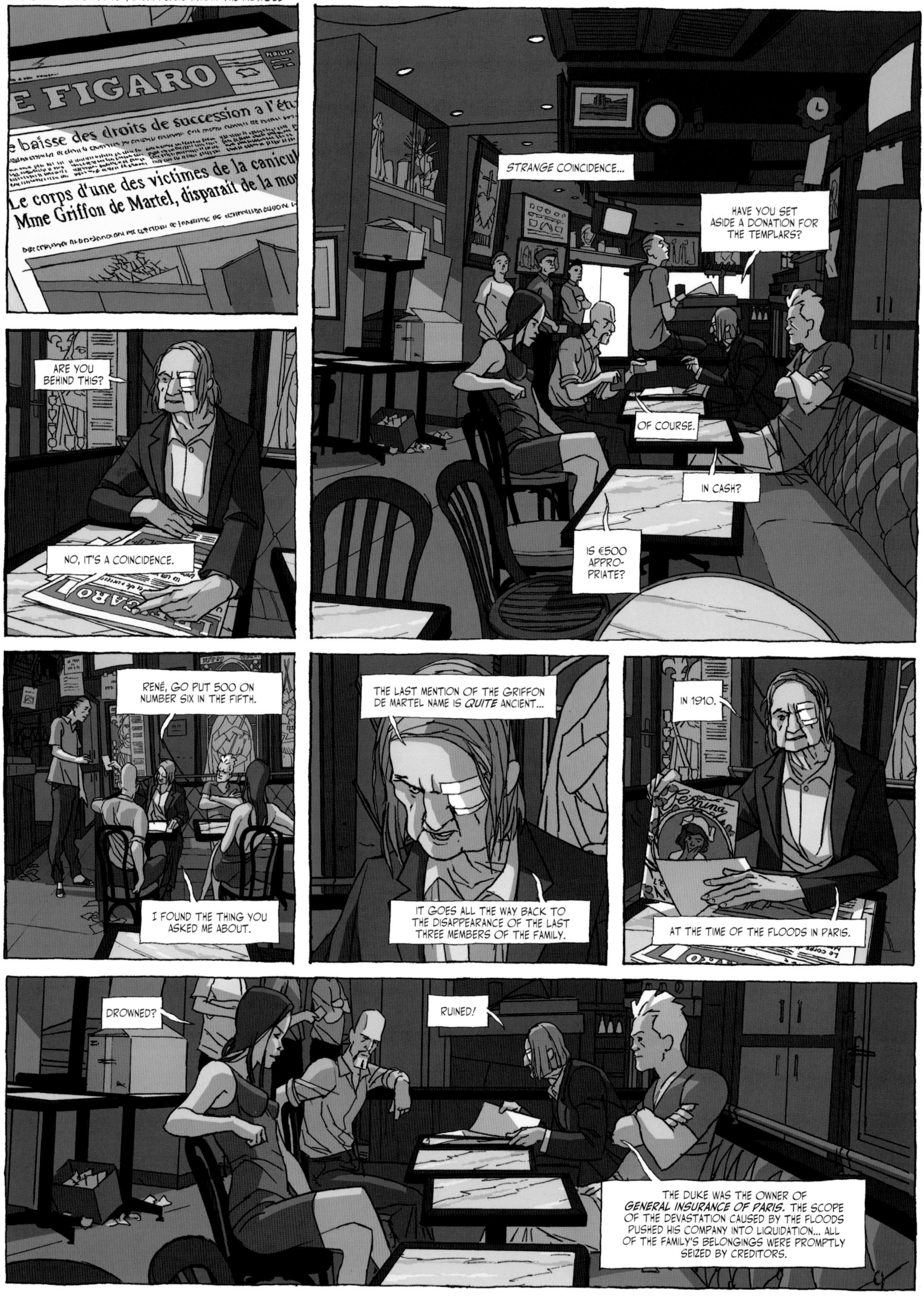
E FIGARO
baisse des droits de succession a l'étu
Le corps d'une des victimes de la canicul
Mme Griffon de Martel, disparait de la mor
ARE YOU BEHIND THIS?
NO, IT'S A COINCIDENCE.
STRANGE COINCIDENCE...
HAVE YOU SET ASIDE A DONATION FOR THE TEMPLARS?
OF COURSE.
IN CASH?
IS €500 APPROPRIATE?
RENÉ, GO PUT 500 ON NUMBER SIX IN THE FIFTH.
I FOUND THE THING YOU ASKED ME ABOUT.
THE LAST MENTION OF THE GRIFFON DE MARTEL NAME IS QUITE ANCIENT...
IT GOES ALL THE WAY BACK TO THE DISAPPEARANCE OF THE LAST THREE MEMBERS OF THE FAMILY.
IN 1910.
AT THE TIME OF THE FLOODS IN PARIS.
DROWNED?
RUINED!
THE DUKE WAS THE OWNER OF GENERAL INSURANCE OF PARIS. THE SCOPE OF THE DEVASTATION CAUSED BY THE FLOODS PUSHED HIS COMPANY INTO LIQUIDATION... ALL OF THE FAMILY'S BELONGINGS WERE PROMPTLY SEIZED BY CREDITORS.

*PORTRAIT OF MADEMOISELLE GRIFFON DE MARTEL /
THE CASE OF THE STRANGE DISAPPEARANCE OF THE GRIFFON DE MARTEL

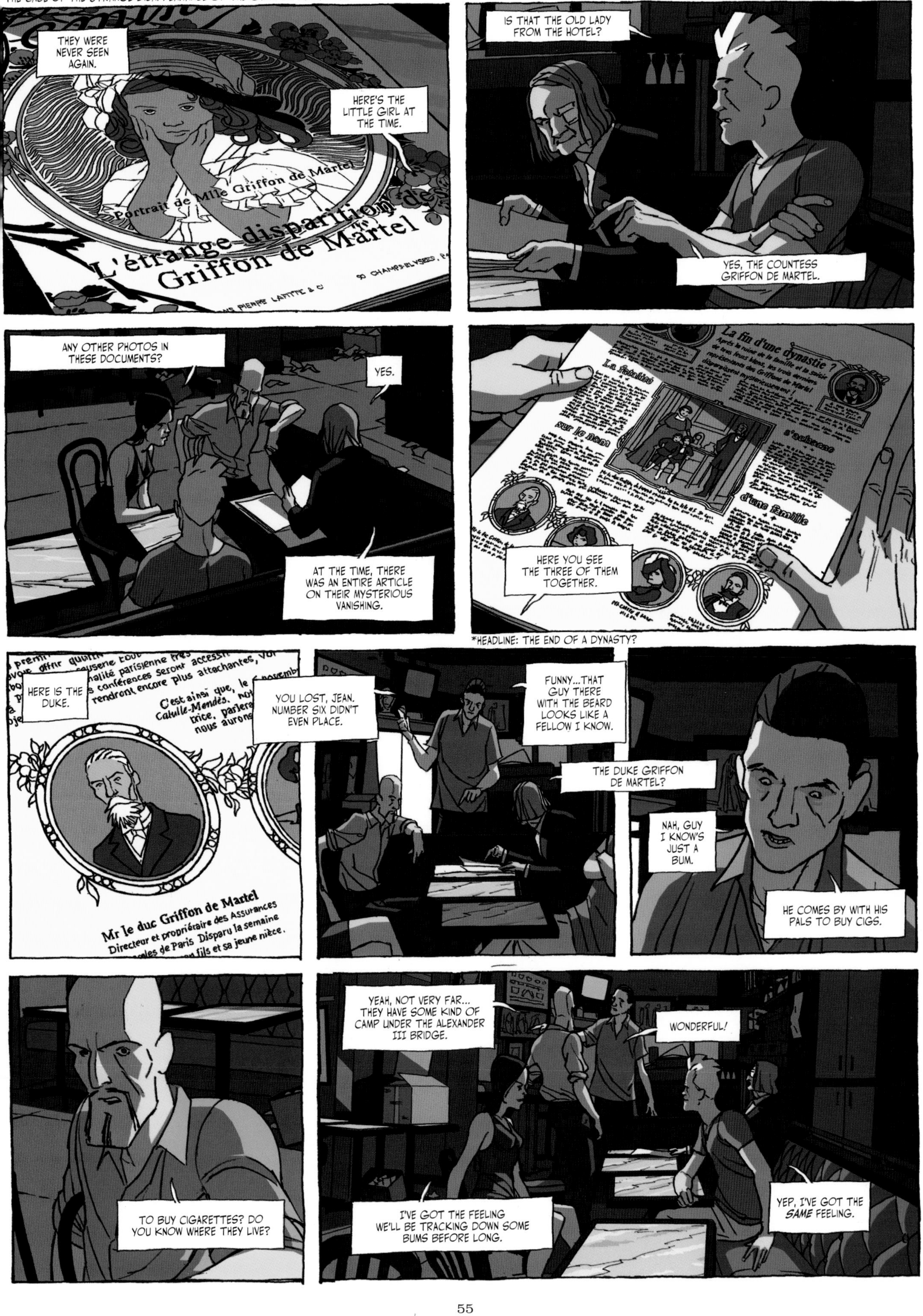
Portrait de Mlle Griffon de Martel
L'étrange disparition de Griffon de Martel
THEY WERE NEVER SEEN AGAIN.
HERE'S THE LITTLE GIRL AT THE TIME.
IS THAT THE OLD LADY FROM THE HOTEL?
YES, THE COUNTESS GRIFFON DE MARTEL.
ANY OTHER PHOTOS IN THESE DOCUMENTS?
YES.
AT THE TIME, THERE WAS AN ENTIRE ARTICLE ON THEIR MYSTERIOUS VANISHING.
La fin d'une dynastie ?
HERE YOU SEE THE THREE OF THEM TOGETHER.
*HEADLINE: THE END OF A DYNASTY?
HERE IS THE DUKE.
Mr le duc Griffon de Martel
YOU LOST, JEAN. NUMBER SIX DIDN'T EVEN PLACE.
FUNNY...THAT GUY THERE WITH THE BEARD LOOKS LIKE A FELLOW I KNOW.
THE DUKE GRIFFON DE MARTEL?
NAH, GUY I KNOW'S JUST A BUM.
HE COMES BY WITH HIS PALS TO BUY CIGS.
TO BUY CIGARETTES? DO YOU KNOW WHERE THEY LIVE?
YEAH, NOT VERY FAR... THEY HAVE SOME KIND OF CAMP UNDER THE ALEXANDER III BRIDGE.
WONDERFUL!
I'VE GOT THE FEELING WE'LL BE TRACKING DOWN SOME BUMS BEFORE LONG.
YEP, I'VE GOT THE *SAME* FEELING.

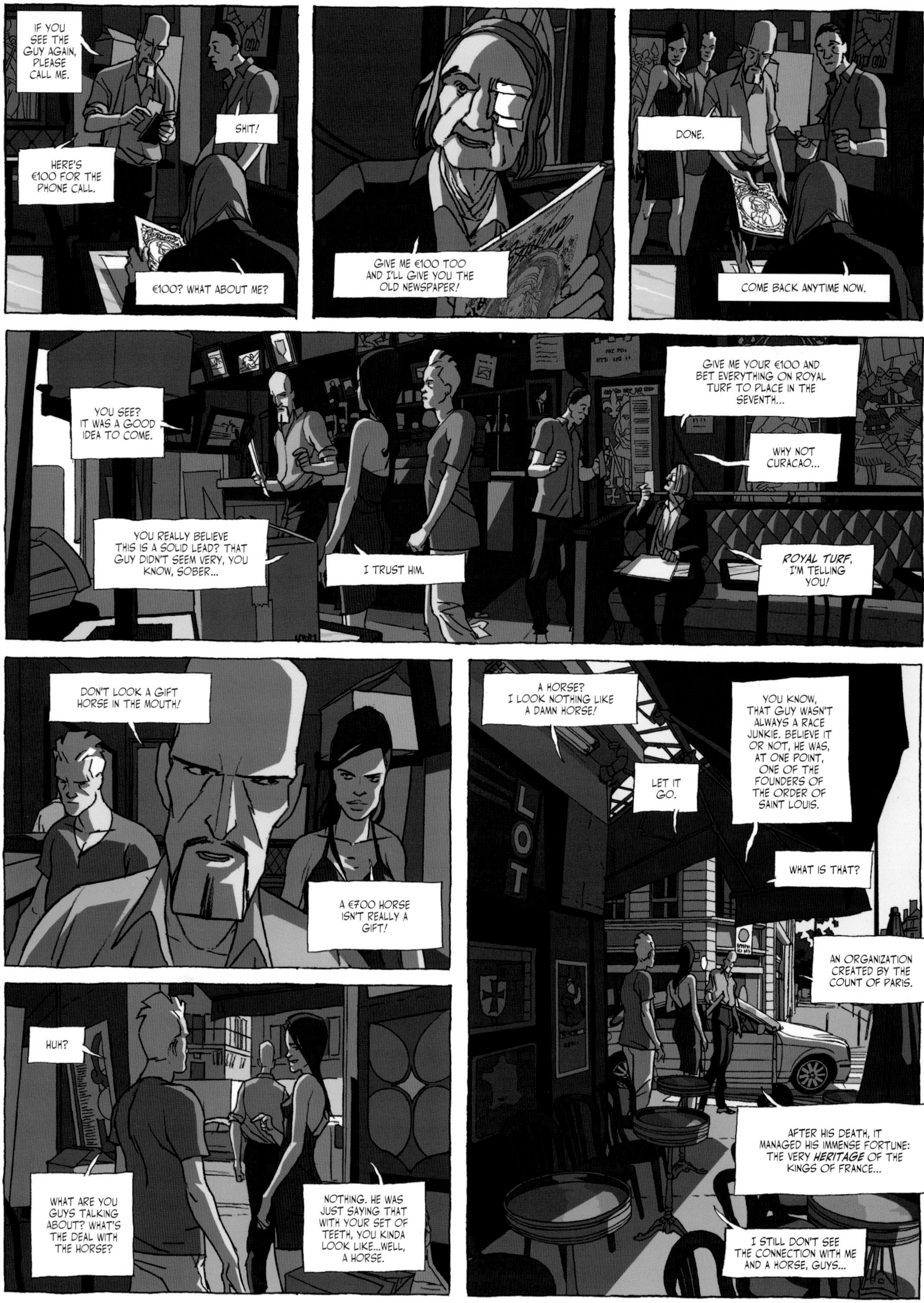

IF YOU SEE THE GUY AGAIN, PLEASE CALL ME.
SHIT!
HERE'S €100 FOR THE PHONE CALL.
€100? WHAT ABOUT ME?
GIVE ME €100 TOO AND I'LL GIVE YOU THE OLD NEWSPAPER!
DONE.
COME BACK ANYTIME NOW.
YOU SEE? IT WAS A GOOD IDEA TO COME.
YOU REALLY BELIEVE THIS IS A SOLID LEAD? THAT GUY DIDN'T SEEM VERY, YOU KNOW, SOBER...
I TRUST HIM.
GIVE ME YOUR €100 AND BET EVERYTHING ON ROYAL TURF TO PLACE IN THE SEVENTH...
WHY NOT CURACAO...
ROYAL TURF, I'M TELLING YOU!
DON'T LOOK A GIFT HORSE IN THE MOUTH!
A €700 HORSE ISN'T REALLY A GIFT!
HUH?
WHAT ARE YOU GUYS TALKING ABOUT? WHAT'S THE DEAL WITH THE HORSE?
NOTHING. HE WAS JUST SAYING THAT WITH YOUR SET OF TEETH, YOU KINDA LOOK LIKE...WELL, A HORSE.
A HORSE? I LOOK NOTHING LIKE A DAMN HORSE!
LET IT GO.
YOU KNOW, THAT GUY WASN'T ALWAYS A RACE JUNKIE. BELIEVE IT OR NOT, HE WAS, AT ONE POINT, ONE OF THE FOUNDERS OF THE ORDER OF SAINT LOUIS.
WHAT IS THAT?
AN ORGANIZATION CREATED BY THE COUNT OF PARIS.
AFTER HIS DEATH, IT MANAGED HIS IMMENSE FORTUNE: THE VERY HERITAGE OF THE KINGS OF FRANCE...
I STILL DON'T SEE THE CONNECTION WITH ME AND A HORSE, GUYS...

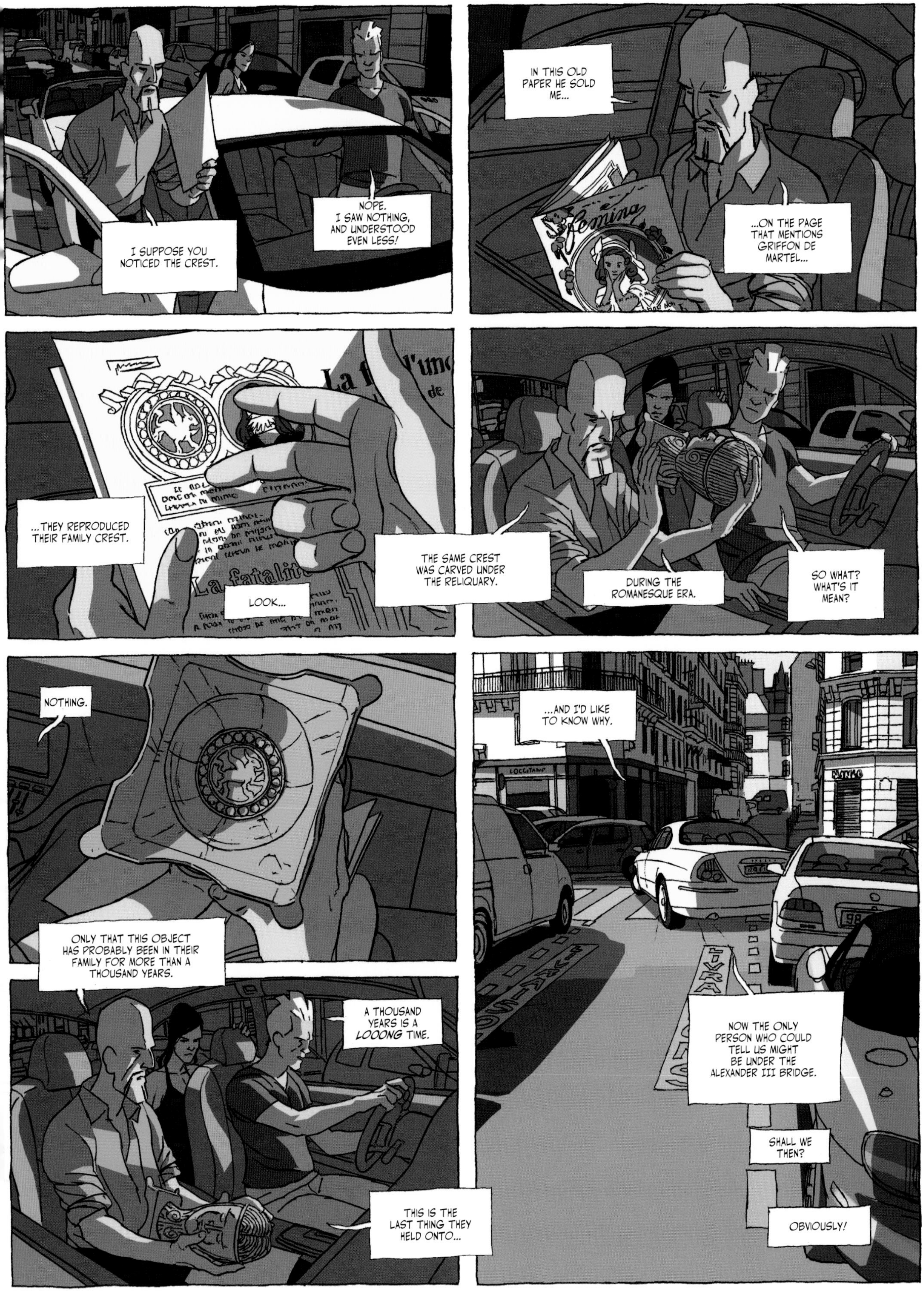
I SUPPOSE YOU NOTICED THE CREST.
NOPE. I SAW NOTHING, AND UNDERSTOOD EVEN LESS!
IN THIS OLD PAPER HE SOLD ME...
...ON THE PAGE THAT MENTIONS GRIFFON DE MARTEL...
...THEY REPRODUCED THEIR FAMILY CREST.
LOOK...
THE SAME CREST WAS CARVED UNDER THE RELIQUARY.
DURING THE ROMANESQUE ERA.
SO WHAT? WHAT'S IT MEAN?
NOTHING.
ONLY THAT THIS OBJECT HAS PROBABLY BEEN IN THEIR FAMILY FOR MORE THAN A THOUSAND YEARS.
A THOUSAND YEARS IS A LOOONG TIME.
THIS IS THE LAST THING THEY HELD ONTO...
...AND I'D LIKE TO KNOW WHY.
NOW THE ONLY PERSON WHO COULD TELL US MIGHT BE UNDER THE ALEXANDER III BRIDGE.
SHALL WE THEN?
OBVIOUSLY!

WHY WOULD I ANSWER YOUR QUESTIONS?

YOU COPS?

DO WE *LOOK LIKE* COPS?

NO.

THAT'S *ONE* POINT IN YOUR FAVOR...

WHAT D'YOU WANT WITH HIM?

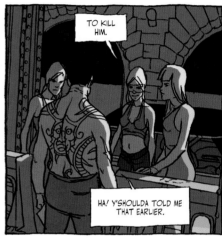

TO KILL HIM.

HA! Y'SHOULDA TOLD ME THAT EARLIER.

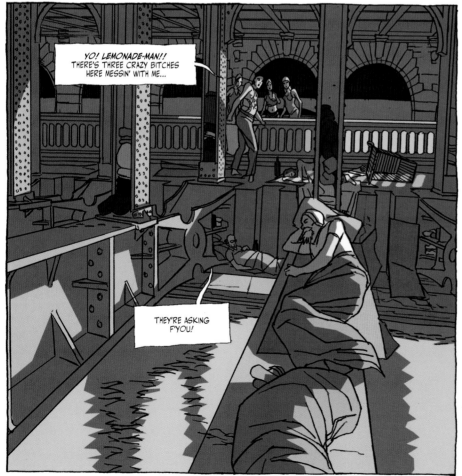

YO! LEMONADE-MAN!! THERE'S THREE CRAZY BITCHES HERE MESSIN' WITH ME...

THEY'RE ASKING F'YOU!

?

AND WHAT MAKES YOU THINK WE'RE MESSING AROUND?

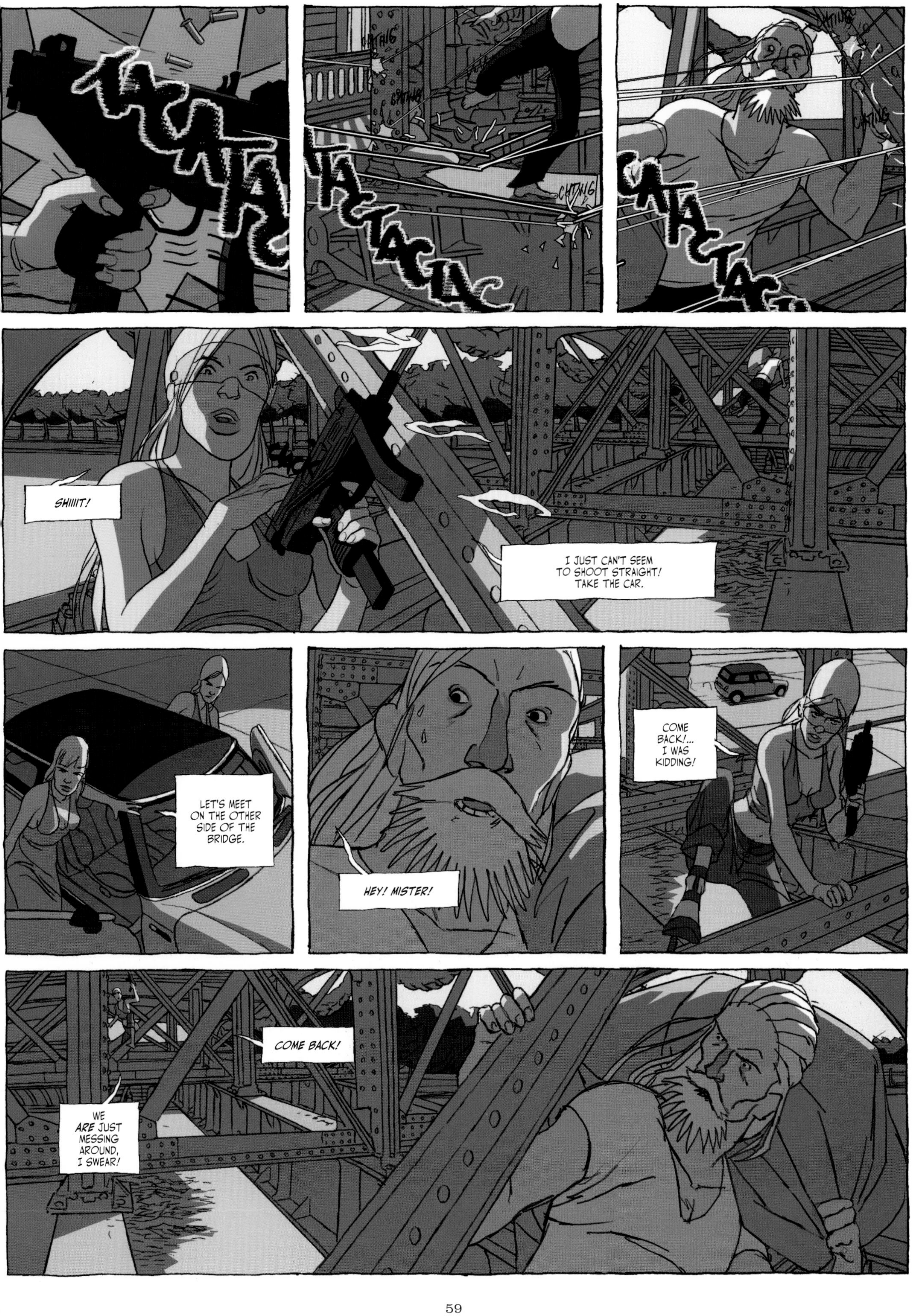
TACATACTAC
CHTING
CHTING
TACTACTACTAC
CHTING
TACATACTACTA
SHIIIIT!
I JUST CAN'T SEEM TO SHOOT STRAIGHT! TAKE THE CAR.
LET'S MEET ON THE OTHER SIDE OF THE BRIDGE.
HEY! MISTER!
COME BACK!... I WAS KIDDING!
COME BACK!
WE ARE JUST MESSING AROUND, I SWEAR!

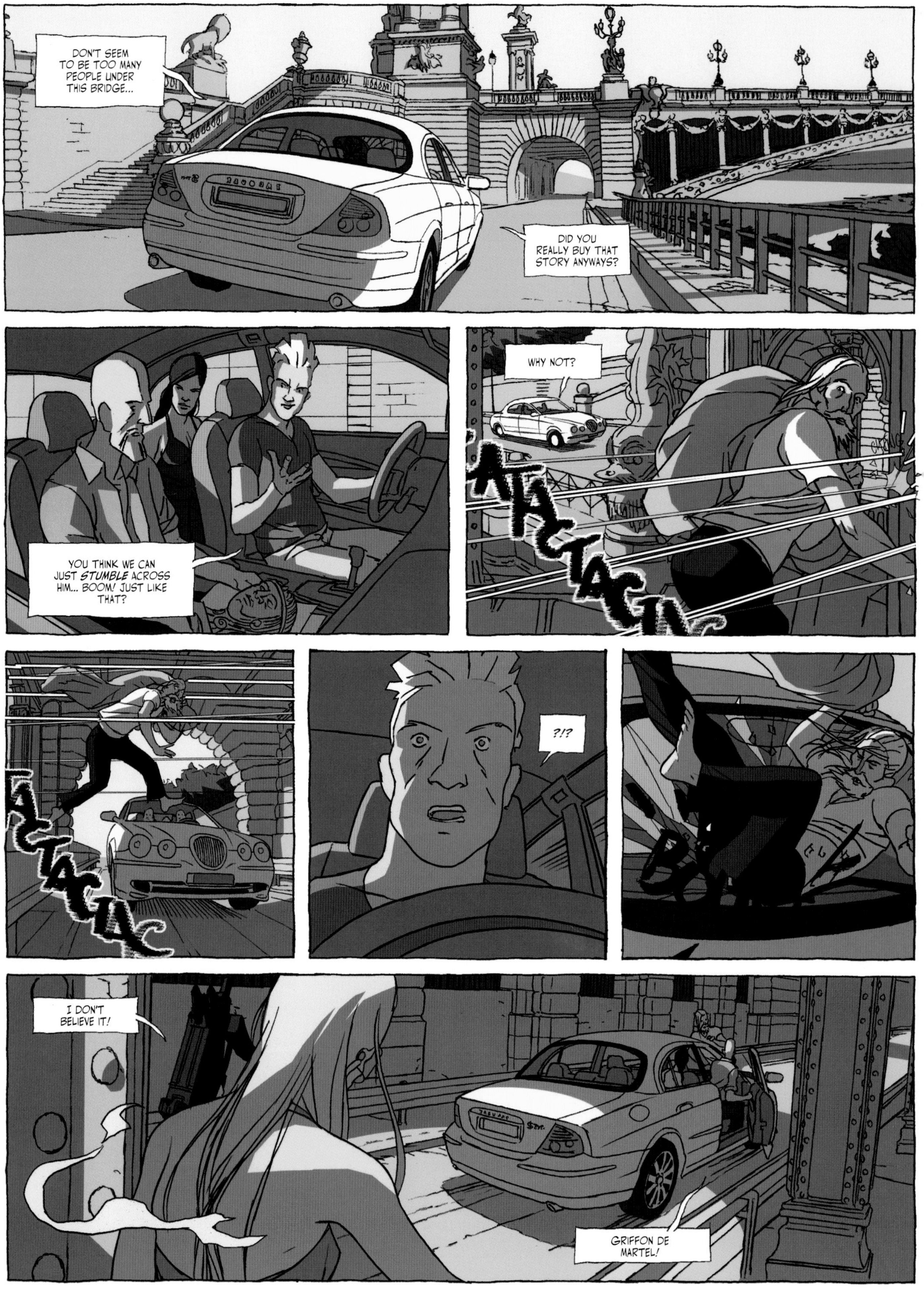
DON'T SEEM TO BE TOO MANY PEOPLE UNDER THIS BRIDGE...
DID YOU REALLY BUY THAT STORY ANYWAYS?
YOU THINK WE CAN JUST STUMBLE ACROSS HIM... BOOM! JUST LIKE THAT?
WHY NOT?
?!?
I DON'T BELIEVE IT!
GRIFFON DE MARTEL!

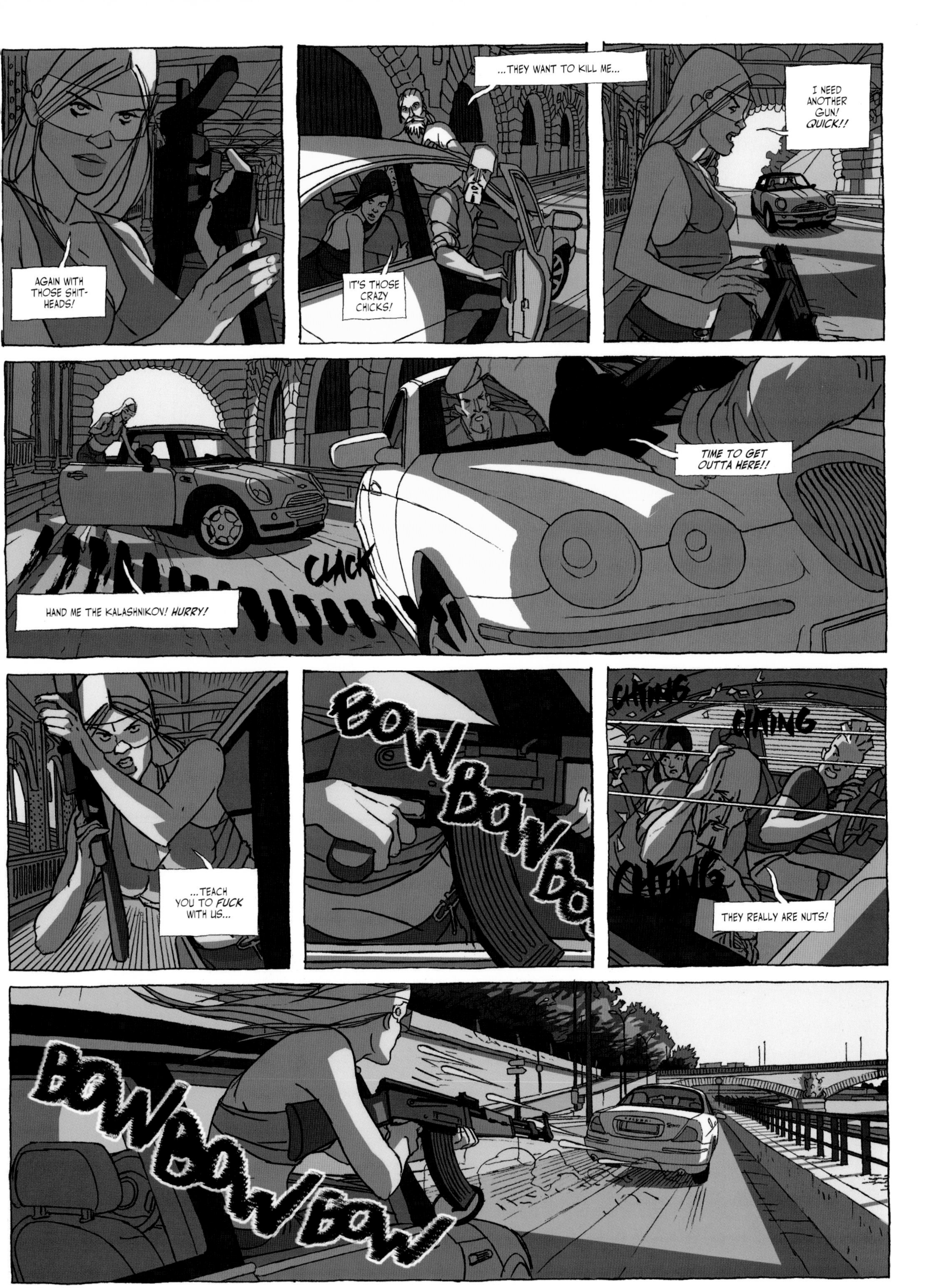
AGAIN WITH THOSE SHIT-HEADS!
...THEY WANT TO KILL ME...
IT'S THOSE CRAZY CHICKS!
I NEED ANOTHER GUN! *QUICK!!*
TIME TO GET OUTTA HERE!!
CLACK
HAND ME THE KALASHNIKOV! *HURRY!*
...TEACH YOU TO *FUCK* WITH US...
BOW BOW BOW BOW
CHING
CHING
CHING
THEY REALLY ARE NUTS!
BOW BOW BOW BOW

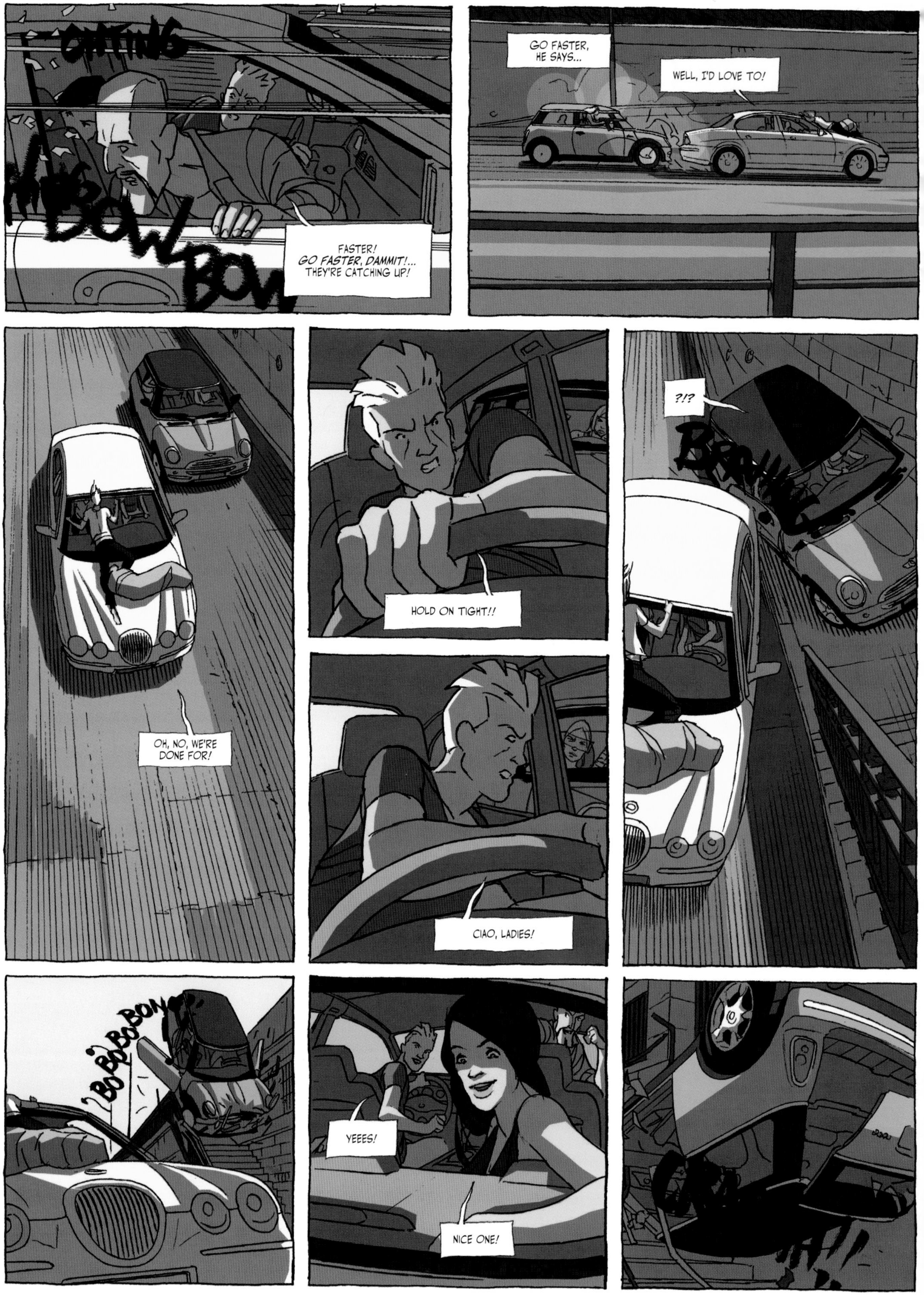
BOW
BOW
FASTER! GO FASTER, DAMMIT!... THEY'RE CATCHING UP!
GO FASTER, HE SAYS...
WELL, I'D LOVE TO!
OH, NO, WE'RE DONE FOR!
HOLD ON TIGHT!!
CIAO, LADIES!
?!?
YEEES!
NICE ONE!

HA! HA! HA!
WE ALMOST--

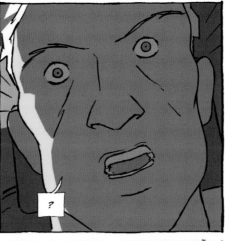

?

THE PROPHECY...

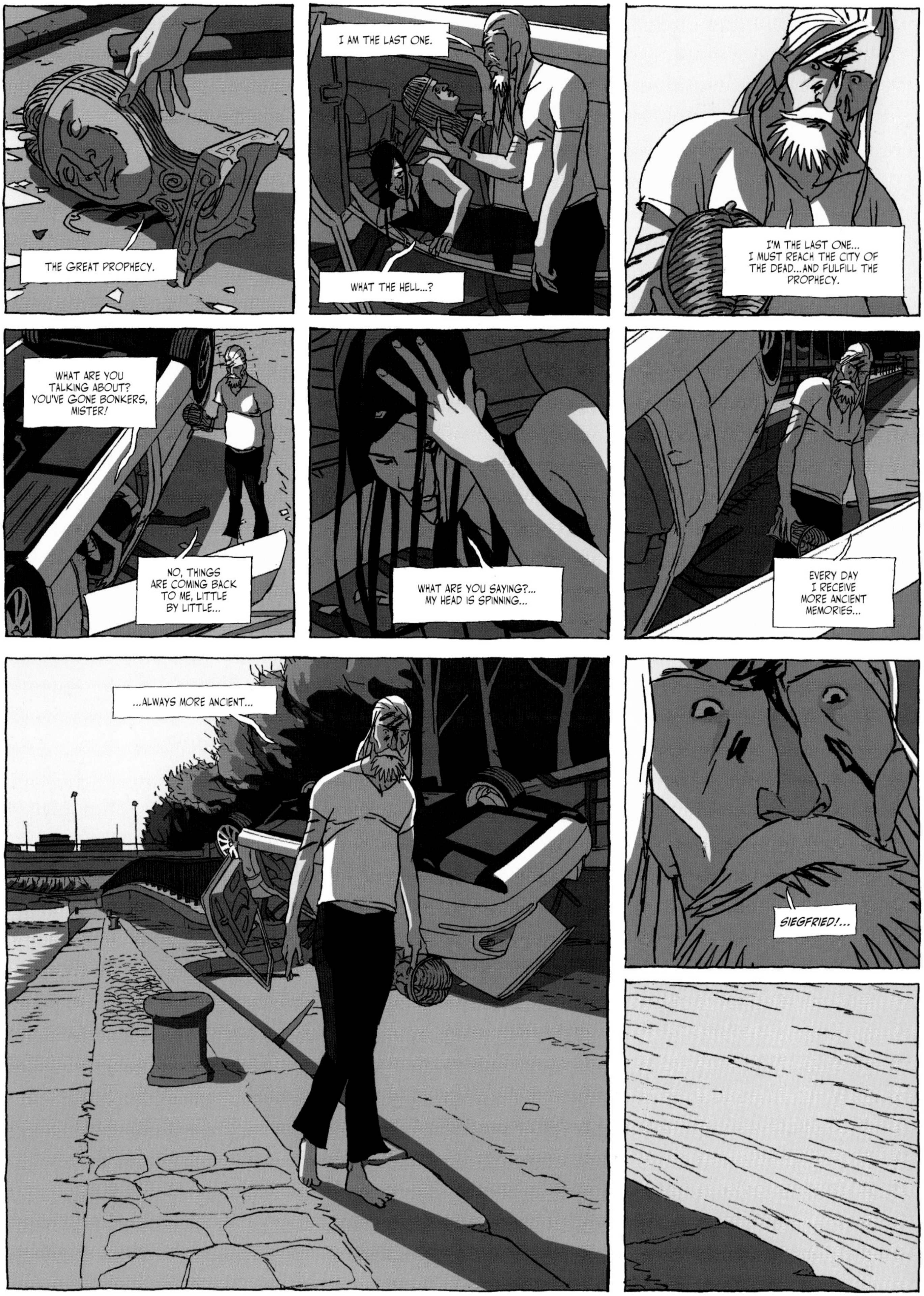
THE GREAT PROPHECY.
I AM THE LAST ONE.
WHAT THE HELL...?
I'M THE LAST ONE... I MUST REACH THE CITY OF THE DEAD...AND FULFILL THE PROPHECY.
WHAT ARE YOU TALKING ABOUT? YOU'VE GONE BONKERS, MISTER!
NO, THINGS ARE COMING BACK TO ME, LITTLE BY LITTLE...
WHAT ARE YOU SAYING?... MY HEAD IS SPINNING...
EVERY DAY I RECEIVE MORE ANCIENT MEMORIES...
...ALWAYS MORE ANCIENT...
SIEGFRIED!...

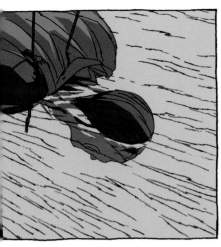

THE FIRST MENTION OF THE NAME
GRIFFON DE MARTEL DATES BACK
TO THE WINTER OF 885...

...WHEN MORE THAN 700 DRAKKARS LED BY
SIEGFRIED HAD PARIS UNDER SIEGE...

FOR WEEKS, THE CITY, PROTECTED BY ITS
HOLY RELICS, REFUSED TO SURRENDER...

...ONE NIGHT, HOWEVER, THE LARGE BRIDGE CONNECTING THE SOUTHERN
ENTRANCE OF THE CITY WAS WASHED AWAY BY A FLOOD...

...12 MEN...

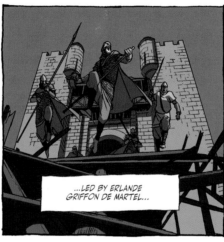

...LED BY ERLANDE
GRIFFON DE MARTEL...

...FOUND THEMSELVES STRANDED ON
THE TOWERS OF THE SMALL CASTLE.

IN A DESPERATE RUSH, THE 12 WARRIORS LEAPT DOWN TO THE REMAINS OF THE BRIDGE...

...AND TRIED TO STAVE OFF THE HORDES OF
NORMANS BY THEMSELVES.

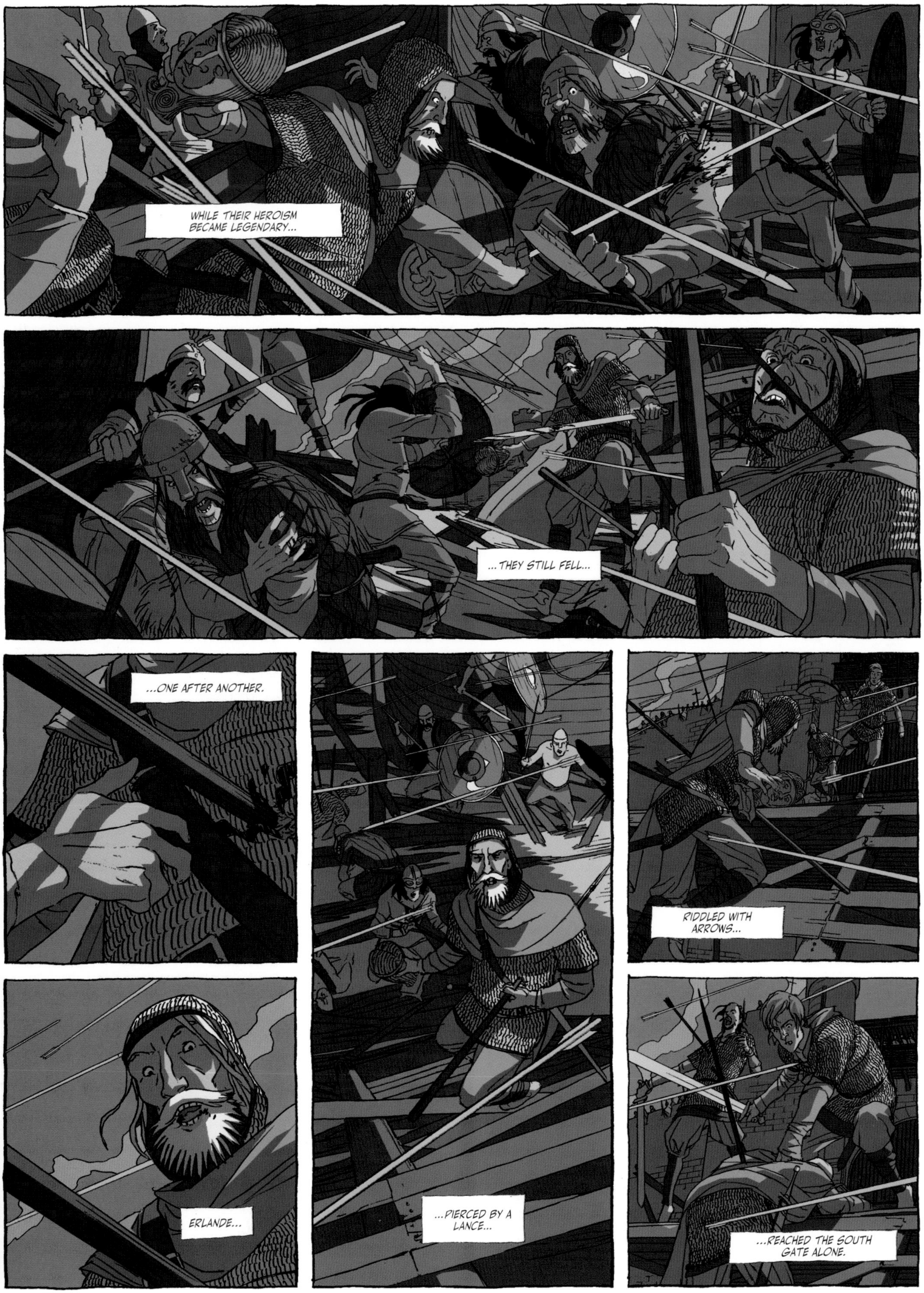
WHILE THEIR HEROISM BECAME LEGENDARY...
...THEY STILL FELL...
...ONE AFTER ANOTHER.
RIDDLED WITH ARROWS...
ERLANDE...
...PIERCED BY A LANCE...
...REACHED THE SOUTH GATE ALONE.

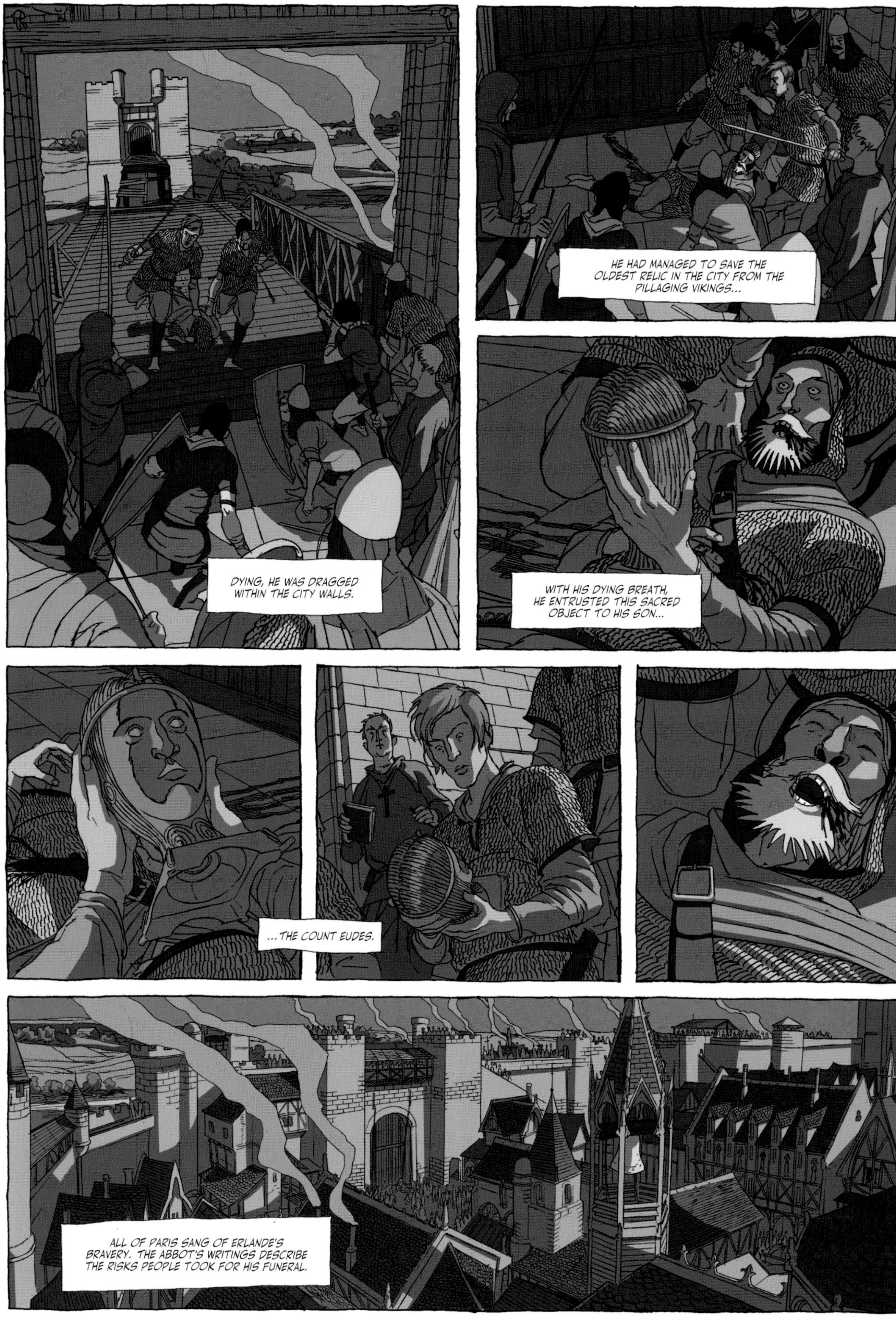
DYING, HE WAS DRAGGED WITHIN THE CITY WALLS.
HE HAD MANAGED TO SAVE THE OLDEST RELIC IN THE CITY FROM THE PILLAGING VIKINGS...
WITH HIS DYING BREATH, HE ENTRUSTED THIS SACRED OBJECT TO HIS SON...
...THE COUNT EUDES.
ALL OF PARIS SANG OF ERLANDE'S BRAVERY. THE ABBOT'S WRITINGS DESCRIBE THE RISKS PEOPLE TOOK FOR HIS FUNERAL.

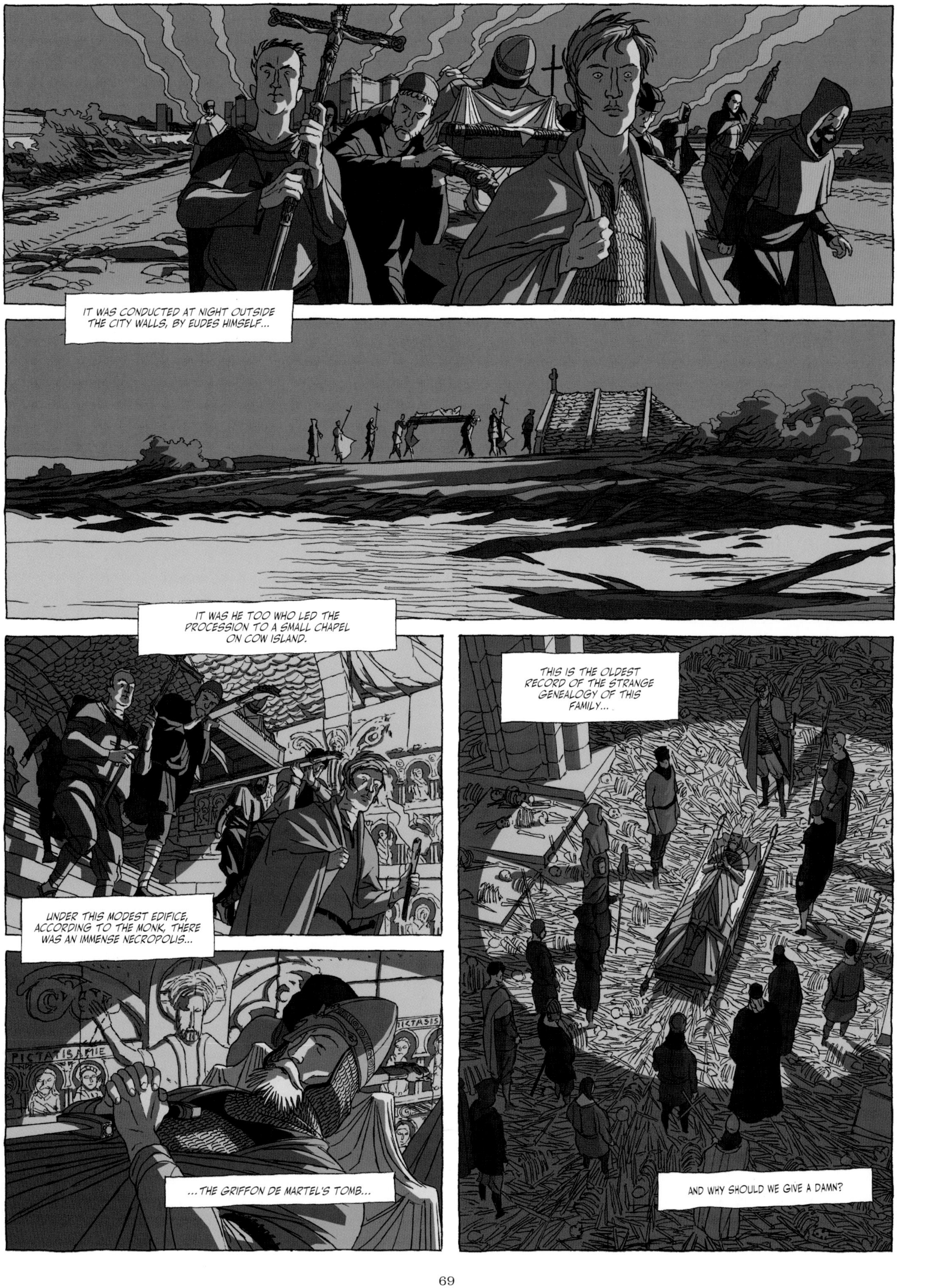
IT WAS CONDUCTED AT NIGHT OUTSIDE THE CITY WALLS, BY EUDES HIMSELF...
IT WAS HE TOO WHO LED THE PROCESSION TO A SMALL CHAPEL ON COW ISLAND.
UNDER THIS MODEST EDIFICE, ACCORDING TO THE MONK, THERE WAS AN IMMENSE NECROPOLIS...
...THE GRIFFON DE MARTEL'S TOMB...
THIS IS THE OLDEST RECORD OF THE STRANGE GENEALOGY OF THIS FAMILY...
AND WHY SHOULD WE GIVE A DAMN?

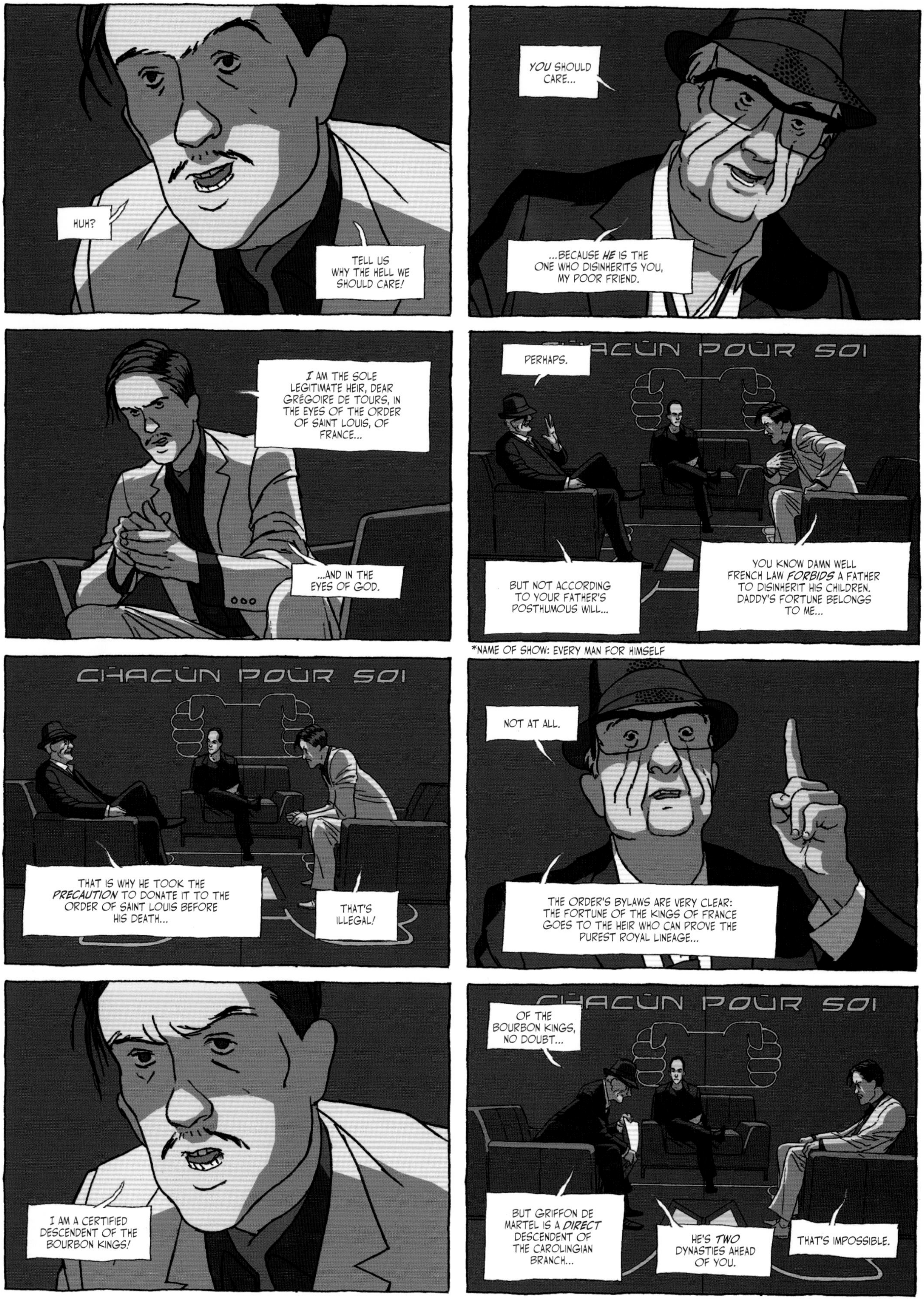
HUH?
TELL US WHY THE HELL WE SHOULD CARE!
YOU SHOULD CARE...
...BECAUSE HE IS THE ONE WHO DISINHERITS YOU, MY POOR FRIEND.
I AM THE SOLE LEGITIMATE HEIR, DEAR GRÉGOIRE DE TOURS, IN THE EYES OF THE ORDER OF SAINT LOUIS, OF FRANCE...
...AND IN THE EYES OF GOD.
CHACÜN POÜR SOI
PERHAPS.
BUT NOT ACCORDING TO YOUR FATHER'S POSTHUMOUS WILL...
YOU KNOW DAMN WELL FRENCH LAW FORBIDS A FATHER TO DISINHERIT HIS CHILDREN. DADDY'S FORTUNE BELONGS TO ME...
*NAME OF SHOW: EVERY MAN FOR HIMSELF
CHACÜN POÜR SOI
THAT IS WHY HE TOOK THE PRECAUTION TO DONATE IT TO THE ORDER OF SAINT LOUIS BEFORE HIS DEATH...
THAT'S ILLEGAL!
NOT AT ALL.
THE ORDER'S BYLAWS ARE VERY CLEAR: THE FORTUNE OF THE KINGS OF FRANCE GOES TO THE HEIR WHO CAN PROVE THE PUREST ROYAL LINEAGE...
I AM A CERTIFIED DESCENDENT OF THE BOURBON KINGS!
CHACÜN POÜR SOI
OF THE BOURBON KINGS, NO DOUBT...
BUT GRIFFON DE MARTEL IS A DIRECT DESCENDENT OF THE CAROLINGIAN BRANCH...
HE'S TWO DYNASTIES AHEAD OF YOU.
THAT'S IMPOSSIBLE.

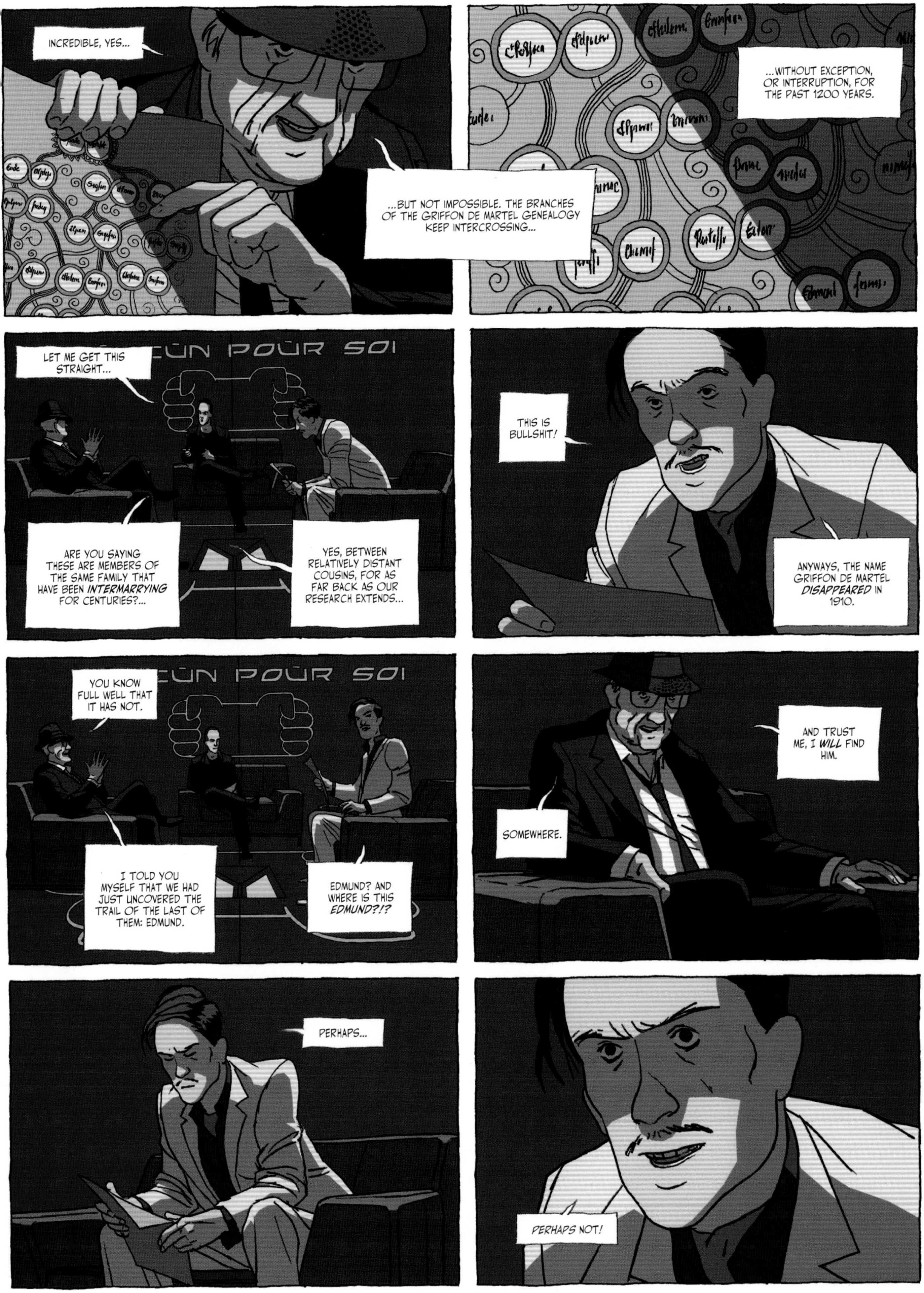
INCREDIBLE, YES...
...BUT NOT IMPOSSIBLE. THE BRANCHES OF THE GRIFFON DE MARTEL GENEALOGY KEEP INTERCROSSING...
...WITHOUT EXCEPTION, OR INTERRUPTION, FOR THE PAST 1200 YEARS.
LET ME GET THIS STRAIGHT...
ARE YOU SAYING THESE ARE MEMBERS OF THE SAME FAMILY THAT HAVE BEEN *INTERMARRYING* FOR CENTURIES?...
YES, BETWEEN RELATIVELY DISTANT COUSINS, FOR AS FAR BACK AS OUR RESEARCH EXTENDS...
THIS IS BULLSHIT!
ANYWAYS, THE NAME GRIFFON DE MARTEL *DISAPPEARED* IN 1910.
YOU KNOW FULL WELL THAT IT HAS NOT.
I TOLD YOU MYSELF THAT WE HAD JUST UNCOVERED THE TRAIL OF THE LAST OF THEM: EDMUND.
EDMUND? AND WHERE IS THIS *EDMUND?!?*
SOMEWHERE.
AND TRUST ME, I ***WILL*** FIND HIM.
PERHAPS...
PERHAPS NOT!

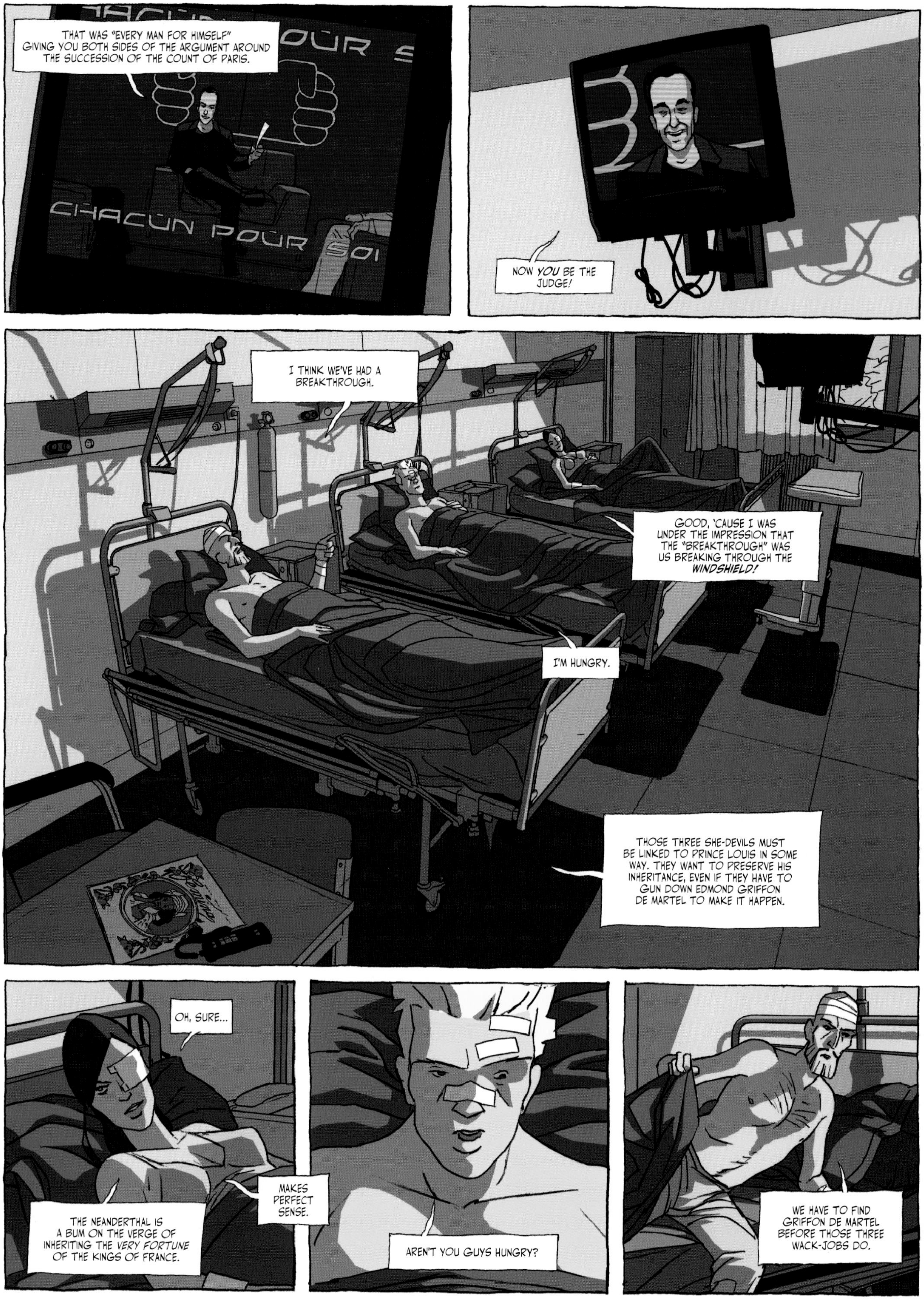
CHACUN POUR S
CHACUN POUR SOI
THAT WAS "EVERY MAN FOR HIMSELF" GIVING YOU BOTH SIDES OF THE ARGUMENT AROUND THE SUCCESSION OF THE COUNT OF PARIS.
NOW *YOU* BE THE JUDGE!
I THINK WE'VE HAD A BREAKTHROUGH.
GOOD, 'CAUSE I WAS UNDER THE IMPRESSION THAT THE "BREAKTHROUGH" WAS US BREAKING THROUGH THE *WINDSHIELD!*
I'M HUNGRY.
THOSE THREE SHE-DEVILS MUST BE LINKED TO PRINCE LOUIS IN SOME WAY. THEY WANT TO PRESERVE HIS INHERITANCE, EVEN IF THEY HAVE TO GUN DOWN EDMOND GRIFFON DE MARTEL TO MAKE IT HAPPEN.
OH, SURE...
THE NEANDERTHAL IS A BUM ON THE VERGE OF INHERITING THE *VERY FORTUNE* OF THE KINGS OF FRANCE.
MAKES PERFECT SENSE.
AREN'T YOU GUYS HUNGRY?
WE HAVE TO FIND GRIFFON DE MARTEL BEFORE THOSE THREE WACK-JOBS DO.

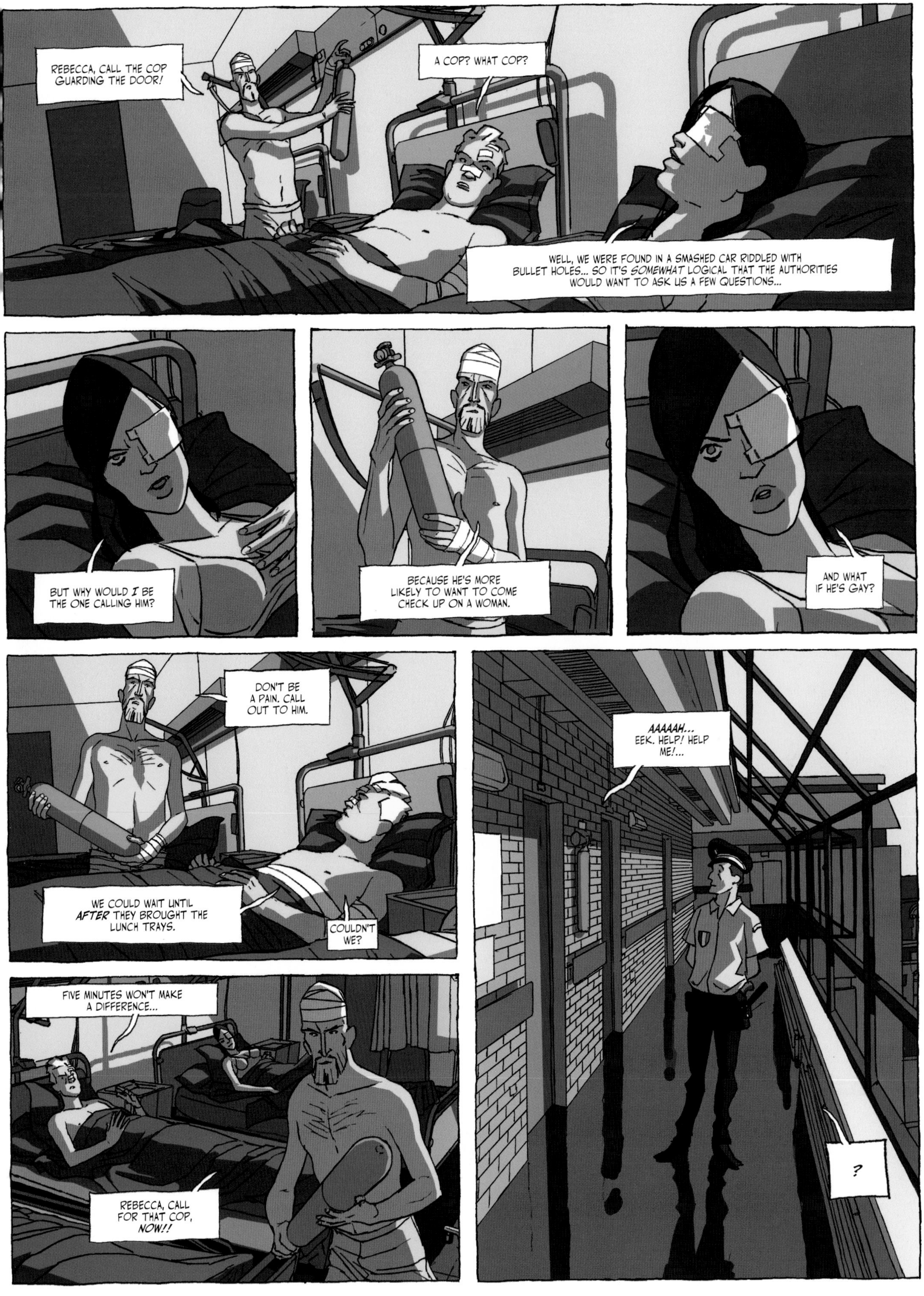
REBECCA, CALL THE COP GUARDING THE DOOR!
A COP? WHAT COP?
WELL, WE WERE FOUND IN A SMASHED CAR RIDDLED WITH BULLET HOLES... SO IT'S *SOMEWHAT* LOGICAL THAT THE AUTHORITIES WOULD WANT TO ASK US A FEW QUESTIONS...
BUT WHY WOULD *I* BE THE ONE CALLING HIM?
BECAUSE HE'S MORE LIKELY TO WANT TO COME CHECK UP ON A WOMAN.
AND WHAT IF HE'S GAY?
DON'T BE A PAIN. CALL OUT TO HIM.
WE COULD WAIT UNTIL *AFTER* THEY BROUGHT THE LUNCH TRAYS.
COULDN'T WE?
FIVE MINUTES WON'T MAKE A DIFFERENCE...
REBECCA, CALL FOR THAT COP, *NOW!!*
AAAAAH... EEK. HELP! HELP ME!...
?

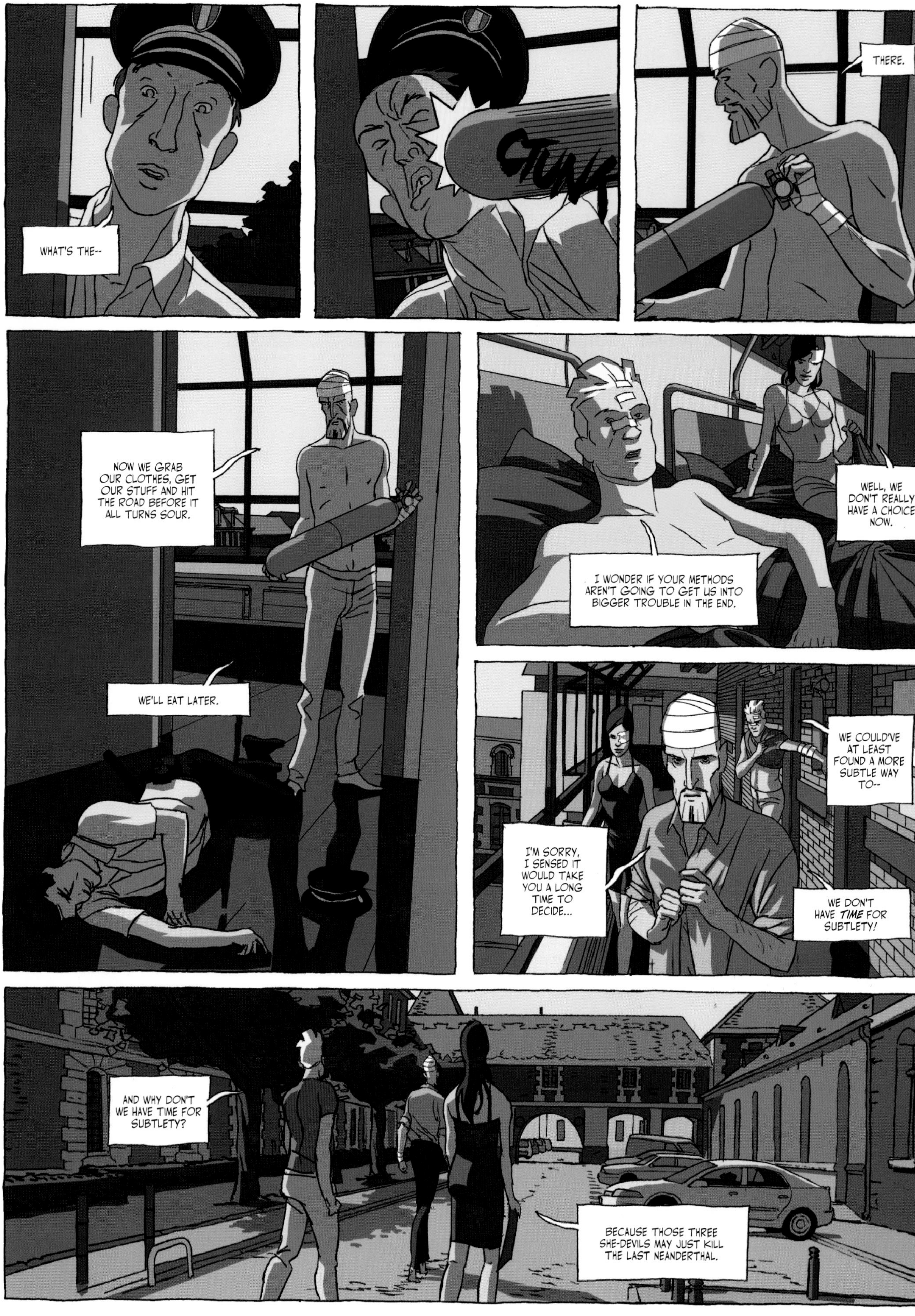
WHAT'S THE--
CTUNK
THERE.
NOW WE GRAB OUR CLOTHES, GET OUR STUFF AND HIT THE ROAD BEFORE IT ALL TURNS SOUR.
WE'LL EAT LATER.
I WONDER IF YOUR METHODS AREN'T GOING TO GET US INTO BIGGER TROUBLE IN THE END.
WELL, WE DON'T REALLY HAVE A CHOICE NOW.
WE COULD'VE AT LEAST FOUND A MORE SUBTLE WAY TO--
I'M SORRY, I SENSED IT WOULD TAKE YOU A LONG TIME TO DECIDE...
WE DON'T HAVE *TIME* FOR SUBTLETY!
AND WHY DON'T WE HAVE TIME FOR SUBTLETY?
BECAUSE THOSE THREE SHE-DEVILS MAY JUST KILL THE LAST NEANDERTHAL.

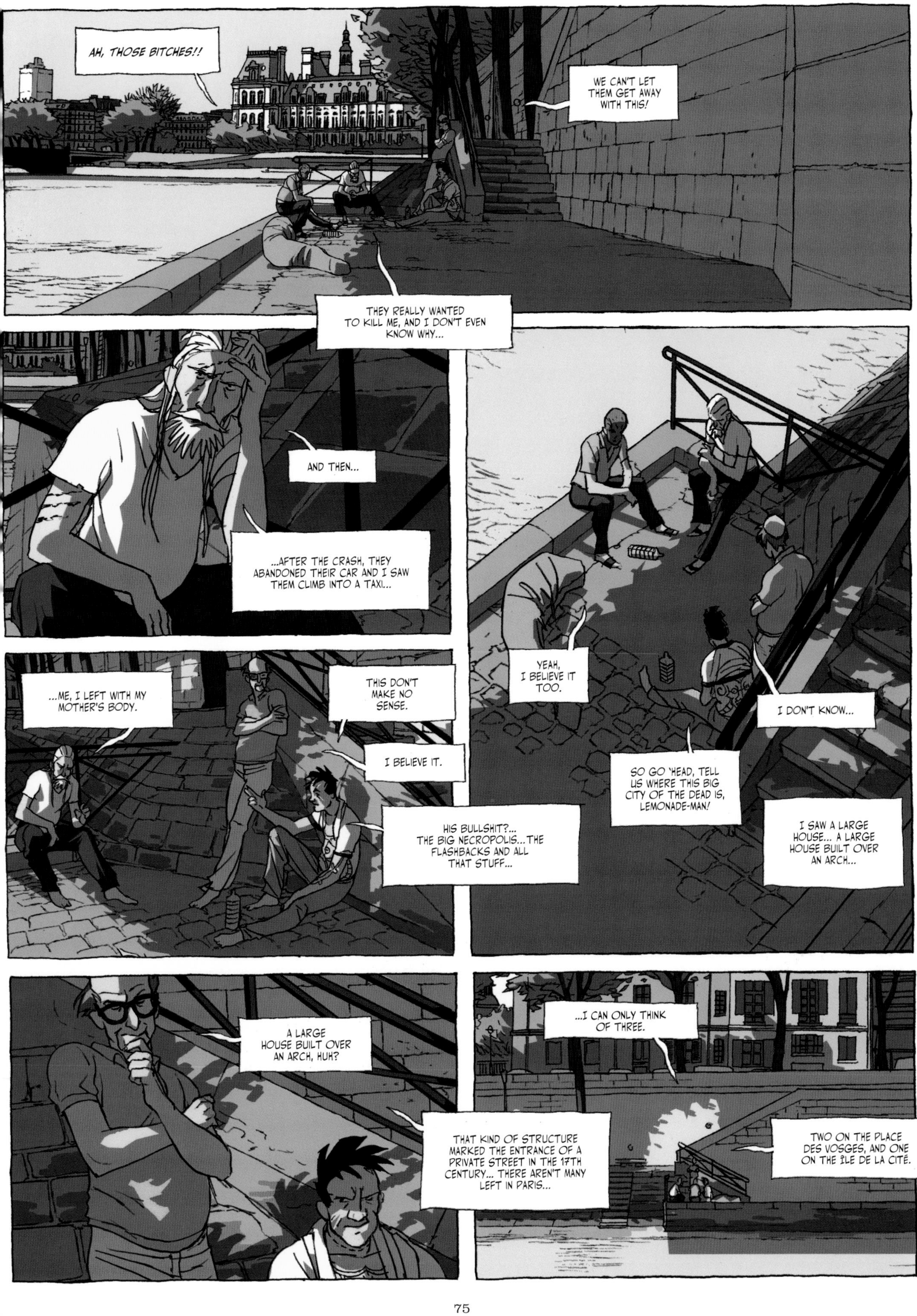
AH, THOSE BITCHES!!
WE CAN'T LET THEM GET AWAY WITH THIS!
THEY REALLY WANTED TO KILL ME, AND I DON'T EVEN KNOW WHY...
AND THEN...
...AFTER THE CRASH, THEY ABANDONED THEIR CAR AND I SAW THEM CLIMB INTO A TAXI...
YEAH, I BELIEVE IT TOO.
I DON'T KNOW...
SO GO 'HEAD, TELL US WHERE THIS BIG CITY OF THE DEAD IS, LEMONADE-MAN!
I SAW A LARGE HOUSE... A LARGE HOUSE BUILT OVER AN ARCH...
...ME, I LEFT WITH MY MOTHER'S BODY.
THIS DON'T MAKE NO SENSE.
I BELIEVE IT.
HIS BULLSHIT?... THE BIG NECROPOLIS... THE FLASHBACKS AND ALL THAT STUFF...
A LARGE HOUSE BUILT OVER AN ARCH, HUH?
THAT KIND OF STRUCTURE MARKED THE ENTRANCE OF A PRIVATE STREET IN THE 17TH CENTURY... THERE AREN'T MANY LEFT IN PARIS...
...I CAN ONLY THINK OF THREE.
TWO ON THE PLACE DES VOSGES, AND ONE ON THE ÎLE DE LA CITÉ.

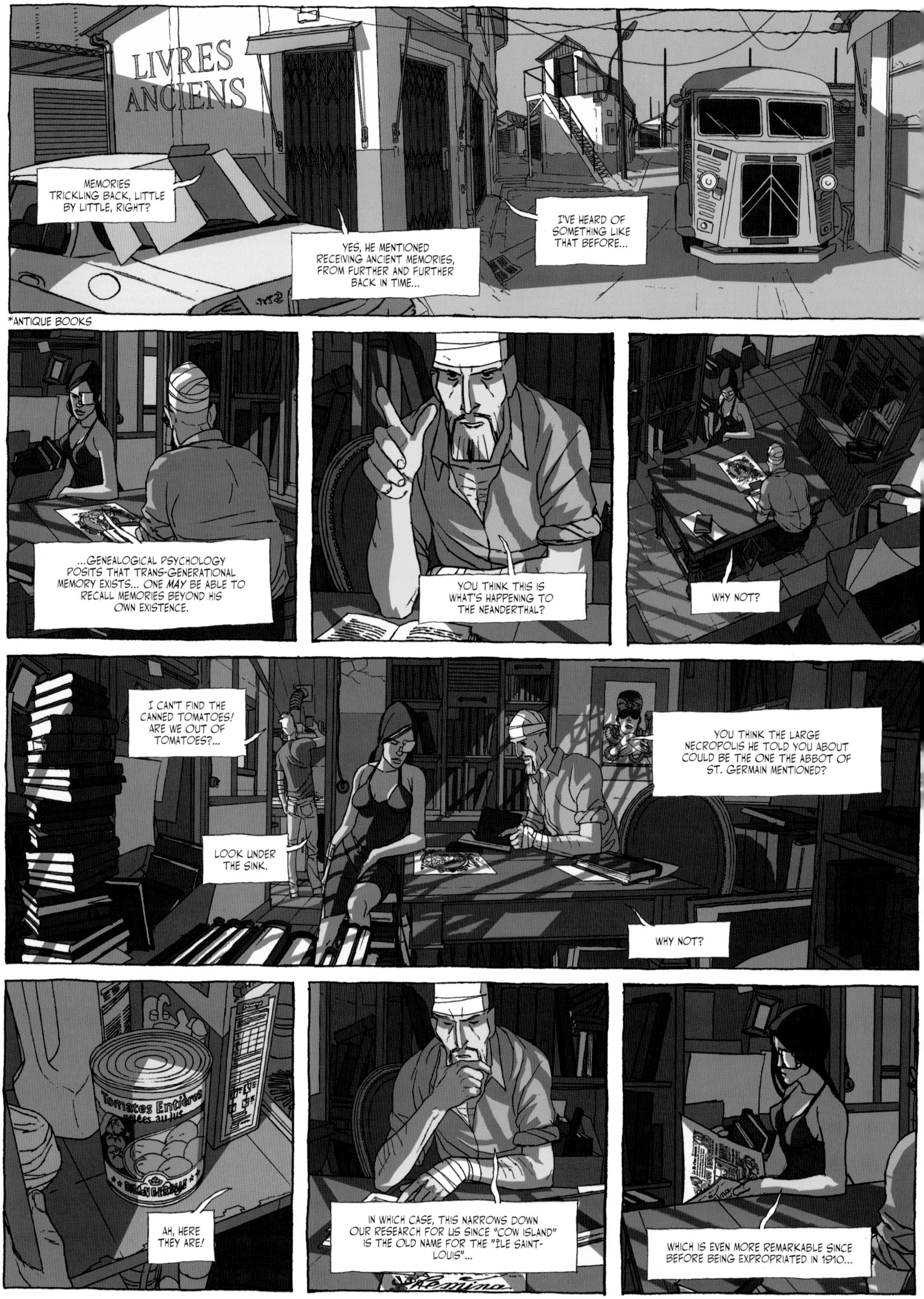
LIVRES ANCIENS
MEMORIES TRICKLING BACK, LITTLE BY LITTLE, RIGHT?
YES, HE MENTIONED RECEIVING ANCIENT MEMORIES, FROM FURTHER AND FURTHER BACK IN TIME...
I'VE HEARD OF SOMETHING LIKE THAT BEFORE...
*ANTIQUE BOOKS
...GENEALOGICAL PSYCHOLOGY POSITS THAT TRANS-GENERATIONAL MEMORY EXISTS... ONE MAY BE ABLE TO RECALL MEMORIES BEYOND HIS OWN EXISTENCE.
YOU THINK THIS IS WHAT'S HAPPENING TO THE NEANDERTHAL?
WHY NOT?
I CAN'T FIND THE CANNED TOMATOES! ARE WE OUT OF TOMATOES?...
YOU THINK THE LARGE NECROPOLIS HE TOLD YOU ABOUT COULD BE THE ONE THE ABBOT OF ST. GERMAIN MENTIONED?
LOOK UNDER THE SINK.
WHY NOT?
Tomates Entières
AH, HERE THEY ARE!
IN WHICH CASE, THIS NARROWS DOWN OUR RESEARCH FOR US SINCE "COW ISLAND" IS THE OLD NAME FOR THE "ÎLE SAINT-LOUIS"...
WHICH IS EVEN MORE REMARKABLE SINCE BEFORE BEING EXPROPRIATED IN 1910...

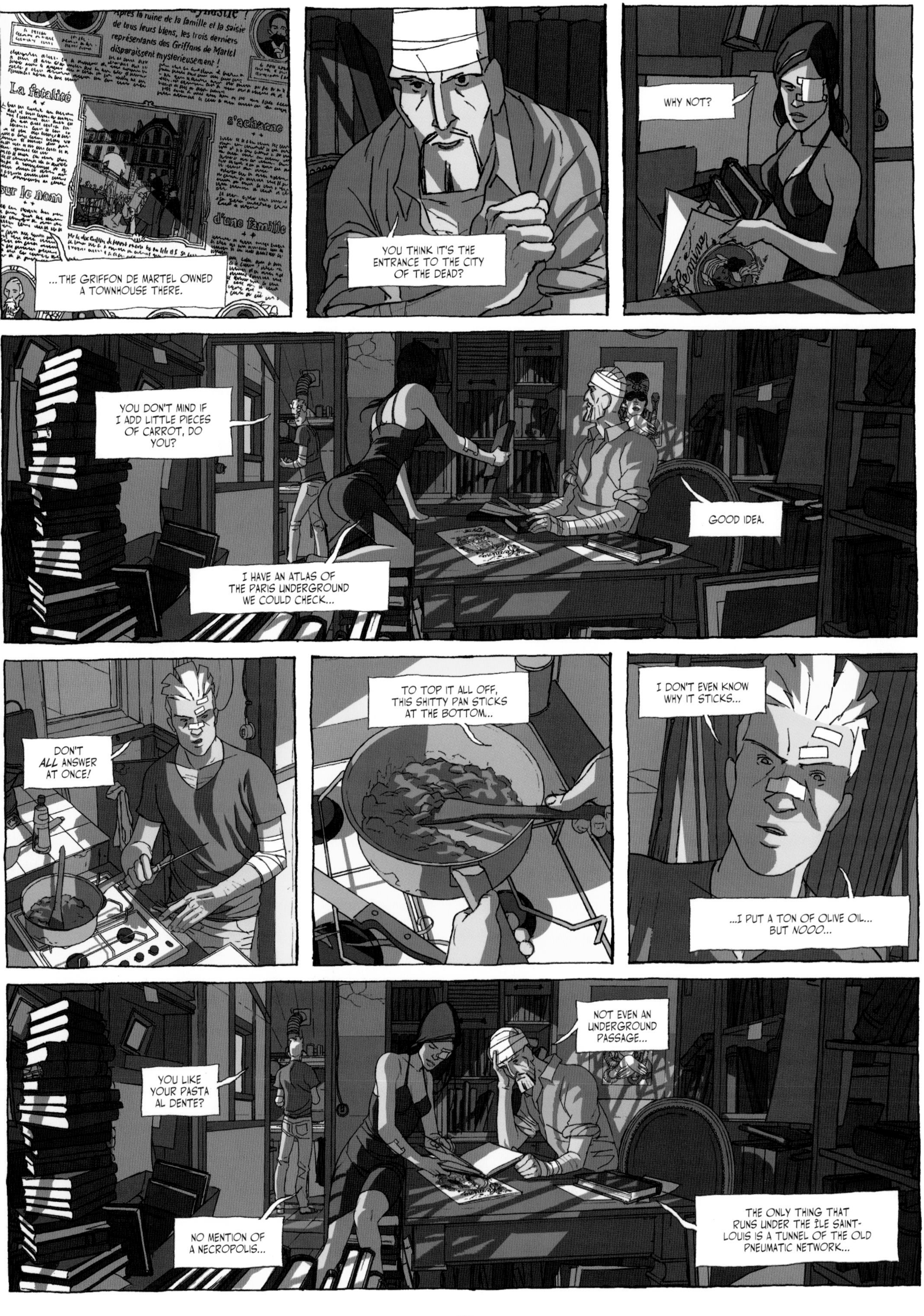
Après la ruine de la famille et la saisie de tous leurs biens, les trois derniers représentants des Griffons de Martel disparaissent mystérieusement !
La fatalité
s'acharne
sur le nom
d'une famille
...THE GRIFFON DE MARTEL OWNED A TOWNHOUSE THERE.
YOU THINK IT'S THE ENTRANCE TO THE CITY OF THE DEAD?
WHY NOT?
YOU DON'T MIND IF I ADD LITTLE PIECES OF CARROT, DO YOU?
GOOD IDEA.
I HAVE AN ATLAS OF THE PARIS UNDERGROUND WE COULD CHECK...
DON'T ALL ANSWER AT ONCE!
TO TOP IT ALL OFF, THIS SHITTY PAN STICKS AT THE BOTTOM...
I DON'T EVEN KNOW WHY IT STICKS...
...I PUT A TON OF OLIVE OIL... BUT NOOO...
NOT EVEN AN UNDERGROUND PASSAGE...
YOU LIKE YOUR PASTA AL DENTE?
NO MENTION OF A NECROPOLIS...
THE ONLY THING THAT RUNS UNDER THE ÎLE SAINT-LOUIS IS A TUNNEL OF THE OLD PNEUMATIC NETWORK...

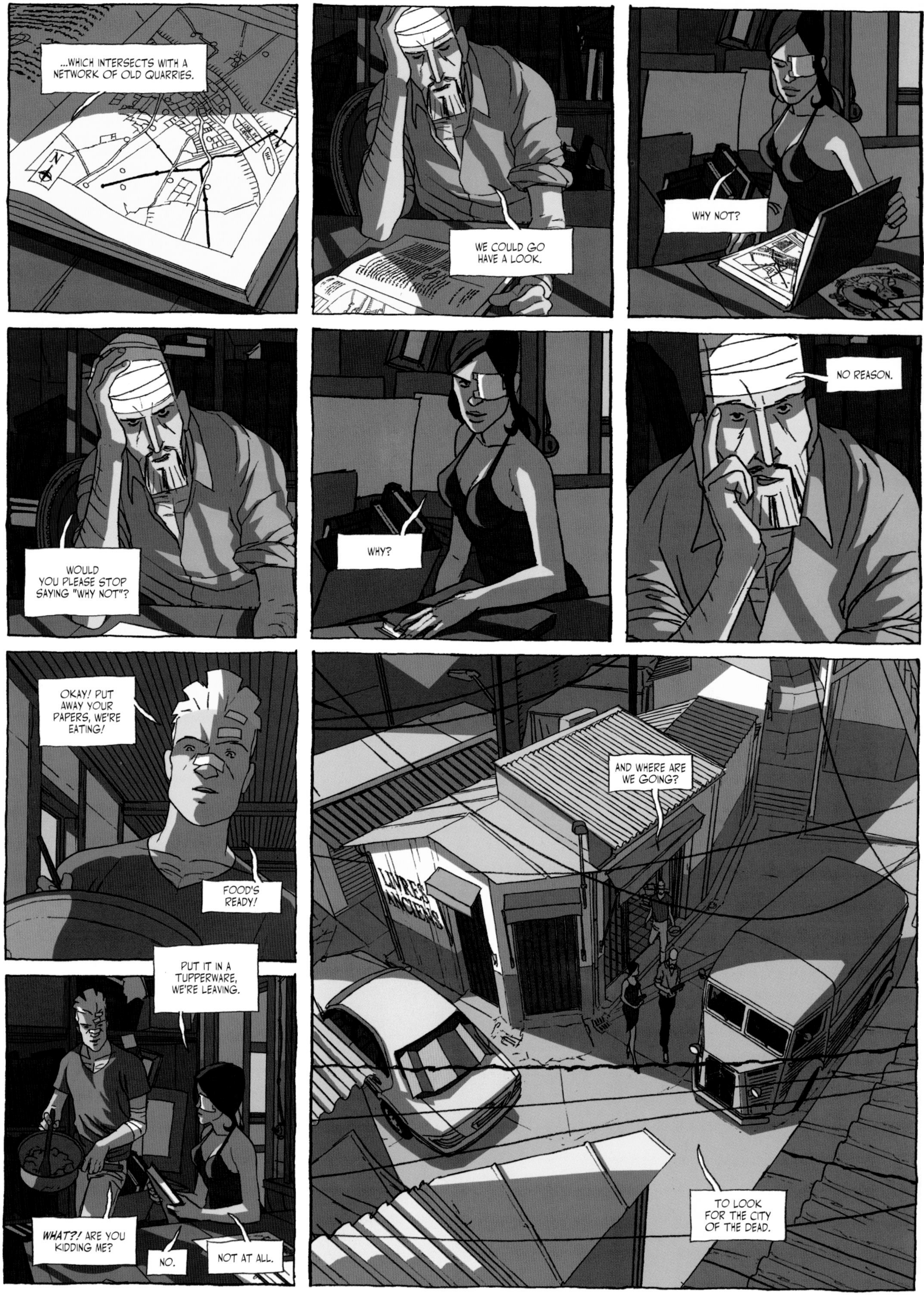
...WHICH INTERSECTS WITH A NETWORK OF OLD QUARRIES.
WE COULD GO HAVE A LOOK.
WHY NOT?
WOULD YOU PLEASE STOP SAYING "WHY NOT"?
WHY?
NO REASON.
OKAY! PUT AWAY YOUR PAPERS, WE'RE EATING!
FOOD'S READY!
PUT IT IN A TUPPERWARE, WE'RE LEAVING.
WHAT?! ARE YOU KIDDING ME?
NO.
NOT AT ALL.
AND WHERE ARE WE GOING?
LIVRES ANCIENS
TO LOOK FOR THE CITY OF THE DEAD.

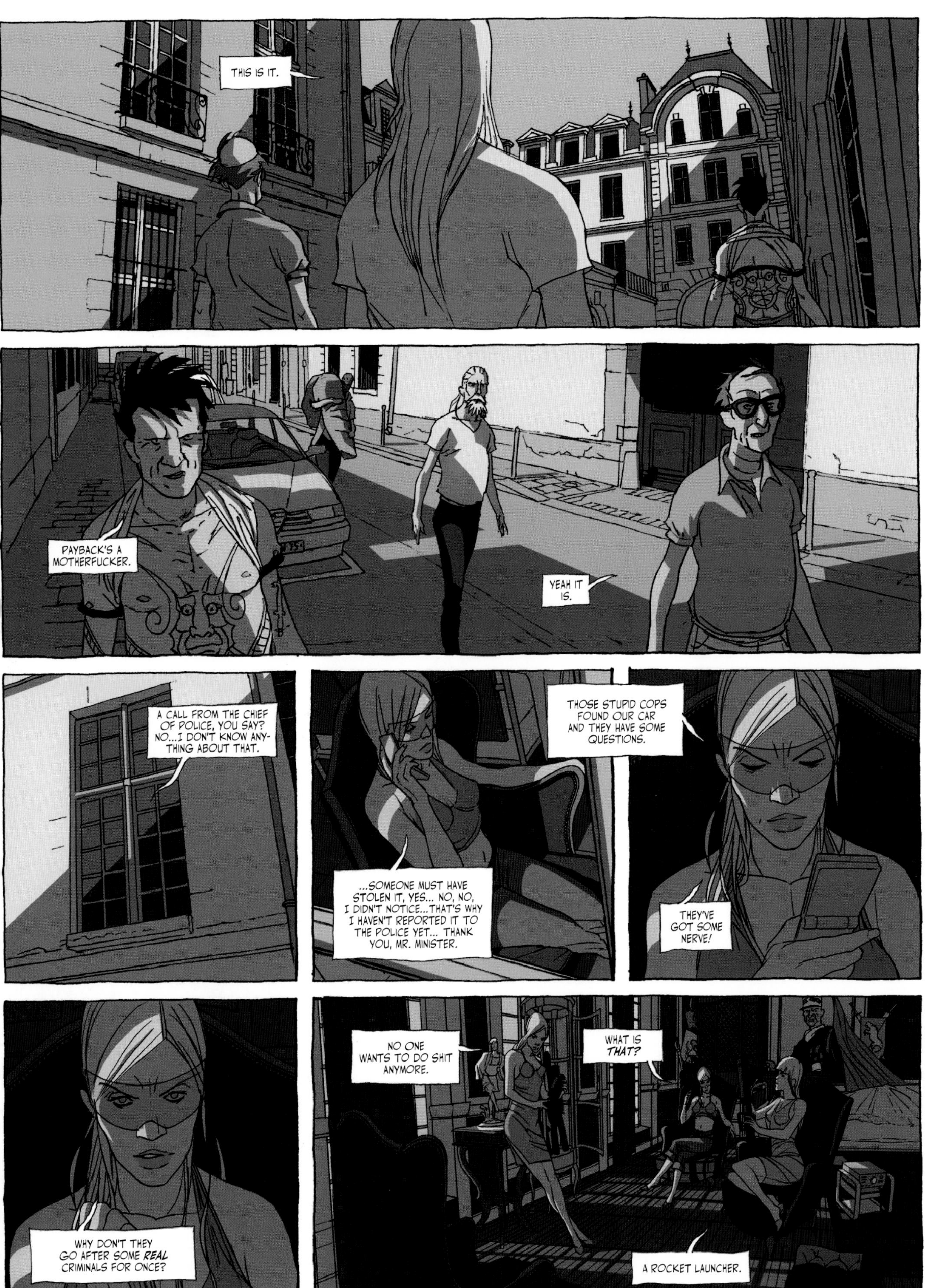

THIS IS IT.
PAYBACK'S A MOTHERFUCKER.
YEAH IT IS.
A CALL FROM THE CHIEF OF POLICE, YOU SAY? NO...I DON'T KNOW ANYTHING ABOUT THAT.
...SOMEONE MUST HAVE STOLEN IT, YES... NO, NO, I DIDN'T NOTICE...THAT'S WHY I HAVEN'T REPORTED IT TO THE POLICE YET... THANK YOU, MR. MINISTER.
THOSE STUPID COPS FOUND OUR CAR AND THEY HAVE SOME QUESTIONS.
THEY'VE GOT SOME NERVE!
WHY DON'T THEY GO AFTER SOME REAL CRIMINALS FOR ONCE?
NO ONE WANTS TO DO SHIT ANYMORE.
WHAT IS THAT?
A ROCKET LAUNCHER.

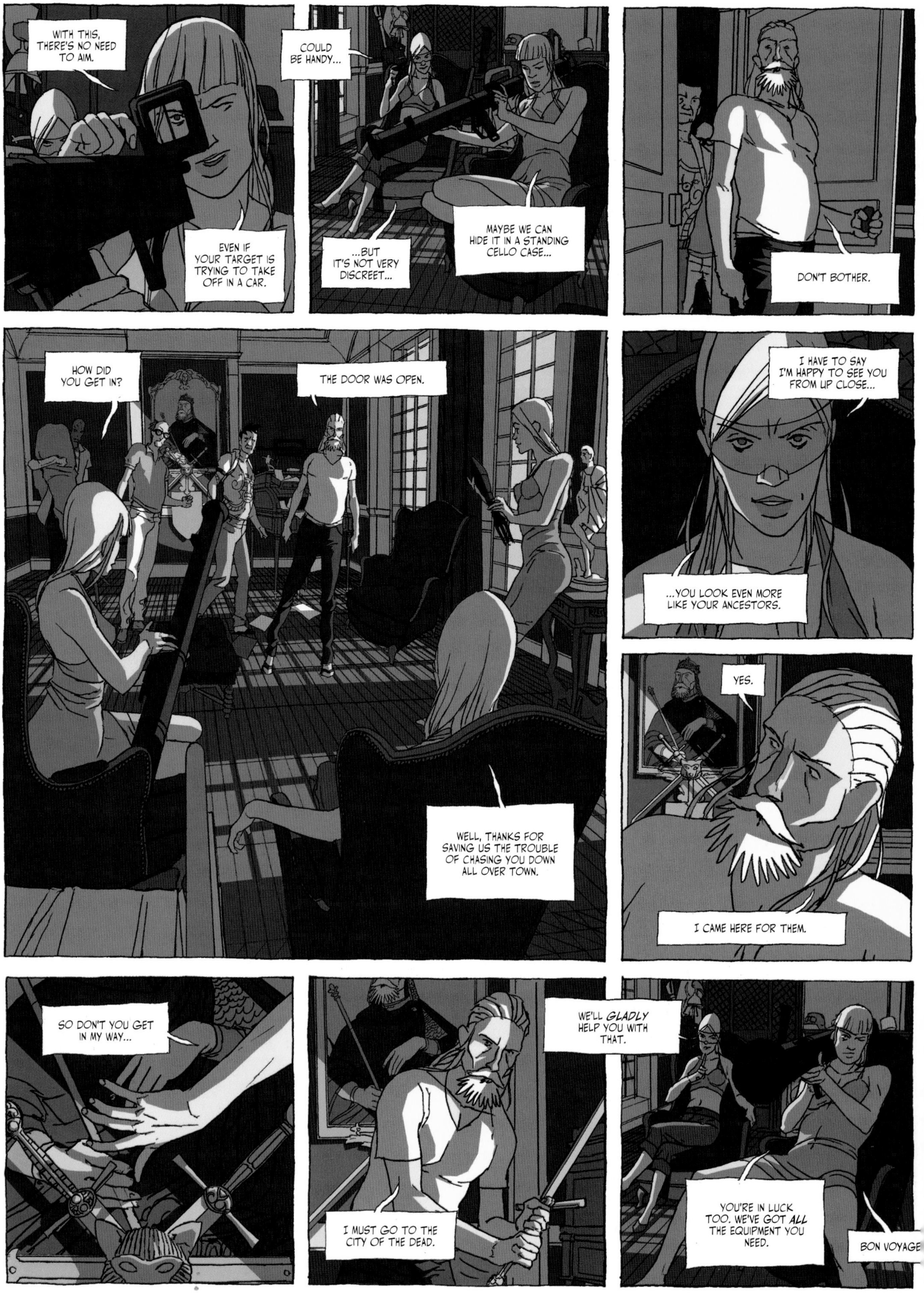

WITH THIS, THERE'S NO NEED TO AIM.
EVEN IF YOUR TARGET IS TRYING TO TAKE OFF IN A CAR.
COULD BE HANDY...
...BUT IT'S NOT VERY DISCREET...
MAYBE WE CAN HIDE IT IN A STANDING CELLO CASE...
DON'T BOTHER.
HOW DID YOU GET IN?
THE DOOR WAS OPEN.
WELL, THANKS FOR SAVING US THE TROUBLE OF CHASING YOU DOWN ALL OVER TOWN.
I HAVE TO SAY I'M HAPPY TO SEE YOU FROM UP CLOSE...
...YOU LOOK EVEN MORE LIKE YOUR ANCESTORS.
YES.
I CAME HERE FOR THEM.
SO DON'T YOU GET IN MY WAY...
I MUST GO TO THE CITY OF THE DEAD.
WE'LL *GLADLY* HELP YOU WITH THAT.
YOU'RE IN LUCK TOO. WE'VE GOT *ALL* THE EQUIPMENT YOU NEED.
BON VOYAGE

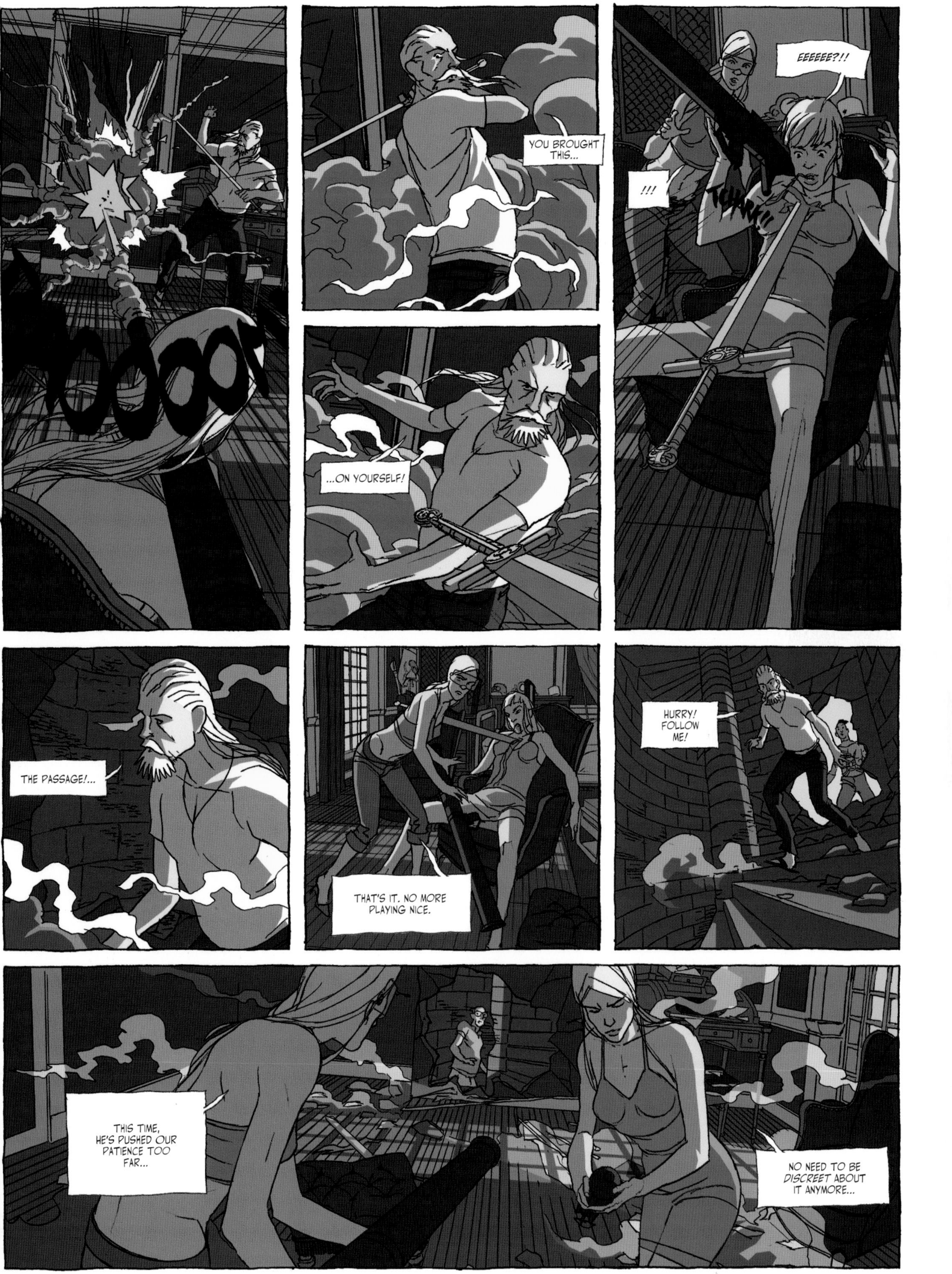
YOU BROUGHT THIS...
EEEEEE?!!
!!!
...ON YOURSELF!
THE PASSAGE!...
THAT'S IT. NO MORE PLAYING NICE.
HURRY! FOLLOW ME!
THIS TIME, HE'S PUSHED OUR PATIENCE TOO FAR...
NO NEED TO BE DISCREET ABOUT IT ANYMORE...

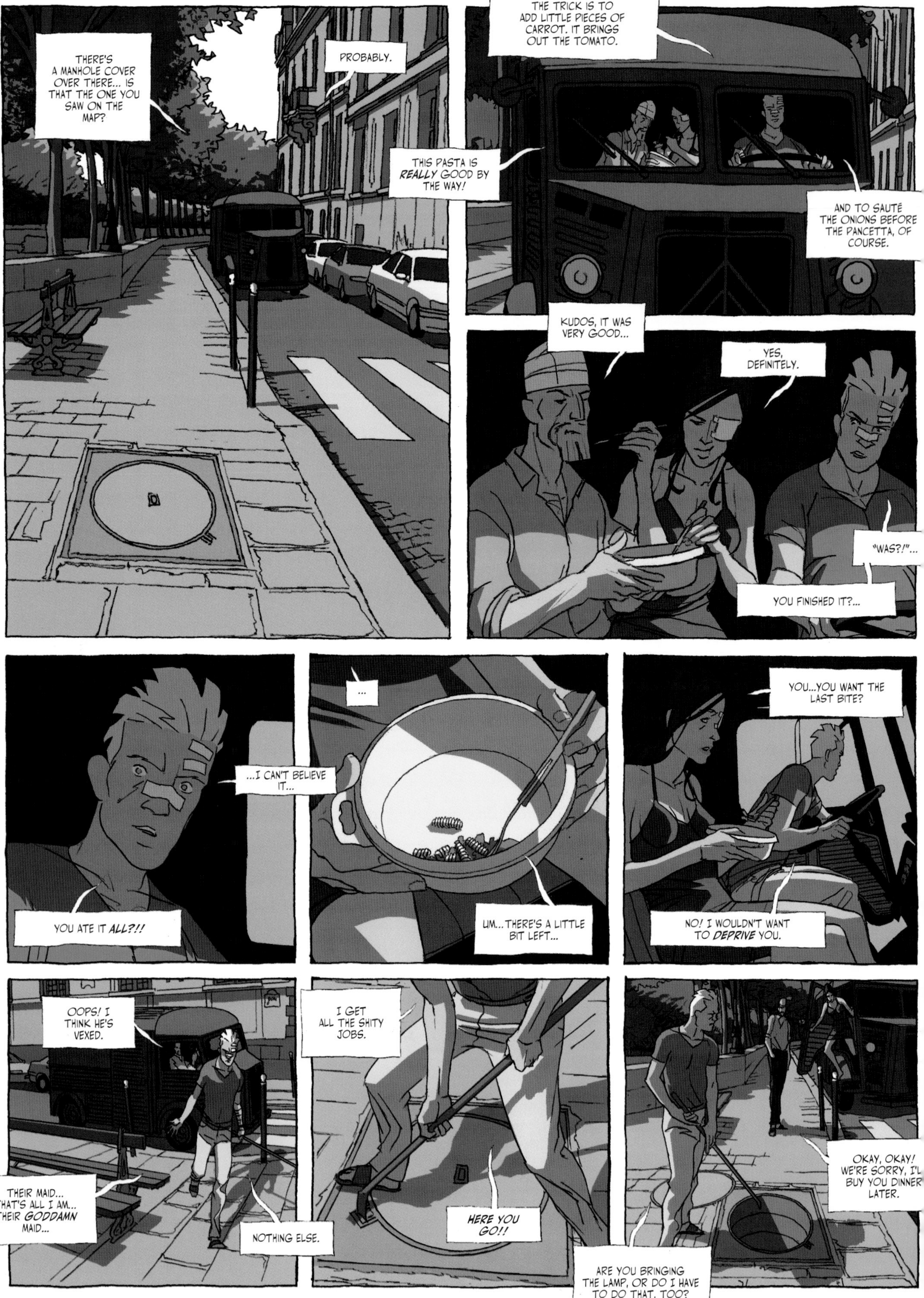
THERE'S A MANHOLE COVER OVER THERE... IS THAT THE ONE YOU SAW ON THE MAP?
PROBABLY.
THE TRICK IS TO ADD LITTLE PIECES OF CARROT. IT BRINGS OUT THE TOMATO.
THIS PASTA IS REALLY GOOD BY THE WAY!
AND TO SAUTÉ THE ONIONS BEFORE THE PANCETTA, OF COURSE.
KUDOS, IT WAS VERY GOOD...
YES, DEFINITELY.
"WAS?!"...
YOU FINISHED IT?...
...I CAN'T BELIEVE IT...
YOU ATE IT ALL?!!
...
UM... THERE'S A LITTLE BIT LEFT...
YOU...YOU WANT THE LAST BITE?
NO! I WOULDN'T WANT TO DEPRIVE YOU.
OOPS! I THINK HE'S VEXED.
THEIR MAID... THAT'S ALL I AM... THEIR GODDAMN MAID...
NOTHING ELSE.
I GET ALL THE SHITY JOBS.
HERE YOU GO!!
ARE YOU BRINGING THE LAMP, OR DO I HAVE TO DO THAT, TOO?
OKAY, OKAY! WE'RE SORRY, I'LL BUY YOU DINNER LATER.

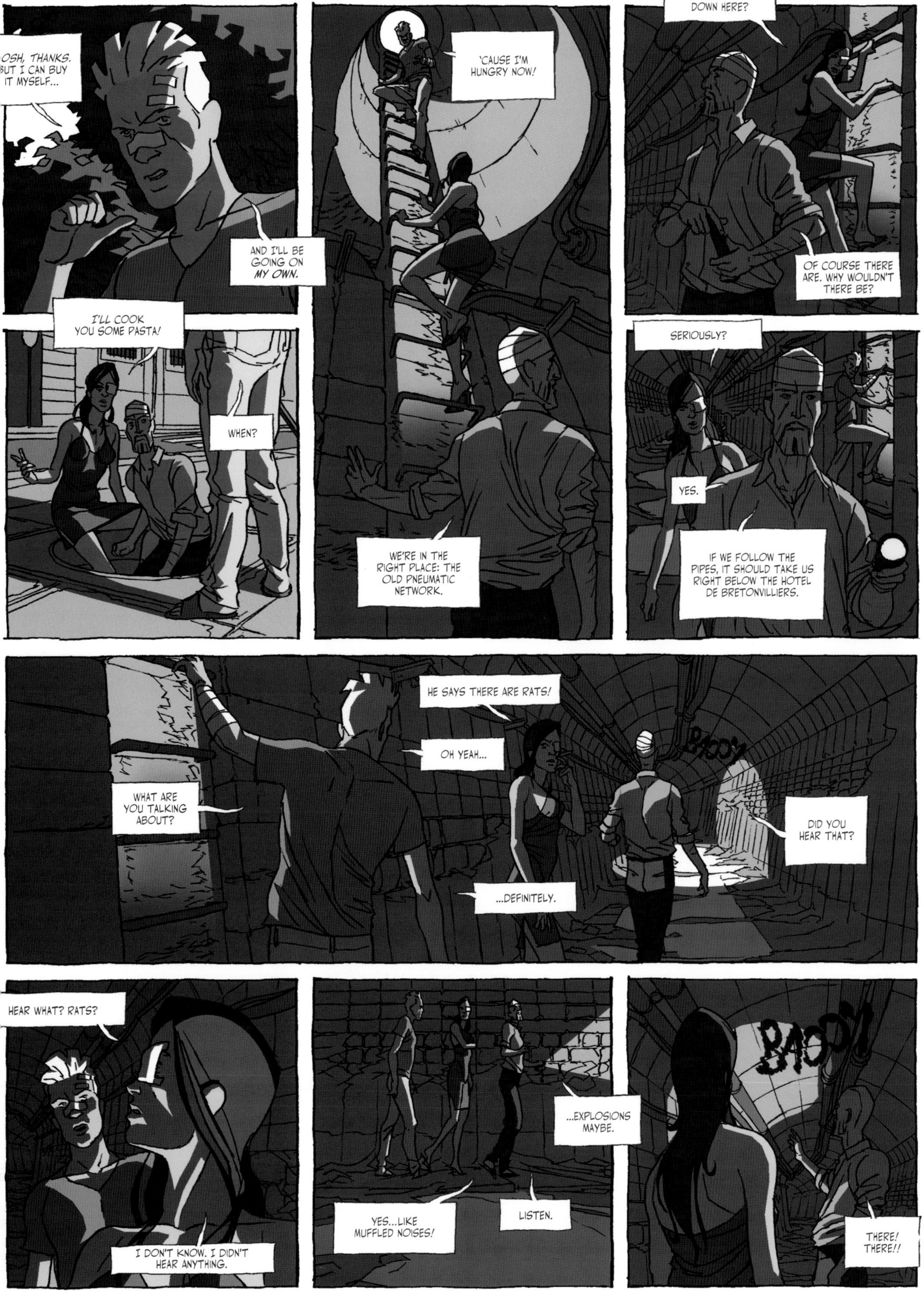
OSH, THANKS. BUT I CAN BUY IT MYSELF...
AND I'LL BE GOING ON MY OWN.
I'LL COOK YOU SOME PASTA!
WHEN?
'CAUSE I'M HUNGRY NOW!
WE'RE IN THE RIGHT PLACE: THE OLD PNEUMATIC NETWORK.
YOU THINK THERE ARE ANY RATS DOWN HERE?
OF COURSE THERE ARE. WHY WOULDN'T THERE BE?
SERIOUSLY?
YES.
IF WE FOLLOW THE PIPES, IT SHOULD TAKE US RIGHT BELOW THE HOTEL DE BRETONVILLIERS.
HE SAYS THERE ARE RATS!
OH YEAH...
WHAT ARE YOU TALKING ABOUT?
...DEFINITELY.
DID YOU HEAR THAT?
HEAR WHAT? RATS?
I DON'T KNOW. I DIDN'T HEAR ANYTHING.
YES...LIKE MUFFLED NOISES!
LISTEN.
...EXPLOSIONS MAYBE.
THERE! THERE!!

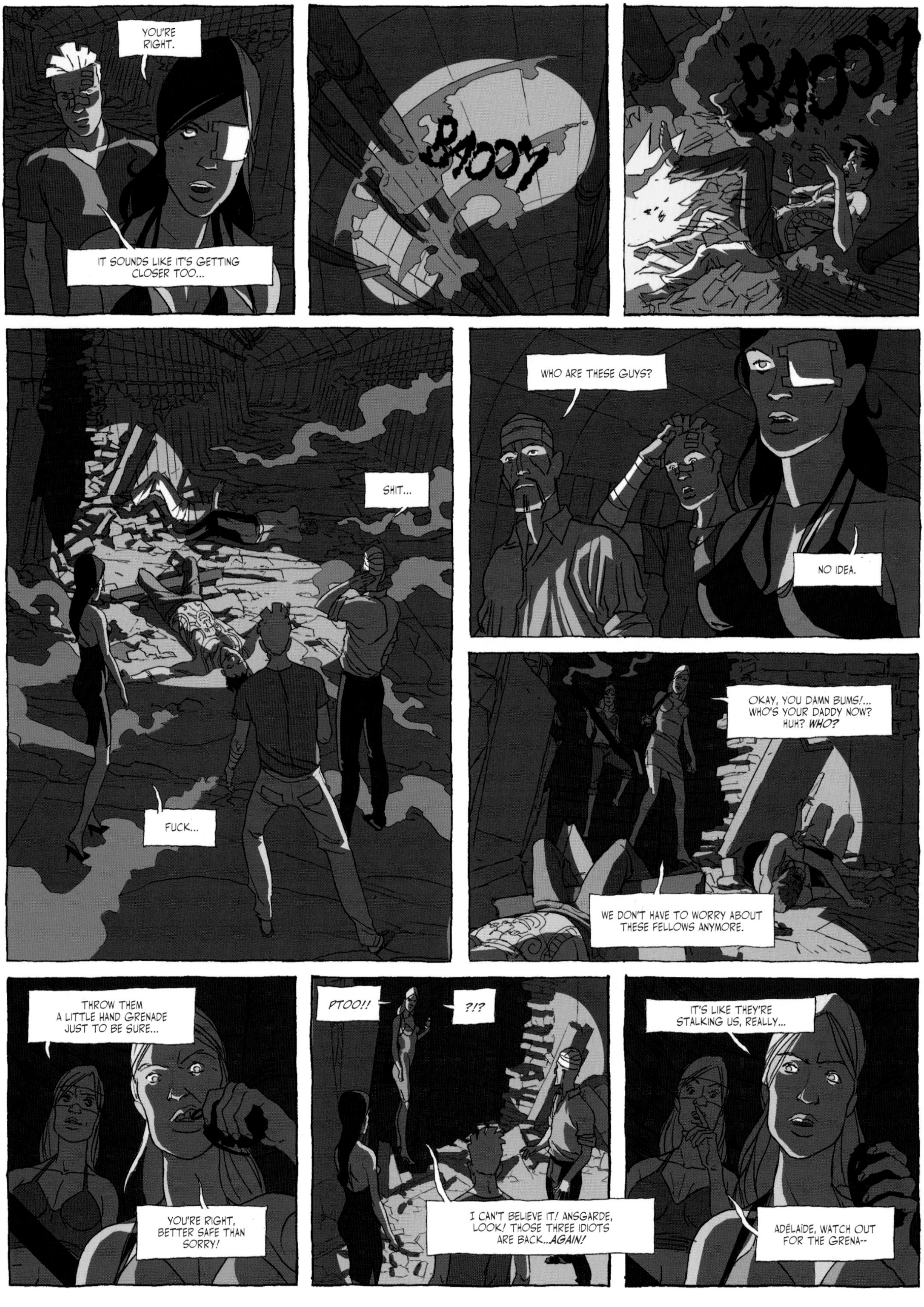

YOU'RE RIGHT.
IT SOUNDS LIKE IT'S GETTING CLOSER TOO...
BAOOM
BAOOM
SHIT...
FUCK...
WHO ARE THESE GUYS?
NO IDEA.
OKAY, YOU DAMN BUMS!... WHO'S YOUR DADDY NOW? HUH? *WHO?*
WE DON'T HAVE TO WORRY ABOUT THESE FELLOWS ANYMORE.
THROW THEM A LITTLE HAND GRENADE JUST TO BE SURE...
YOU'RE RIGHT, BETTER SAFE THAN SORRY!
PTOO!!
?!?
I CAN'T BELIEVE IT! ANSGARDE, LOOK! THOSE THREE IDIOTS ARE BACK...*AGAIN!*
IT'S LIKE THEY'RE STALKING US, REALLY...
ADÉLAÏDE, WATCH OUT FOR THE GRENA--

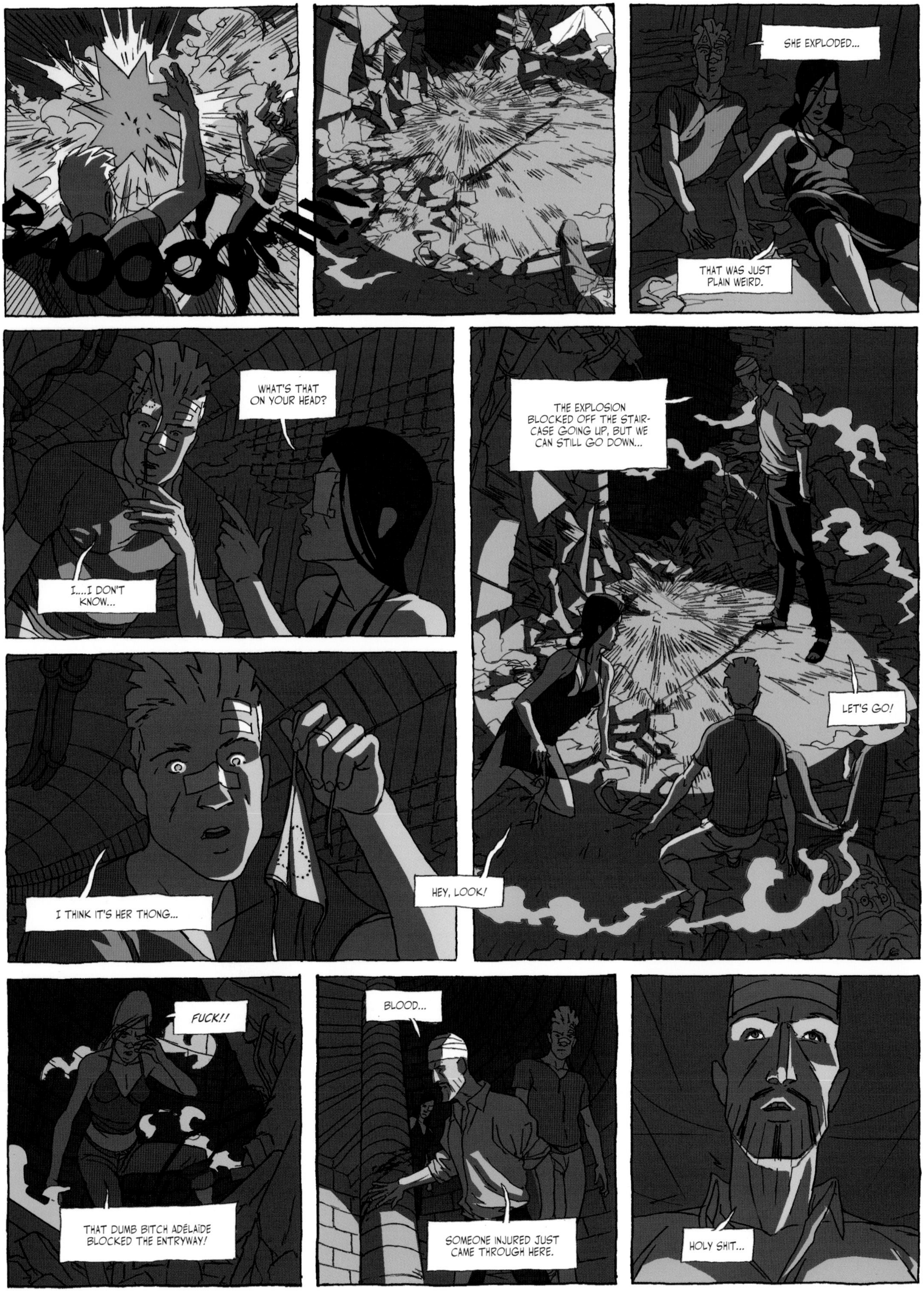
BROOOM!!!
SHE EXPLODED...
THAT WAS JUST PLAIN WEIRD.
WHAT'S THAT ON YOUR HEAD?
I....I DON'T KNOW...
I THINK IT'S HER THONG...
THE EXPLOSION BLOCKED OFF THE STAIR-CASE GOING UP, BUT WE CAN STILL GO DOWN...
LET'S GO!
HEY, LOOK!
FUCK!!
THAT DUMB BITCH ADÉLAÏDE BLOCKED THE ENTRYWAY!
BLOOD...
SOMEONE INJURED JUST CAME THROUGH HERE.
HOLY SHIT...

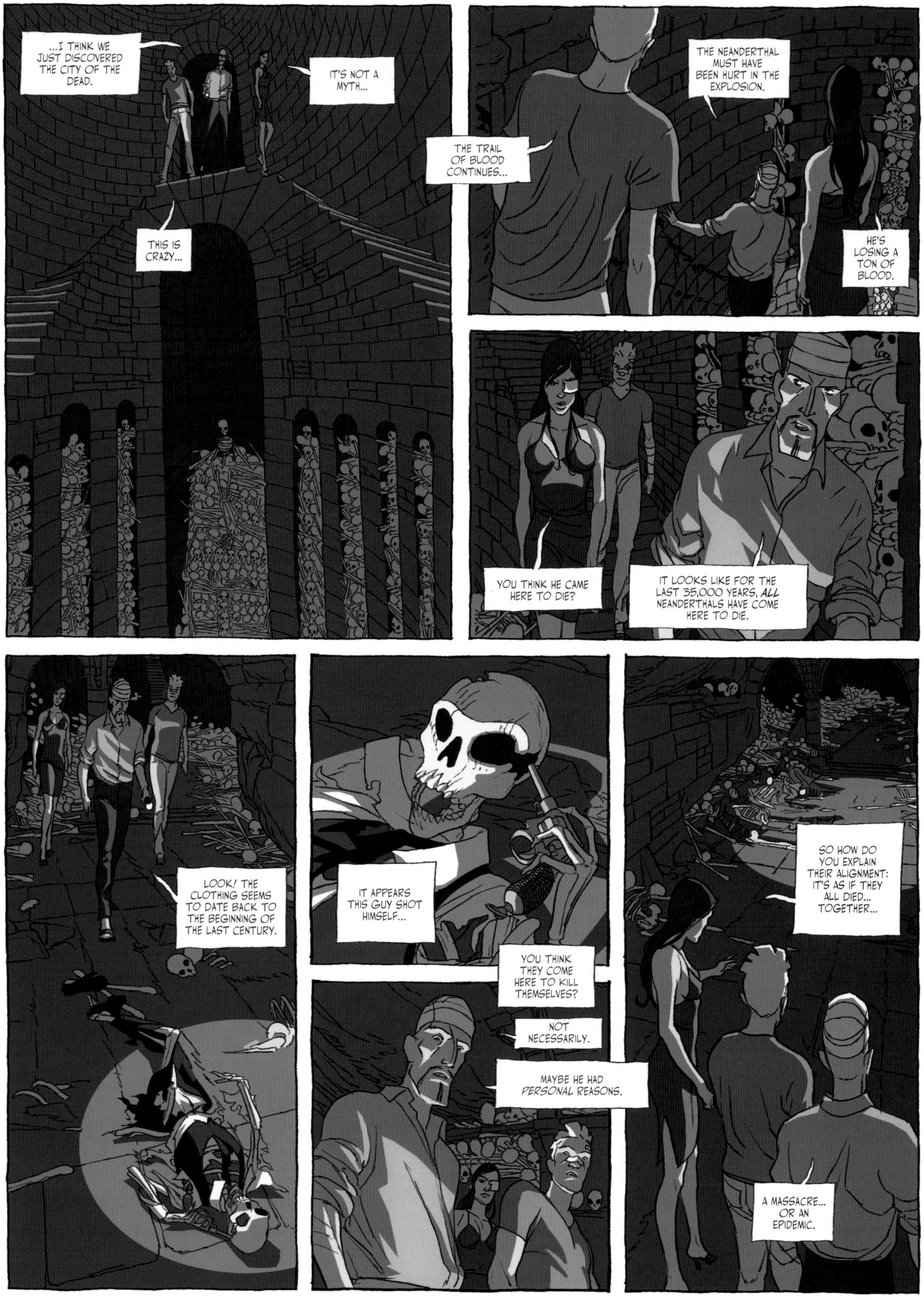
...I THINK WE JUST DISCOVERED THE CITY OF THE DEAD.
IT'S NOT A MYTH...
THIS IS CRAZY...
THE NEANDERTHAL MUST HAVE BEEN HURT IN THE EXPLOSION.
THE TRAIL OF BLOOD CONTINUES...
HE'S LOSING A TON OF BLOOD.
YOU THINK HE CAME HERE TO DIE?
IT LOOKS LIKE FOR THE LAST 35,000 YEARS, *ALL* NEANDERTHALS HAVE COME HERE TO DIE.
LOOK! THE CLOTHING SEEMS TO DATE BACK TO THE BEGINNING OF THE LAST CENTURY.
IT APPEARS THIS GUY SHOT HIMSELF...
YOU THINK THEY COME HERE TO KILL THEMSELVES?
NOT NECESSARILY.
MAYBE HE HAD *PERSONAL* REASONS.
SO HOW DO YOU EXPLAIN THEIR ALIGNMENT: IT'S AS IF THEY ALL DIED... TOGETHER...
A MASSACRE... OR AN EPIDEMIC.

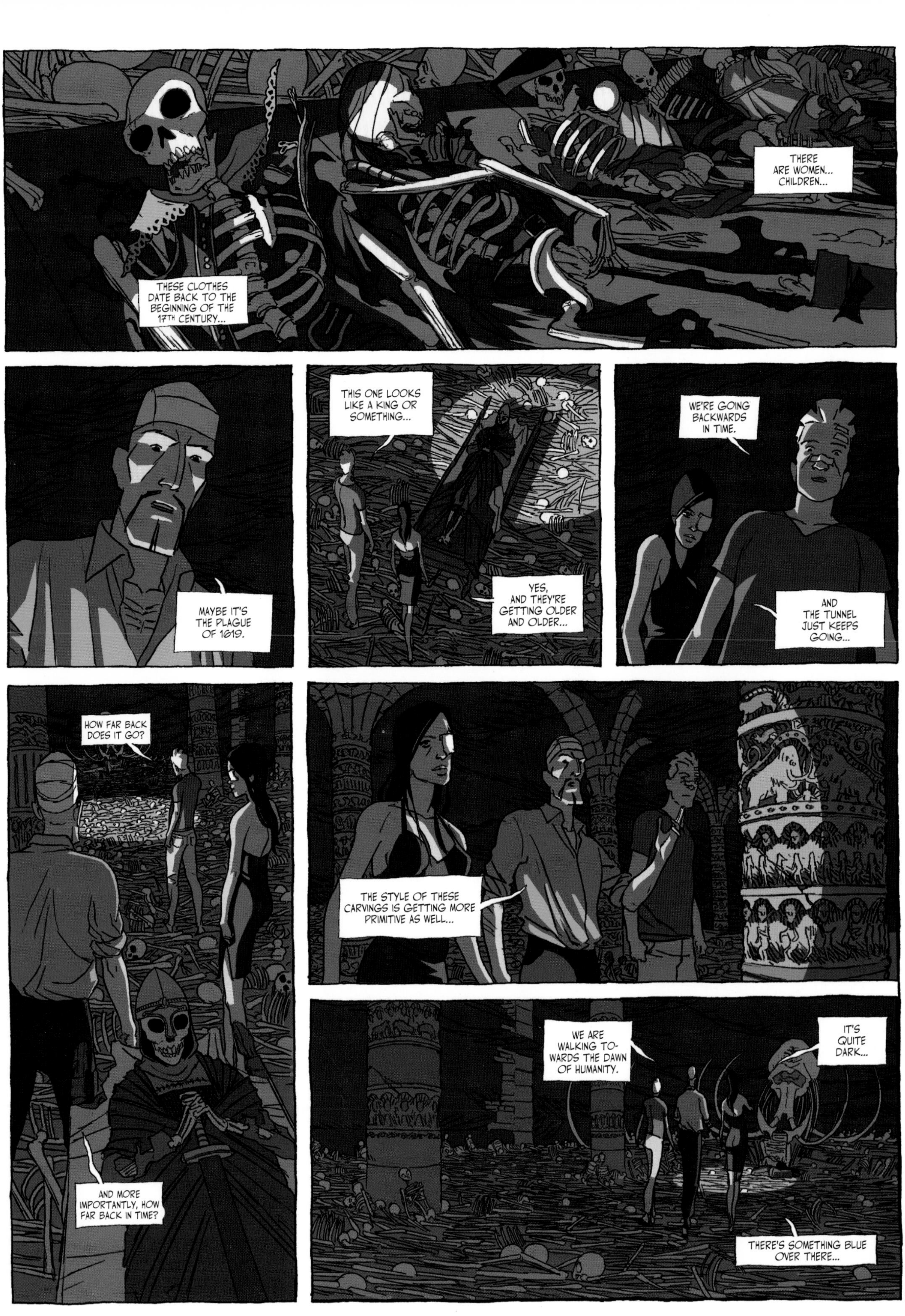

THERE ARE WOMEN... CHILDREN...
THESE CLOTHES DATE BACK TO THE BEGINNING OF THE 17TH CENTURY...
MAYBE IT'S THE PLAGUE OF 1619.
THIS ONE LOOKS LIKE A KING OR SOMETHING...
YES, AND THEY'RE GETTING OLDER AND OLDER...
WE'RE GOING BACKWARDS IN TIME.
AND THE TUNNEL JUST KEEPS GOING...
HOW FAR BACK DOES IT GO?
AND MORE IMPORTANTLY, HOW FAR BACK IN TIME?
THE STYLE OF THESE CARVINGS IS GETTING MORE PRIMITIVE AS WELL...
WE ARE WALKING TOWARDS THE DAWN OF HUMANITY.
IT'S QUITE DARK...
THERE'S SOMETHING BLUE OVER THERE...

I'M THE LAST ONE...

THE NEANDERTHAL!!

THE GREAT PROPHECY MUST COME TRUE...

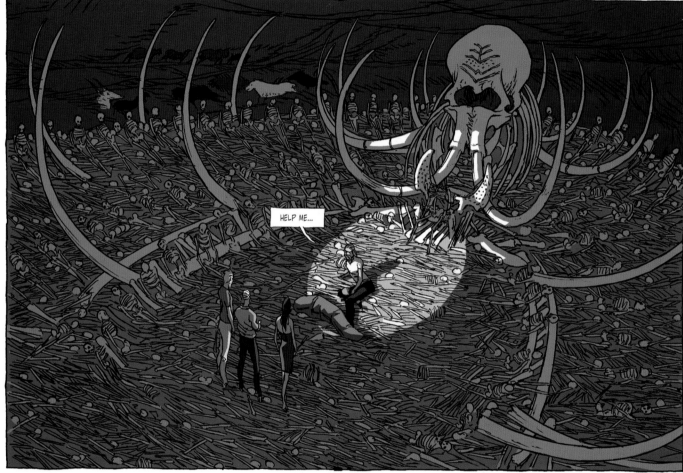

HELP ME...

THE PROPHECY *MUST* COME TRUE.

WHAT'S THIS PROPHECY?

YES, SINCE WE SURE KEEP HEARING ABOUT IT.

THE PROPHECY OF THE ARMY OF THE DEAD!

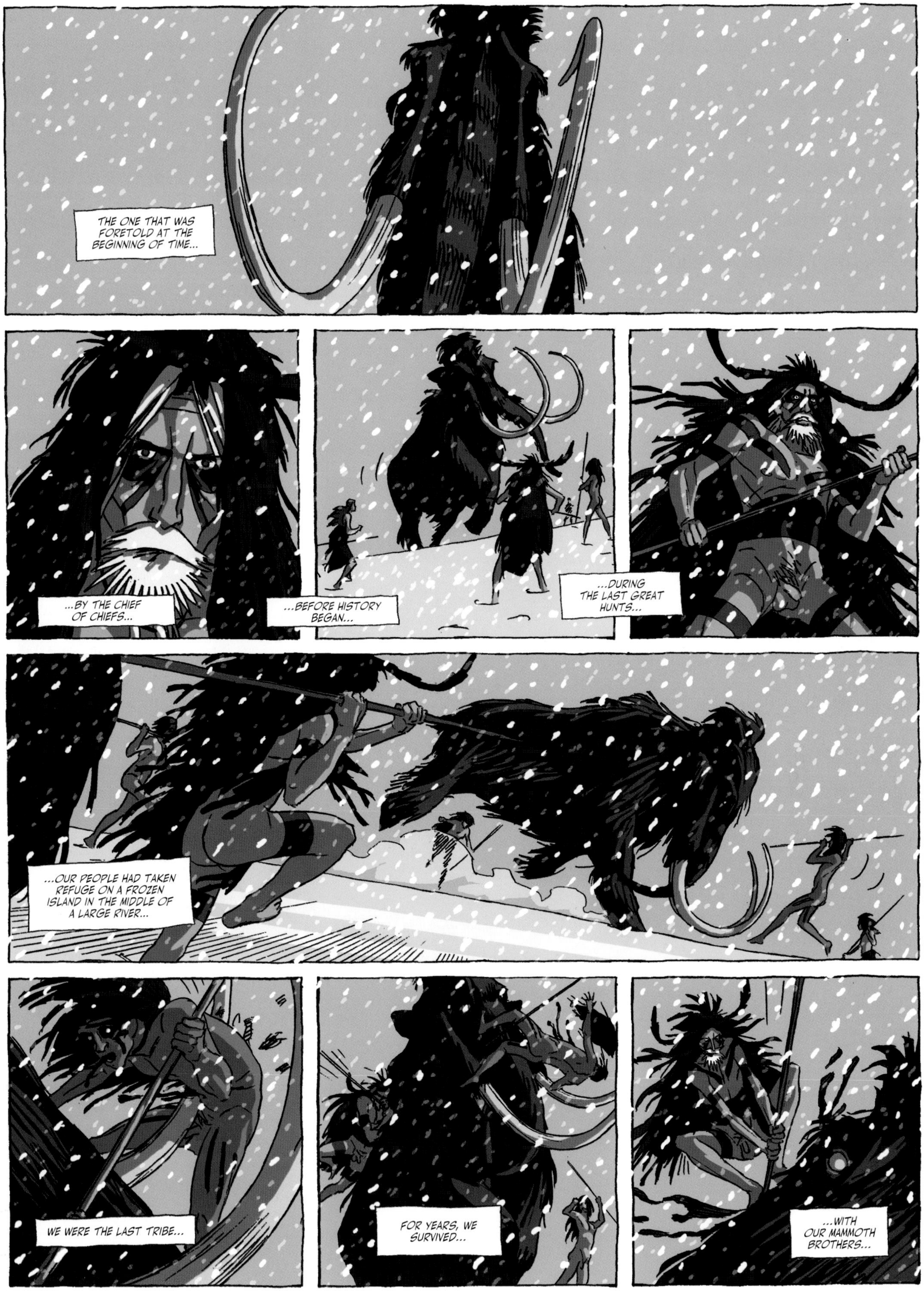
THE ONE THAT WAS FORETOLD AT THE BEGINNING OF TIME...
...BY THE CHIEF OF CHIEFS...
...BEFORE HISTORY BEGAN...
...DURING THE LAST GREAT HUNTS...
...OUR PEOPLE HAD TAKEN REFUGE ON A FROZEN ISLAND IN THE MIDDLE OF A LARGE RIVER...
WE WERE THE LAST TRIBE...
FOR YEARS, WE SURVIVED...
...WITH OUR MAMMOTH BROTHERS...

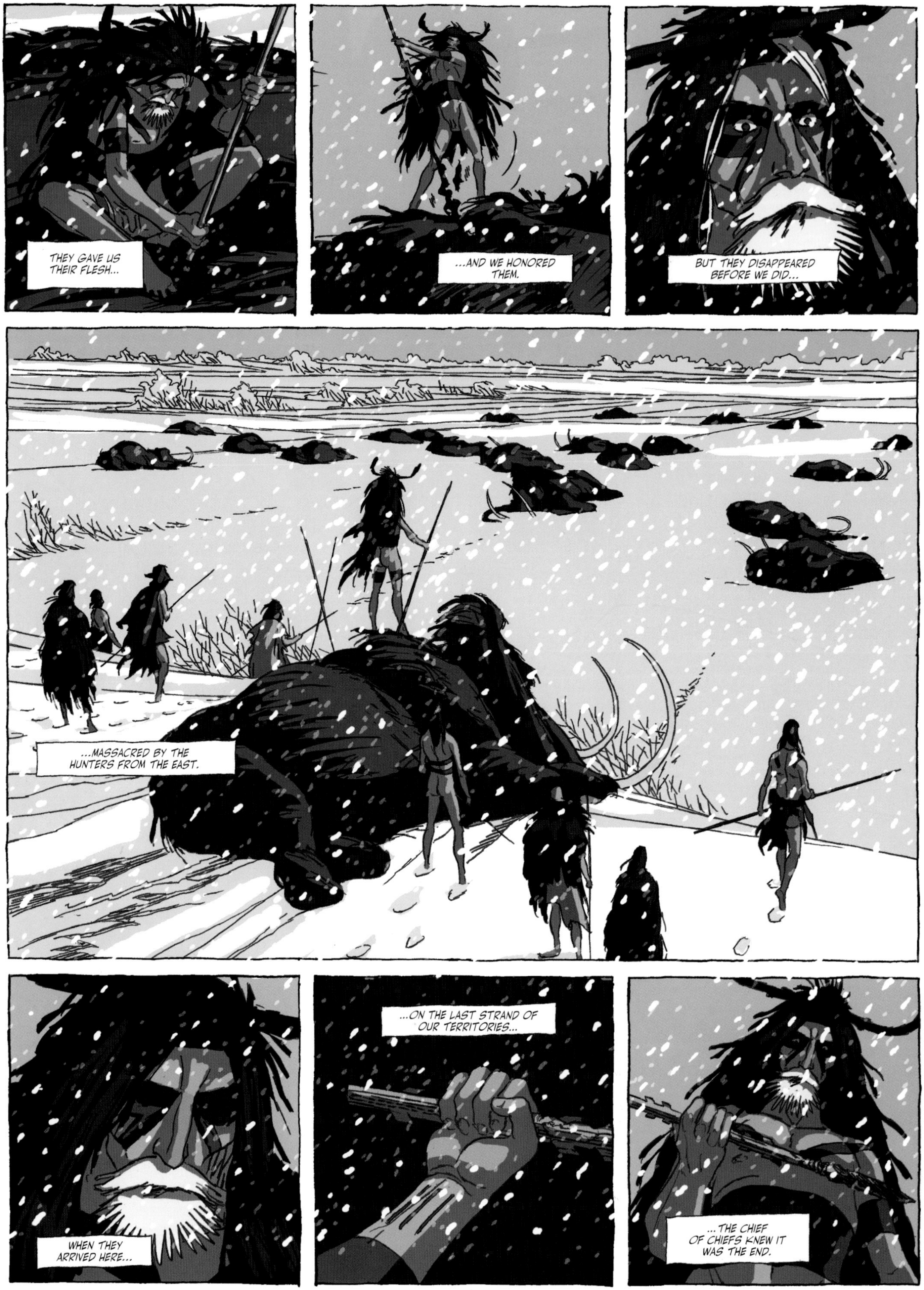
THEY GAVE US THEIR FLESH...
...AND WE HONORED THEM.
BUT THEY DISAPPEARED BEFORE WE DID...
...MASSACRED BY THE HUNTERS FROM THE EAST.
WHEN THEY ARRIVED HERE...
...ON THE LAST STRAND OF OUR TERRITORIES...
...THE CHIEF OF CHIEFS KNEW IT WAS THE END.

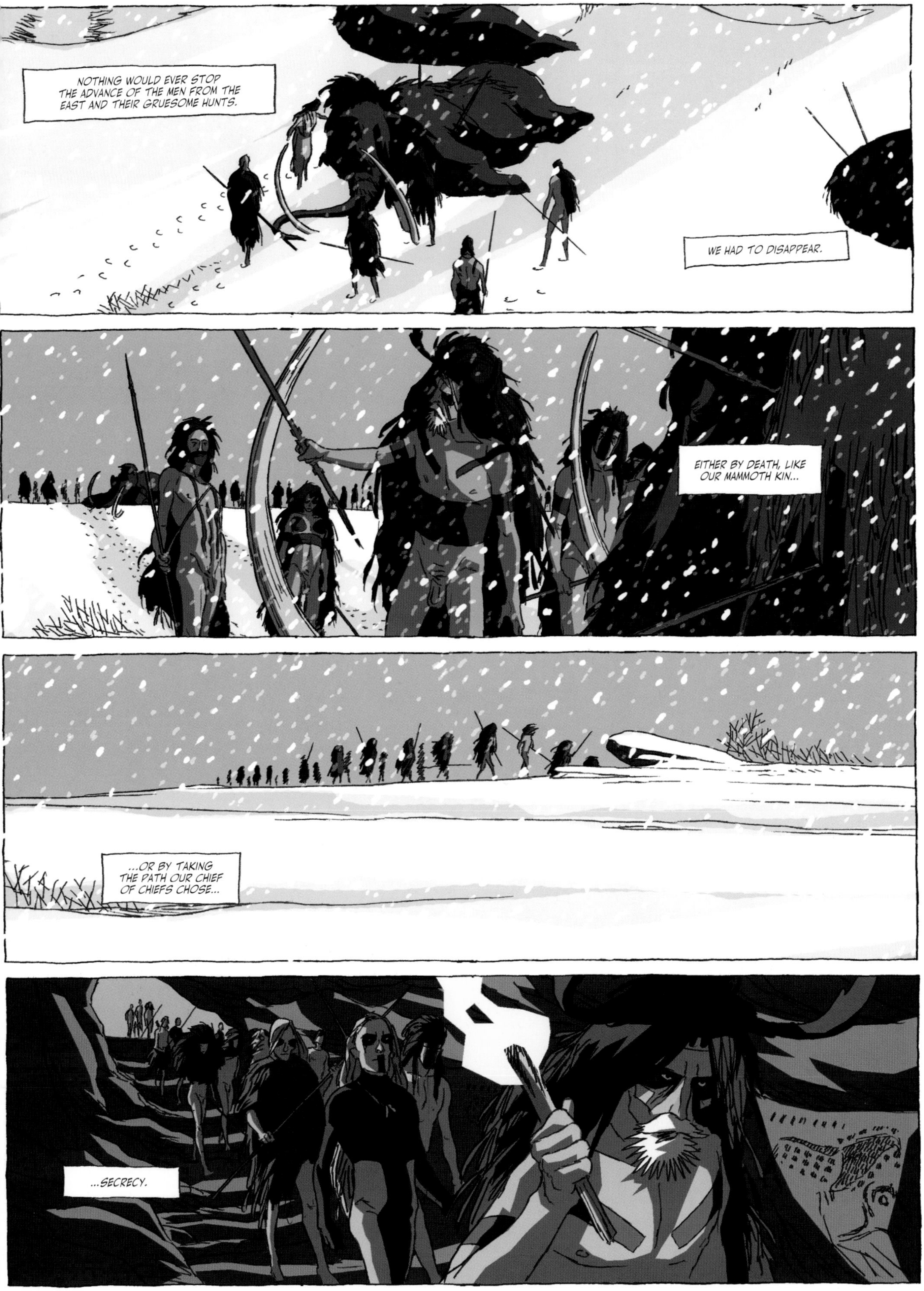
NOTHING WOULD EVER STOP THE ADVANCE OF THE MEN FROM THE EAST AND THEIR GRUESOME HUNTS.
WE HAD TO DISAPPEAR.
EITHER BY DEATH, LIKE OUR MAMMOTH KIN...
...OR BY TAKING THE PATH OUR CHIEF OF CHIEFS CHOSE...
...SECRECY.

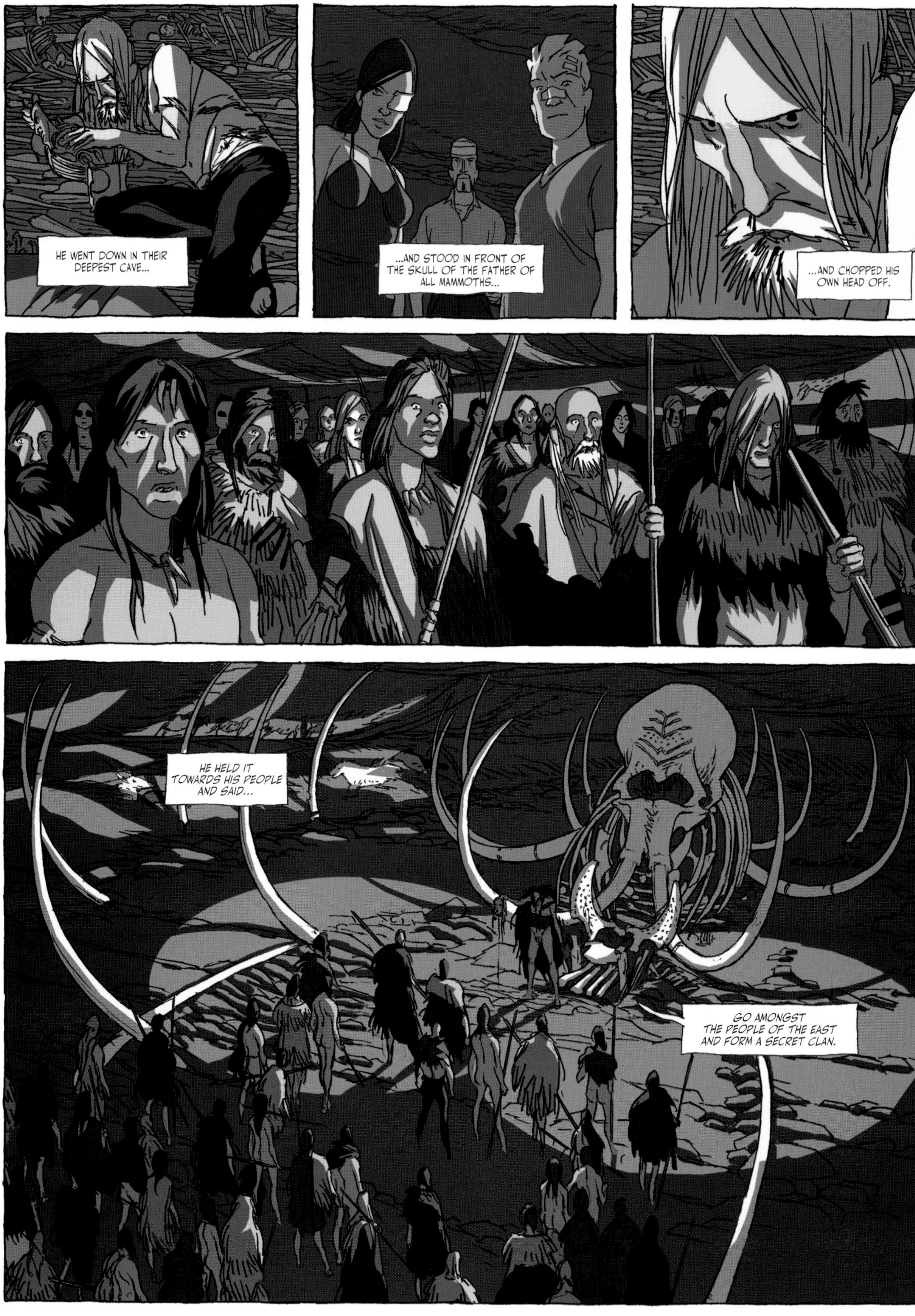
HE WENT DOWN IN THEIR DEEPEST CAVE...
...AND STOOD IN FRONT OF THE SKULL OF THE FATHER OF ALL MAMMOTHS...
...AND CHOPPED HIS OWN HEAD OFF.
HE HELD IT TOWARDS HIS PEOPLE AND SAID...
GO AMONGST THE PEOPLE OF THE EAST AND FORM A SECRET CLAN.

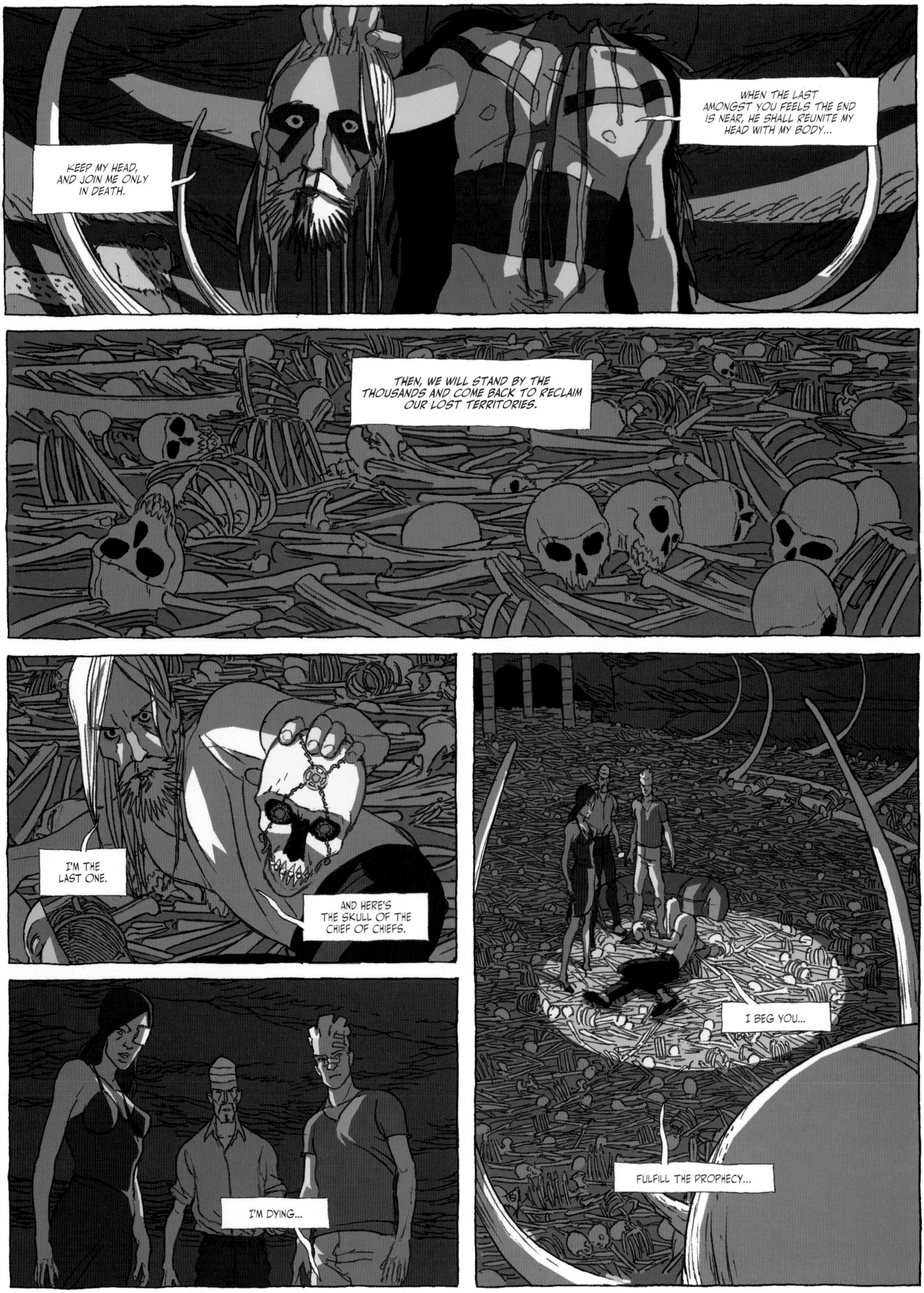
KEEP MY HEAD, AND JOIN ME ONLY IN DEATH.
WHEN THE LAST AMONGST YOU FEELS THE END IS NEAR, HE SHALL REUNITE MY HEAD WITH MY BODY...
THEN, WE WILL STAND BY THE THOUSANDS AND COME BACK TO RECLAIM OUR LOST TERRITORIES.
I'M THE LAST ONE.
AND HERE'S THE SKULL OF THE CHIEF OF CHIEFS.
I'M DYING...
I BEG YOU...
FULFILL THE PROPHECY...

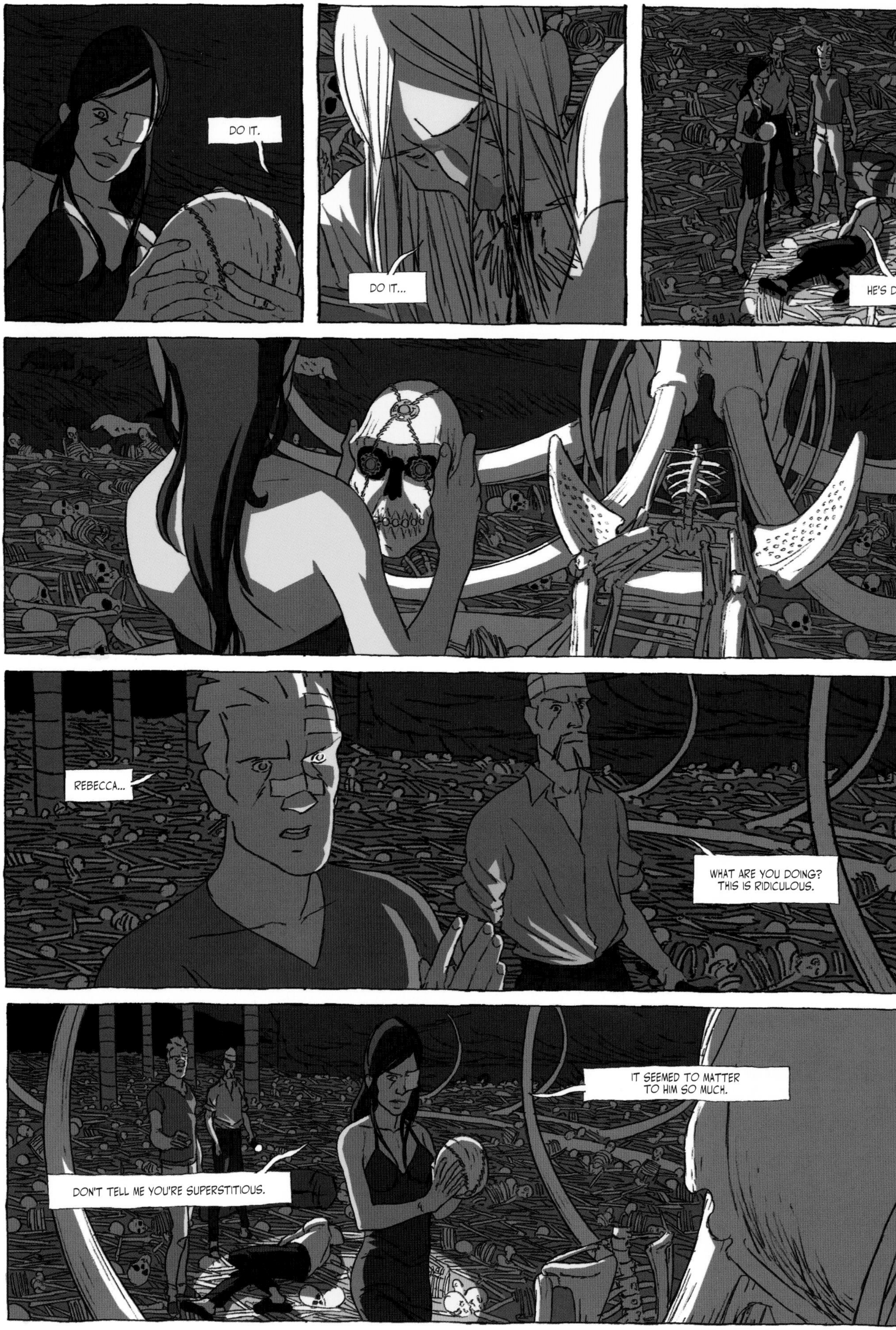

DO IT.
DO IT...
HE'S DEAD.
REBECCA...
WHAT ARE YOU DOING? THIS IS RIDICULOUS.
DON'T TELL ME YOU'RE SUPERSTITIOUS.
IT SEEMED TO MATTER TO HIM SO MUCH.

AND WHAT IF IT WAS TRUE?

HUH?

YES, WHAT IF IT WERE TRUE.

THERE'S ONLY ONE WAY TO FIND OUT...

IF IT *WAS* TRUE, LET ME POINT OUT THAT WE WOULD BE IN A SHIT-LOAD OF TROUBLE.

...

YES.

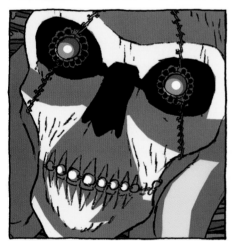

EH, WHAT THE FUCK.

AFTER ALL, I DIDN'T PROMISE HIM ANYTHING.

YEAH... THIS WHOLE PROPHECY THING ISN'T ANY OF OUR BUSINESS.

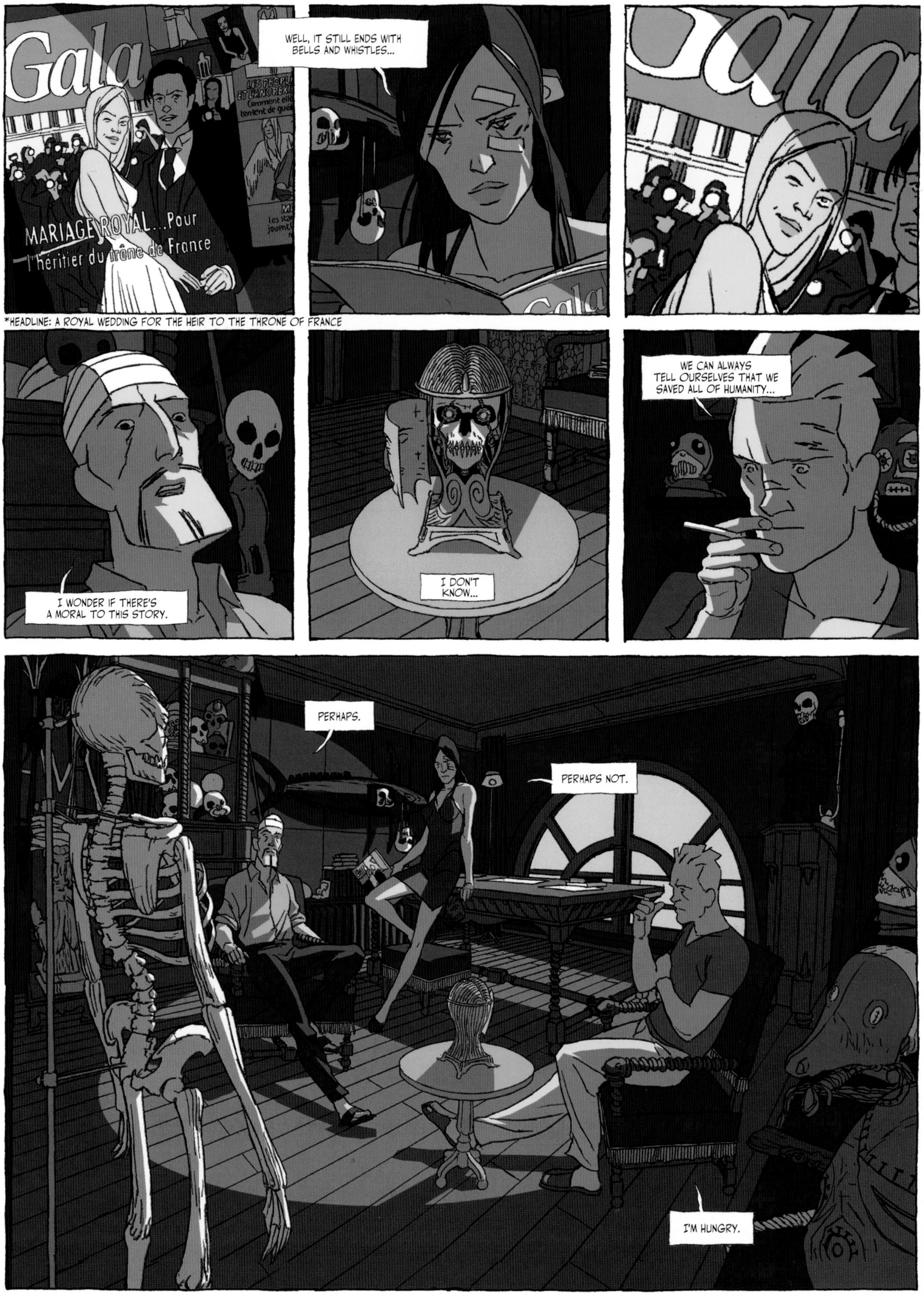
Gala
MARIAGE ROYAL...Pour l'héritier du trône de France
WELL, IT STILL ENDS WITH BELLS AND WHISTLES...
*HEADLINE: A ROYAL WEDDING FOR THE HEIR TO THE THRONE OF FRANCE
I WONDER IF THERE'S A MORAL TO THIS STORY.
I DON'T KNOW...
WE CAN ALWAYS TELL OURSELVES THAT WE SAVED ALL OF HUMANITY...
PERHAPS.
PERHAPS NOT.
I'M HUNGRY.

THE END